DATE DUE

4-97 Dockery			
1-13-99 DN			
4-21-99 J.C.			
Cather			
E.H.D.			
4-11-04-J. Chap.			
WEF 1-25-05			
B			
Owens			
T.H.			
5-07 W.R.C			
K.Lilz 10-30-07			
D. Jenkins			
J.C.B.-2-7-13			
Starcher			

DEMCO 38-296

Legend in the Dust

Legend in the Dust

DWIGHT BENNETT NEWTON

Sagebrush
Large Print Westerns

Library of Congress Cataloging in Publication Data

Newton, D. B. (Dwight Bennett), 1918 –
    Legend in the dust / Dwight Bennett Newton.
    p.   cm.
    ISBN 1-57490-020-X (alk. paper)
    1. Large type books. I. Title.
[PS3527.E9176L44   1996]
813'.54—dc20   96-19311
                                                              CIP

Cataloguing in Publication Data is available from
the British Library and the National Library of Australia.

Copyright © 1970 by Dwight Bennett Newton.
Copyright © 1973 by Dwight Bennett Newton in the British
Commonwealth.
Published by arrangement with Golden West Literary
Agency. All rights reserved.

Sagebrush Large Print Westerns are published in the
United States and Canada by Thomas T. Beeler, Publisher,
Box 659, Hampton Falls, New Hampshire 03844-0659.
ISBN 1-57490-020-X

Published in the United Kingdom, Eire, and the Republic of
South Africa by Isis Publishing Ltd, 7 Centremead, Osney
Mead, Oxford OX2 0ES England. ISBN 0-7531-5131-6

Published in Australia and New Zealand by Australian
Large Print Audio & Video Pty Ltd, 17 Mohr Street,
Tullamarine, Victoria, 3043, Australia. ISBN 1-86340-600-X

Manufactured in the United States of America

Legend in the Dust

CHAPTER I

The young man's name was Rim Adams, and the day in 1869 when he left the steam cars at Kansas City he was encumbered by a hungry, restless urge and not much else. Almost before he gave a glance to the town itself he found himself turning to stare along the river whose slow and muddy current, a burnished copper color in the sunset, swept majestically toward him here in a broad bend out of the north and west. A wind, blowing from over Kansas way, touched his brooding face and narrowed the pale eyes that slanted a little above highset cheeks. It brought him the raw scent of prairie warmed by a spring sun, hinting of wildness and stretching miles.

The inner voice of a constant, troubling dialogue with himself suggested restlessly, Maybe yonder?...

Meanwhile here was the town, sprawling up the Missouri's steep south bluff; and here was Rim Adams in an ill-fitting derby and a suit bought off a St. Louis merchant's bargain table, its pockets lighter now by the price of his railroad fare. The grime of engine smoke seemed ground into him. In a barber shop equipped with a public bath he tortured his skin with the yellow lye soap, and paid a dollar to have two days' wiry, blue-black stubble scraped from his cheeks. Afterward came a meal—the first real one since St. Louis, aside from sandwiches and apples purchased from a candy butcher who worked the swaying cars.

By the time he left the restaurant, twilight was turning smoky and the Kansas City night was tuning up. He had no actual plans. The course of wisdom

1

would seem to be that he make his money last—find cheap lodgings and dole out each penny while he looked around for something to suggest itself. There was a rebel in Rim Adams, however—a streak of pure, reckless stubbornness. He had slept, many a time, in crummy flophouses like those he saw crowding the waterfront; in every likelihood, he would again. But tonight he still had a few dollars in his pocket, and a halfway presentable suit of clothes on his back. Time enough to worry when the money was gone.

Tonight he had a feeling—call it a hunch—and he would not be satisfied until he followed it. He followed it, accordingly, through Market Square and the gaudier end of the city, down toward the foot of Main. And at last his hunch led him up a flight of stairs and through the polished, hardwood door at the head of them.

The room beyond was no waterfront dive. It had more the air of a gentleman's club. Crowded as it was, wine-colored velvet curtains and a deep-napped carpet of the same color sopped up most of the noise. Chandeliers spread a mellow glow over white shirtfronts and the bare shoulders of women; tall mirrors caught and splintered the light and bounced it in jewels off the lineup of bottles along the polished backbar. From an area at the rear, raised a couple of steps and set off behind looping velvet ropes, came the click of chips and rattle of dice and the whir of a roulette wheel. The drifting fog of tobacco smoke had the taste, even at second hand, of expensive cigars.

A big, bullet-headed man with shoulders so wide as to make him look faintly grotesque lounged just within the doorway, half hidden by a potted palm. He eyed the newcomer but Rim Adams challenged

2

him with a bold look, settling the hang of his cheap suitcoat; the bouncer shrugged and let him pass. He strolled nonchalantly into the place; for all the world as though he belonged there.

At the bar he caught the eye of one of the attendants and ordered whiskey, frowning at the price he was charged for it. It was good stock, though, and he drank slowly, one elbow on the wood, a young man aloof from the tide of people around him. A bar girl swung her hips past him, pausing just long enough to size him up with a look that quickly lost interest. As she prowled on in search of more promising material, he thought, The hell with you!

Rim Adams knew what he looked like, against this wellheeled crowd. Just now as it happened his interest didn't lie in women, or in whiskey; rather, it was on the platform beyond those velvet ropes. Having finished his glass he set it aside, threaded his way over there, with unhurried deliberateness, and mounted the carpeted steps.

When it came to gambling, he had one liking and so he passed up the faro and blackjack dealers and the roulette wheel, and made instead directly for the felt-lined dice table. Here he found room for himself between a thick-chested, heavily bearded man in a plug hat and another who had the sallow look of a lunger. In the bright cone of light put down by a reflected lamp overhead he watched the hypnotic dance of the ivory cubes, venturing to cover a small bet now and then but mainly waiting for the dice to come round to him—he had a fatalist's belief in good or bad fortune, but with it also a faith in the signs which would tell him which to expect.

At last the man in the plug hat missed his point, swearing savagely into the black tangle of beard.

3

The houseman shoved the dice across the felt toward Adams. Someone said roughly, "They're yours, kid. What can you do with them?"

"I ought to do *that* well," he said calmly, and picked them up and rolled them slowly between his palms, getting the feel.

They felt right. An instinct told him they were going to work for him; a tightness of excitement began to form inside his chest, and his hands trembled slightly. "Get your money ready," he told the crowd. "I'm about to take some of it!"

Just beginning to warm the dice for his first cast, he paused and his lifted hand went still.

Across the velvet ropes and the crowd along the bar, Adams had caught sight of a man who entered through the big mahogany door. He knew him instantly; at least he was certain he should recognize the handsome, hawklike face with the downcurving mustache, the sweep of tawny hair that fell below his shoulders, the eyes whose hard glitter one could sense through the smoke haze of the long room. This odd sense of familiarity held him until one of the other players demanded impatiently, "All right! You going to hold onto those bones all night? Or, are you going to roll 'em?"

Ignoring him, Adams pointed. "Anybody tell me who that is?"

The one in the plug hat said, "Why, hell! That's Frank Keyhoe."

"Keyhoe..."

He'd never before encountered a celebrity, or seen a face translated from the lines of a woodcut engraving into living flesh and blood. The bearded man apparently mistook his silent stare for ignorance. "You ain't heard of Frank Keyhoe? You read the papers, don't you? Or *can* you read?"

He chose to ignore that as he watched the gunfighter move across the room, heads beginning to turn now as others became aware of him. Here and there a hand was lifted and a greeting spoken, which this Frank Keyhoe acknowledged with no more than a nod; his stare continued restlessly to range the place.

Someone in back of Rim Adams said, "I hadn't heard he was in town. Thought he was out in Kansas somewhere—maybe scouting for the military...."

Despite the lowcrowned, roundbrimmed hat, the long coat and frilled white shirtfront, anyone would surely have known another milieu better suited this man. It showed in the swing and set of his shoulders; in the prowling movement—toes in, knees slightly sprung—that seemed more fitting to moccasins than to high-polished, bench-fitted boots. Rim Adams looked at the lean waist, wondering if that coat concealed the famous pearl-handled presentation Colts—the gift, he had read somewhere, of a big wheel in the Union Pacific organization in recognition of end-of-track hells this man had tamed all the way from Omaha to Promontory Point.

The house man said, "Shoot the dice, kid, or pass them on. You're holding up this game!"

Keyhoe had disappeared among the crowd at the bar, Adams turned back to the table and the impatient players. He shook the dice and let them go, with a snap of the wrist that sent them flashing down the cloth and bouncing against the table's deep rim. The house man's bored voice called his point.

It was a five. Somehow he was not at all surprised when, on the third roll, he made it. He pulled in his winnings, tried again and rolled a seven. Then

5

again, for a ten that he made almost immediately.

In a matter of minutes he knew his hunch was right, and the dice were going for him. The rest of the table soon began to know it, too. By now the man in the plug hat was riding with him, sweating and shouting as he urged him on, both fists full of crumpled bills; the electricity of a winning streak began to sweep the platform, and already players were leaving their own games to crowd around and watch the young fellow make point after point.

Rim Adams had had lucky streaks before, and he knew better than to trust this one too far. Suddenly, from feeling right it began to feel wrong. The low ceiling of the room seemed to press too close over his head, the cone of lamplight above the table was too blinding, the crowd too oppressive. He felt he would strangle on tobacco smoke—if the bearded man bawling in his ear didn't deafen him first.

Quietly he laid down the dice, "gathered in the bills that lay in a drift before him. "That's enough," he said, and turned to leave.

They didn't want that. Hands caught and pushed him back to the table, angry voices protested. Still he shook his head, doggedly, until someone at last exclaimed, "Let him alone, then. He's smart enough to know when they've cooled off for him. That ended it. The wall of bodies separated and he shouldered free.

He didn't know how much he had in his pockets but he judged it close to four or five hundred—more money than he had ever owned. It would do.

As he started down the steps to the bar area, his two companions at the table—the man with the beard, and the consumptive—fell in step on either side of him. The bearded one showed his angry frustration—plug hat pushed back, cheeks shining

6

with sweat above the tangle of whiskers. He thought Rim Adams had quit too soon, just when he might have made a killing for both of them. But apparently seeing his argument had no effect, the fellow quickly changed his manner; by the time ·they reached the bar he was laughing and slapping the young man's shoulder in friendly fashion, as he signaled the bartender for drinks.

Rim Adams took the drink but put down his own money to pay for it. Irritated, he first made an easy movement that dislodged the hand from his shoulder. When it promptly returned, he simply reached up, took the wrist and slammed it down, hard, upon the counter.

"I'm no friend of yours," he said coldly. "Go find somebody else with a lucky streak to ride with."

The other's face went tight and red; a gust of breath, sour with the whiskey he had drunk, burst from his bearded lips. But he seemed to decide not to push matters for he merely scowled and, after a moment, shrugged and turned away; the crowd swallowed him.

The consumptive had already vanished somewhere. But looking into the bar mirror Adams discovered a pair of cold eyes reflected there, resting on him: Frank Keyhoe, it appeared, had been watching. At first a little startled, and then made bold by his attention, Adams picked up the bar bottle and slid it along the counter until they were face to face.

The gunfighter, he could see now, stood some five inches taller than himself. Beneath the predatory beak of a nose, and only partly disguised by the silken yellow mustache, Keyhoe's upper lip appeared curiously short—you might almost have thought it gave his face a look of petulance, if you missed the message in the amber-colored eyes. He had an empty glass beside him, a thin cheroot between his lips. A bar girl pressed close with his arm across her powdered shoulders.

Rim Adams said, "I'll buy you a drink, Mister Keyhoe."

The stare that considered him was entirely without friendliness. "Why?" the tall man said bluntly.

He frowned, suddenly less sure of himself. "Why, it would be my pleasure…"

The other canted his head, keeping Adams waiting while he considered the offer. At last, in a tone almost of contempt, he answered indifferently, "I guess not," and turned away, dismissing the stranger—just as Adams, in his turn, had brushed off the loud man in the plug hat.

Rim Adams could feel the heat beat up into his face, clear to the edge of his hairline. He saw the knowing leer the girl gave him, the tilt of amusement on her rouged lips; in his angry humiliation, the air of that place seemed all at once too thick to breathe. Needing escape, he turned and shouldered blindly through the crowd. The bouncer gave him the briefest glance as he pulled the big door open and went out of there, to blunder down the steep flight of stairs and into the cool obscurity of the street.

He was still too young—only twenty, plus a year or two—to have learned to take a rebuff and shrug it aside. This affront from Keyhoe had to be worked off; he walked it off, prowling the muddy streets, jostling and being jostled. Even the feel of the money in his pockets meant very little to him now. He had been made a fool of, and he told himself he hated this Frank Keyhoe—a man he had been

8

prepared to admire.

Still brimming with furious energy, he climbed a hill and turned and without warning found himself standing upon a point of bluff, with the Missouri bottoms spread before him. Abruptly, he caught his breath as he saw the river under the moon.

The streets of the city ran steeply down to the water's edge, where the riding lanterns of a couple of sternwheelers made oily reflections. For the rest, there was deep moon-shadow and the bright mesh of stars overhead. A night wind brought him the river's dark scent.

He forgot Frank Keyhoe, forgot the smirk of the girl in the gambling house, as he was caught up once again in thought of the untamed land stretching westward. The plains: He had never seen them, but the very word could conjure pictures of emptiness and distance, of burning sun and steady wind and the pull of the unknown that drew at his imagination....

Suddenly he realized he was not alone here.

A clumsy scrape of bootleather against a stone brought his head around; immediately he was turning, with the alarm bells beating high inside, to discover the pair who had come almost upon him. There were no lighted buildings along this section of the bluff, but by moonglow he recognized them even before one spoke with a familiar voice: "All right, kid. We'll take what you got in your pockets."

He made no answer. He set himself, watching them bulk nearer. "Hand it over," the voice said. "Don't give us any trouble..." Then, as they closed with him, he was suddenly lunging straight forward, a fist swinging.

It struck, sinking into the soft bulge of a waistcoat. There was a "grunt of surprise and pain and Rim Adams struck again, this time feeling wiry beard scrape his knuckles as the blow rocked the man's head, dislodging his plug hat. At the same moment he heard a muttered exclamation and a sound of metal sliding over cloth. Sweat broke out on him, for he knew that was a gun. He turned, and caught the faint gleam of starlight on the muzzle of a derringer.

Desperate, he went after it. With luck his fingers closed over a bony wrist; when he tried to twist it and force its owner to drop the gun, the consumptive's wasted frame was flung instead in a half circle, stumbling and scrambling over the stony ground, before his own momentum jerked him free from Adams' grasp. In the next breath the whole weight of the first attacker landed full upon the young man's shoulders and an elbow clamped about his throat.

His knees buckled. His head and shoulders bowed forward, and he thought his neck would snap when the one on his back rolled on over in a heavy, sprawling spin. Half strangled, Adams staggered and managed somehow to retain his feet. But now he felt the bearded man's hand pawing at his ankle, trying to pull him down. Adams deliberately kicked him in the jaw and ran over him, as he went searching for his remaining enemy—the one with the gun.

There wasn't any silhouette of him against the stars. Casting about, a little frantic, Rim Adams found his man then—almost tripped over him. The consumptive was down on hands and knees, crawling about over the rough ground as he emitted wheezing sounds of exertion and anxiety. It occurred to Adams the man must have lost his derringer and was hunting for it.

Just as he discovered the gun and pounced upon it, Adams got him by arm and coat collar and, without ceremony, yanked him up and simply flung him aside. Stooping and sweeping his hand in a half circle, Adams located the weapon himself and he straightened, holding it.

"On your feet!" he panted. "The pair of you—Or I might just try this thing and see how straight it shoots!"

When they realized he actually had the little gun, the fight left them. There was a hasty scramble, and they stood before him and he heard the bearded one exclaim breathily, "Take it easy, kid! We never hurt you—and damn if you didn't near break my jaw!"

"Good!" He added, "Now, maybe you'd better find out how far away you can be by the time I count to three…"

"One!" he gave them, and they turned, and bolted.

Adams stood listening to the frantic noise they made leaving the place; he was pretty sure he heard one of them trip and go sprawling and pick himself up again. After that the sounds faded, leaving only the strengthening night breeze that rattled dry brush along the edge of the bluff.

He was angry and shaking, but coming out on top filled him with a heady exhilaration as well. His toe touched something, it was his derby. He leaned for it, popped a dent out of the crown and placed it upon his head.

And then the nearby snap and flare of a sulfur match set him whirling, lifting the derringer. That time there had been no warning at all. With a startled exclamation he slowly lowered the gun, to stand watching the match flame glow on hawklike features as, behind cupped palms, Frank Keyhoe

11

calmly drew fire into the end of a cigar.

CHAPTER 2

Rim Adams said harshly, "That's a hell of a good way for a man to get himself shot!"

Keyhoe spoke between puffs of smoke. "I suppose." Satisfied with the way he had his cigar burning, he shook out the match and flipped it aside. After that there was only the moonlight, settling upon them and upon the river bottoms that spread away below the bluff where they stood.

The younger man's bewilderment was edged with sharp suspicion, and with resentment still over his rebuff earlier, at the bar. Gruffly he demanded, "What are you doing here?"

"Why, when I saw that pair leave right behind you, I had a hunch what they might be after. I knew you'd won quite a roll at the crap table. I followed them."

"To keep them from taking it? I can look out for myself!"

"So I noticed," Frank Keyhoe said, and added, "What would you say to a drink?"

"Maybe you'll remember," Adams reminded him stiffly, "I made you the same offer. You same as told me to go to hell!"

Keyhoe didn't pretend to deny it. "That was before," he pointed out blandly. He drew deep on cigar smoke, and the glow spread itself across his cheeks and struck faint pinpoints of light from the eyes that regarded the smaller man. "What do you call yourself?"

Rim Adams told him.

"That's an odd one."

"Rimmer," the young fellow explained shortly. "A family name. I don't like it much either."

"Where would you be from?"

"Easterly. Illinois, to begin with. Saint Looie, last stop—stevedoring on the levee."

"Ah. That's where you learned to shoot crap?"

"No, I picked that up in the army. But, manhandling cargo you learn to handle trouble. Like that pair that jumped me, just now."

"I'd say you learned well....I'll buy you that drink," Keyhoe added. "I imagine you could use one."

"I'm all right," Adam said gruffly. "But I'll take the drink...."

A few steps brought them again into the heart of town. Now that he had settled down after his fight with the pair on the bluff, Rim Adams could look on this man beside him and feel the full strangeness of crossing paths with someone like Frank Keyhoe. Stranger still, he had a feeling—as lights along the street showed him the chiseled features, the predatory carriage of the head with its tawny, flowing mane—that Keyhoe had some purpose that he would reveal in his own good time. For the moment he gave no hint of it, speaking but once and then only to say, "My hotel's about a block from here. We'll have a bottle sent up. A better place for a talk, than some saloon...."

The room was a good one, though impersonal as only a hotel room can be. Only a worn leather bag standing open on the bed, a razor and a few other articles on the washstand, carried the identity of its present occupant. The two men settled in comfortable chairs, with the opened bottle on the

13

table and the muted glow of the lamp lying upon them. Somewhere beyond and below a pair of curtained windows, that reached nearly from floor to high ceiling, lay the raucous Kansas City night.

Keyhoe held his glass between both palms and peered intently at his guest. "You were in the army," he said suddenly. "During the war, I suppose?"

"The last year of it. I was eighteen when I went in."

"You saw action?"

"Some—on the road to Richmond. Then all at once it was over. Too soon, almost."

Keyhoe nodded as though it were an old story to him. "I've run into a lot of you fellows: restless, not worth a damn to yourselves or anyone else. The war tore up your roots, and afterward you couldn't seem to get them set again..."

Adams corrected him. "I'd have been glad enough to settle—but I found out a lot of things can happen in a year. My pa had died, and my older brother had got married and took over the farm, and he made it clear there wasn't going to be any place for me. I guess he got into the habit of thinking I wouldn't be coming back, and by God he wasn't too pleased to see me when I did. Him or his wife, either." He shrugged. "So I let them have the place and I drifted. I'm still at it."

"After four years?" Keyhoe shook his head. "If you were serious about it, you should have found something by this time."

"Like what?"

"There's always the army..."

"No. No thanks! I never did learn to love them bugles, or the damn saluting, or getting up and setting down because somebody with gold on his shoulder straps tells you!"

14

"They've got a word for that," the other murmured dryly. "It's called 'discipline.' But maybe you never heard."

"You've made your opinion of me clear," Rim Adams retorted angrily. "I don't know why you're drinking with me!"

Frank Keyhoe didn't answer at once. He finished his glass and leaned to set it on the table. Doing so he moved full into the glare of the lamp and it brought out the windwhipped toughness of his cheek, the tiny net of wrinkles fanning out toward cheek and temple from the corner of his eye. Rim Adams found himself wondering at the age of this man. There was no trace at all of gray in the flow of hair that swept back toward his shoulders. But when you considered the legend—from the early years in the wild Colorado gold camps, through the time as Army scout and meat hunter and Yankee spy, and railroad trouble shooter since the war—it was hardly possible that could all have been crowded into less than forty years at the outside.

Settling back again into his chair, Keyhoe built tapered fingers into a steeple. He asked abruptly, "Ever hear of a place called Chase Center?"

Adams looked at him. "Am I supposed to have?"

"Perhaps not. It's a couple hundred miles west of here—the last station on the Kansas Pacific, which happens to make it the northern terminus of the Santa Fe trade. It's also a supply center for the buffalo hunters. Just at the moment the 11th Cavalry is stationed at Fort Chase, guarding the road."

"The 11th? Sutter's outfit?"

Keyhoe nodded. He didn't make a face, but somehow gave the impression without actually doing it. "Yes, that would be Colonel Jeff Sutter, all right. Remains to be seen how he takes to garrison

15

duty, after a winter spent chasing the Comanches all over West Texas: Not many headlines to be got, I'm afraid, holding down a railroad line in Kansas.

"Anyway, there's the setup at Chase Center. And it promises to be a rather lively summer, because the buffalo hunters and the military never did get along, and those Santa Fe bullwhackers have damned little respect for anybody. The town's decided it needs a law officer, a marshal to help keep things in line. They asked me."

Rim Adams commented, "Sounds like it's made for you."

"Yes, since they've agreed to my price. I have a problem, though. I've been looking around for the right person to take along as my chief deputy."

The stare of amber-colored eyes, directed at him, caused the young man's head to lift with a jerk. "You offering *me* the job?"

"Let's say I'm considering. I saw how you handled yourself against that pair tonight. They were really nothing much, of course; still, you kept your head and you showed up very well indeed. How are you with a hand gun?"

"Just fair, I guess. I generally hit close to what I aim at. With a rifle, I'm better."

"One thing I don't want, is the hardened kind of killer I could find hanging around any of these K.C. saloons. I'd much rather have a younger man, with quick reactions and flexible enough to learn my methods. The city will pay fifty a month. For the right man, I'll add twenty-five out of my own pocket."

Rim Adams considered, pale eyes narrowed. Seventy-five dollars a month was fabulous wages, for a young fellow who had lately been breaking his back on the St. Louis waterfront, at a stevedore's pay. The size of the money was fair warning, of course, of the size of the job that went with it. But he remembered the vague feelings of expectancy and invitation, that came as he stood up there on the dark bluff with the scent of the plains in the river wind. An omen, perhaps, telling him his destiny lay yonder?

"I'll take the job," he said.

He waited for the man to show some hint of satisfaction, but he was wrong. The look Frank Keyhoe gave him was unchanging, utterly without warmth. "You haven't been offered it yet. First, it's got to be understood that I'll take no insolence and no argument. Whoever serves under me, I guarantee will learn discipline—even if the army couldn't teach it to him. He'll take my orders, without question. He'll breathe when I tell him and stop when I say to!"

Rim Adams was on his feet, setting his glass on the table with a hand unsteadied by temper. "By God, maybe you figure to buy a man's soul for seventy-five dollars—and the chance to serve under Frank Keyhoe! Well, maybe I don't think it's all that great a privilege. From the minute you cut me dead, at that bar this evening, I had my doubts the two of us would ever get along!"

The seated man met his stare, calmly enough. "Suit yourself," he said. "It will have to be on my terms, or not at all. So if you've finished your drink, I won't keep you."

"Thanks!" Adams retorted. He got his battered derby off the table and strode to the door and dropped his hand upon the knob.

But there he hesitated.

Every instinct told him the smartest thing would be to open that door and walk out of it and not look

17

back. The man seated by the table was a legend, of course; but his legend was one of violence and Adams wasn't sure he wanted any part of it. And yet—he thought, with a downward twist of his mouth—just who was Rim Adams? Nobody at all, with no past and no real future. If he could go to Chase Center as the protégé of Frank Keyhoe, how could he afford to throw away such a chance, especially when blind fortune tossed it into his lap?

His hand fell from the doorknob; he turned back. From this angle, only Keyhoe's profile was visible as the gunfighter leaned to take bottle and glass from the table. Rim Adams drew a breath.

"All right...Your terms!"

Deliberately Keyhoe poured his drink and set down the bottle, as though indifferent or unaware of the other's presence. Anger heated up in Adams and his voice rose. "Damn it, did you hear me? I said I'll take your terms! I'm your man if you want me."

Slowly Keyhoe turned his head and peered at Adams for a long moment, without speaking. He took part of his drink, and touched the thumb of the hand that held the glass to a drooping mustache.

He nodded, then. "Very well," he said curtly. "Stay out of trouble, if you can, till morning. Get back here by seven o'clock. The train leaves an hour later. I mean to be on it."

"Seven o'clock," Rim Adams said, and nodded. It was settled as briefly as that.

CHAPTER 3

Up toward the front of the day coach some

enlisted men returning to duty at Fort Chase had an interminable poker game going, to the accompaniment of arguments that seemed always on the verge of breaking into violence. Rim Adams, dozing with hat tilted over his eyes, was roused from time to time by outbursts of guardroom language and by the swaying of the coach, that threw him off balance and started brake cords slapping against its creaking walls.

His fellow passengers were a sorry-looking lot. The civilians, bearded and roughly dressed, included one straggle-haired old fellow in buckskins whose face had weathered to the color of his leather shirt. Pipesmoke and the smells of tobacco juice and sweat mingled with pungent clouds from the engine, that swept from time to time through the open windows. A rifle leaned against nearly every seat.

Frank Keyhoe had warned that they could expect this trip to last a couple of days, since for some reason the Kansas Pacific didn't choose to run its trains at night and they would be laying over somewhere, probably at Ellsworth. Keyhoe had a bottle of whiskey, from which he now and then poured drinks for them both. He had also brought along a stack of newspapers and was reading through them; that hawklike profile, silhouetted against the window and, seemingly absorbed in a day-old Kansas City *Journal of Commerce,* appeared oblivious to everyone else in the car.

Yet even by now Rim Adams had learned that this new employer of his never for a moment let down his guard. In a man like Frank Keyhoe wariness was a learned reflex.

Looking past him through the window, Adams could watch the Kansas earth wheel by. For a considerable distance he'd been able to see no real difference from the country they'd left across the Missouri line. The train threaded a land of rolling hills and farms, dotted with prosperous-looking towns dating back a dozen years or more—some of them still raw, but others already boasting brick streets and solid blocks of business houses, and residences set behind iron pickets and shaded by maple and elm and catalpa trees.

But as the diamond-stacked engine pounded steadily westward, Kansas began to change. The hills leveled out; the timber became more scattered and the towns and the homestead holdings, with their crude log and sod houses, fewer and farther between. On either hand, beyond this shallow river bottom the railroad followed, the horizons opened out and fled toward the distance. Adams was beginning to see something more nearly resembling the plains that he had pictured....

In late afternoon the conductor came through calling yet another station: "Abilene, next..." Immediately Rim Adams stood, reaching for his derby—this was a place he had heard of, and he was curious to get a look at it. Frank Keyhoe glanced up, folded his newspaper and laid it aside. "Think I'll be getting off here myself, for a minute," he said. "A man needs to stretch the cramps out of his leg muscles."

A few mean-looking buildings slid past the windows, and a spread of empty stock pens. Brake shoes grabbed; they jerked to a halt beside a sorry-looking depot. Stepping down onto trackside cinders, Keyhoe explained the absence of activity: "It's early yet. Give Abilene another month, when the trail herds begin to arrive, and she'll put on a lively show for you—I was here for a week last summer, and I know. The Texas longhorn trade is

20

only a couple of years old but already it's big business, and it will get bigger as some of these other towns along the K.P. catch onto a good thing."

Rim Adams said nothing. He hardly knew what he had expected but he could see little enough in this collection of ramshackle buildings, scoured by sun and steady wind. As they stood there a stronger gust than usual came along, carrying a freight of blinding yellow dust and papers and cinders from the roadbed. It caught a young woman in the act of alighting from a buggy drawn up beside the station platform, and staggered her, making her clutch at hat and skirt while the grayhaired man who was helping her down seized her elbow.

The two men turned their backs to the stinging dust curtain and walked along the track a little distance, beside this train that consisted of the single day coach, a couple of freight cars and the express car and caboose. Rim Adams' companion pointed out the saloons and crude store buildings that lined the south side of the right of way.

"Texas Street. Anyway, that's what they call it, during shipping season; the rest of the year, it has some other name nobody ever remembers. After three months of eating trail dust, those Texas yahoos hit this town really loaded for bear. After all, less than four years ago most of them were in the Rebel army, shooting Yankees on sight—and these Kansas towns are full of Yankees. Once they get a few shots of busthead under their belts, the boys are liable to forget the war ever ended. They make Abilene lively!"

"Will we run into this, where we're headed?"

Keyhoe shook his head. "No trail crews, at Chase Center. The herds go where the buyers and the shipping pens are. Just now that means Abilene—

though there's a half dozen other places studying how to take the trade away from her."

"The devil! They all that anxious to have their towns torn to pieces?"

"Who thinks of that, when there's a profit to be had in Texas longhorns?" The tall man touched a finger to his silky mustache. "They'll just hire somebody like me, to come in and paste the pieces back together. Might be an interesting job, at that..."

The conductor's warning shout turned them back. Rim Adams saw the girl, again, saying hurried goodbye to the elderly couple who had brought her to the station. Traveling cloak over her arm and a couple of pieces of luggage at her feet, she embraced the woman warmly and gave the man a kiss on the cheek.

Adams caught a glimpse of a good figure and of light yellow hair beneath a bonnet that had a stuffed bird pinned to it; but she turned to mount the coach steps before he was near enough to see what her face looked like. As it would with any normal young fellow, this only served to intrigue him. The woman continued to fill his mind, after he'd returned his seat and they were rolling again.

The conductor had found her a place by herself, piling her luggage on the adjoining empty seat as a way to discourage strangers; but to Rim Adams watching from across the aisle, she appeared to be terrified. She could hardly help but be—all alone and surrounded by the smells, the loud male talk, the weapons leaning against the seats. She sat there with her face turned to the window as though too frightened of her surroundings to move.

He couldn't help wondering who she was, and what she was doing traveling by herself like this, and who would be waiting when she got there....

Every man on that car was aware of her, of course. Once he even caught Frank Keyhoe staring, above the folded page of his newspaper, while up forward the poker game appeared to have lost some of its interest. There was one big fellow in particular—not a soldier, but a redheaded civilian with massive shoulders and wind-whipped, ruddy features, that Adams judged most likely a muleskinner or a bullteam handler. He was an ugly one, with a lopsided jaw that looked as though it had been smashed by a shod hoof, or by some weapon in the hands of an adversary, and never mended properly. He had plopped himself down into a seat directly across the aisle from the girl where he eyed her openly—plainly it would take little to encourage him. But she took one uneasy glance and deliberately turned away again, and it gave Rim Adams considerable pleasure to see the way she cut him dead.

Finally his own curiosity got Adams onto his feet and sent him forward, through the swaying car, ostensibly to have a look at how the card game was coming. As he loomed above their seats the players glanced up, with the enlisted man's ready hostility for a civilian. One demanded, scowling, "Something you wanted, buster?"

"Just watching," he said, and braced himself with a hand against the wall.

"Maybe we don't like being watched!"

Adams only grinned at him, and casually turned his head for a first head-on look at the girl.

He had been prepared for disappointment, the way lonely men always are when they look at strange women. But she was pretty, remarkably so— he almost forgot where he was for a moment as he stared at the pale, heartshaped face, the handsome brow above a pair of wideset blue eyes…. Then suddenly someone in the car let out a yell. On the instant, men were scrambling to their feet, snatching rifles and hand guns; the girl was abruptly swallowed from sight in a headlong rush that jammed the narrow aisles.

Windows were run up, gunbarrels dropped across sills and began an enthusiastic banging. Leaning to look through the dirtstreaked glass beside him Rim Adams saw a band of running antelope, flowing and vanishing across a swell of land in the middle distance. Even when they were gone from sight the firing continued, until these men had had their fill of wasting lead and powder or else their guns were empty.

Adams was quite sure no one could have hoped to make a hit; but they turned back from their sport amid a slamming of windows and swearing and noisy chaffing:

"I got me one—I seen him kicking."

"Like hell you did!"

"You bastard, you call me a liar?"

The aisle finally emptied. And Rim Adams, who hadn't moved from where he stood, looking quickly to the girl.

She was staring up at a man who had halted to speak to her, smoking rifle in his hand. It was the redhead, and apparently he thought he had found an opening. As she drew away he simply leaned closer, letting an arm slide easily along the top of the seat. Adams swore under his breath and, without pausing to think what he was doing, started toward them.

Wading through the stink of burnt powder, he came squarely up against the big man and felt the woman's stare lift to him as he asked, with cold

24

politeness, "This your seat, friend?"

The luggage piled in it gave obvious proof that it wasn't. As the man jerked about, Rim Adams suggested, "If it ain't, maybe you'll move along and give me a chance to get to mine...."

The redhead slowly straightened. He was every bit as big as he'd looked, standing a good half head taller than Adams. He said, scowling, "I reckon you can get past, all right."

"I'd like it better," Adams told him, "if you were to quit blocking the aisle!"

"Maybe you'd like to try moving me!"

They stood confronted, shifting their weight to the sway of the car. The big man's battered face took on a leer of pure malice. Deliberately he lifted the flat of one huge palm against Rim Adams' chest and let it rest there.

Then the rear door of the coach opened, briefly, letting in a roar of sound and closing it away again. A brakeman came bustling through, on business of his own; coming up behind the redhead he said, "All right, gents. Do you mind? I have to get by you."

He would probably never know what he interrupted. For a moment longer the big redhead glowered at Adams and then, as a sudden lurch of the car flung him off balance, broke stance. That ended it. Adams drew aside and the man shrugged and bulled his way past, carrying the rifle, and dropped into a vacant seat.

The brakeman seemed to have got some wind of trouble. He frowned, looking at Adams. "Anything wrong, here?"

Rim Adams shook his head. "How soon do we hit Ellsworth?"

"Maybe another hour. We're running late as usual." The man hurried on, and Adams looked at

25

the girl and found the whole weight of her blue eyes resting on him; he read a solemn gratitude in the tentative smile that curved her lips.

He was afraid she might try to thank him, and hurriedly indicated the window. "Would you like that closed? It's a pretty strong wind."

She nodded. She wet her lower lip with the tip of her tongue. "If it isn't too much trouble..."

"No trouble at all."

He worried the stubborn window shut. The sun was dropping toward the horizon; dusk would soon be climbing out of the hollows to spread across this faintly rolling land. Rim Adams glanced anxiously toward the redhead but the latter showed no sign, just now, of wanting to pick up the thread of the encounter.

Breathing more easily he turned to the woman. "Another hour to Ellsworth. I understand we lay over there tonight. Should be a welcome break, anyway."

"Yes," she said.

As soon as the train jolted to a halt Adams had his belongings down off the overhead rack—a few purchases made in Kansas City, wrapped in brown paper—and was on his way across the aisle to help the woman with her own luggage; she gave him a long and faintly disturbing look, before thanking him with a smile. They stood aside to wait while the car emptied out. The redhead came by, jostling and swearing, and flung Adams a scowl but still no open challenge.

Then the young man caught sight of Frank Keyhoe and watched him prepare to disembark.

No question, there was a manner about this Keyhoe—an unhurried deliberateness in every move as he settled the hang of his coat precisely, and drew on the roundbrimmed hat, and reached down his worn leather bag from the rack above the seat. Watching the tall, straight figure make its way toward the door at the car's end, Adams heard the woman ask, "That man—didn't I see you with him?"

"Yes, ma'am," he answered as they started through the now deserted car. "You may have heard of him. His name's Frank Keyhoe."

She drew a quick breath. "Keyhoe!" Not the gunman, who's supposed to have killed so many men?"

"I suppose he's killed a few," Adams admitted. "But that doesn't need to make him a gunman, since it was all in line of duty. Just now he's on his way west to take a town marshal's job."

She looked into his face as he opened the door for her. "And are you traveling together?"

"That's right, ma'am. I work for him...."

At the foot of the iron steps they looked to see what they could of Ellsworth, in the rapidly settling dusk. What there was to the town sat well back on either side of the tracks, a few first lights blinking across a wide expanse of mud. Puddles left by recent rains reflected the blank, steel color of a fading sky.

Rim Adams asked, "Was someone to meet you?"

"I don't know a soul in Ellsworth." She sounded dubious and a little frightened. "I was told there'd be a hotel...."

A figure emerged from the shadows beside the coach. "It's yonder," Frank Keyhoe's voice told them.

Adams made out now the squat hulk of a building, with some of the men from the train straggling toward it. Keyhoe added dryly, "I've been

27

keeping an eye on your redheaded friend. He made for the nearest saloon. If you're lucky you might not be running into him right away."

Before there was a chance to stammer out any thanks, Keyhoe was gone, carrying the leather bag and moving off through the dusk in his easy, pantherish stride. So Rim Adams shoved his own parcel beneath his arm and picked up the woman's suitcase. He left her to manage the hatbox and a reticule and with his free hand he took her elbow, to help her across the mud toward the hotel.

It looked like even less, at a nearer view—a steep-roofed slab of a building, put together from raw and unplaned lumber. They entered past a silent clot of loafers gathered by the door, and Adams felt his companion tremble slightly as their stares followed her. Inside, the walls had been finished with canvas tacked directly to the unplastered boards. The forward end of the long, low-ceilinged room contained a bar and billiard layout; to the rear was a trestle table where men were busily wolfing food from china plates. A rough flight of steps led up to a loft where Rim Adams supposed the sleeping quarters would be.

The landlord, a beefy person with a black spitcurl plastered across his forehead, entered from the kitchen bringing a bowl of boiled potatoes and a platter of meat which he slapped down on the table. Afterwards he came waddling forward, rubbing his hands on his shirt. Adams asked, "Would you have a room for this young lady tonight?"

A glance raked her from head to foot, then lifted to her companion. "The two of you ain't together?"

Rim Adams answered hastily, "No."

This was accepted without comment. "Yeah, I got a room. Come along." As the landlord turned

28

abruptly away, the woman gave Adams a despairing look which he tried to answer with a smile of reassurance.

They had nearly reached the stairs when an argument broke out at the long table, a burst of foul profanity. At this the fat man stopped and whirled so quickly the woman nearly collided with him. "Shut that up, damn it!" he roared. "We got a lady present!" This did silence them for a moment. But the hubbub began to swell again as the three climbed the steep and creaking stairs.

The loft was low-roofed and nearly windowless, without light at the moment except for what fanned up the stairwell and through wide cracks between the floor boards. Rim Adams saw rows of army cots, as many as could be crowded into a space twenty feet square. Now the fat man opened a door in a partition at the head of the stairs and after he had found a lamp and got it lighted, ushered them inside.

"You couldn't do better than this!" he said grandly. "Nowhere in Ellsworth."

Rim Adams watched the woman look about her at the cramped and dingy space, the two sagging brass beds, the cheap dresser and chair. A raucous burst of laughter came up to them, hardly muffled at all by the intervening partitions. The door fastening—a single hook-and-eye—looked none too secure.

"How much do you intend to charge her?" Adams demanded.

The landlord was quickly belligerent. "I get three dollars a night for this room—in advance. Ain't my fault if she's got no other lady to split it with."

"I'm sure it will do nicely," the woman said, and opened her reticule.

As soon as his hamlike fist engulfed the money

29

she dug out for him, their host became genial enough. "Meals included, of course. Grub's on the table." He bowed himself out and they heard him easing his bulk down the steep staircase as though his feet hurt him.

Adams scowled at the wash of sound coming up the stairwell. "You don't want to have to face that crowd. Look! You stay here I'll fetch you up something...."

When he returned, minutes later, she opened to him as soon as she recognized his voice through the door. She had put aside the little hat with the bird, and had opened her bag and begun laying out the articles she would need for the night. She took the plates, looking askance at the watery potatoes and what Adams thought must be charred buffalo steaks. "It's all they have," he apologized. "I wish it was better."

"You're taking too much trouble on my account," she said seriously. "I really wish you wouldn't."

"No trouble at all." And having said that he stood for a long moment, observing what the warm patina of lamplight did to the face turned up to his.

She was really only a girl, certainly no older than himself. Her eyes were like a blue stain, above cheeks molded with a delicate hint of shadow that deepened when she smiled. The pale mass of her hair, freed from the pins that held the little hat in place, looked fine enough that a man might almost shove his hands deep into it and never feel a thing. Her voice was softly modulated, with a sound in it of education and breeding. In his lifetime Rim Adams had had few dealings with the sort of females who could be described as ladies, but most surely this girl was one of them.

He drew a breath, cracking the spell she placed on

30

him. Gruffly he said, "Keep your door on the hook, and you ought to be safe enough for the night. I was wondering, though, if you'd mind if I leave my stuff here with you? I don't see any other good place to store it."

He indicated the brown paper parcel he'd laid on one of the beds. "But of course," she said quickly. "It's the least I could do."

"Then, I'll bid you good evening." He touched a finger to the derby's brim, and would have turned to go except that a thought stopped him. "Maybe," he said, frowning, "there's something I'd do well to take with me...."

As she watched he turned back, undid the string and opened the bundle. From the center of it he drew a long-barreled Smith & Wesson. He tried not to see the look she gave him. Without comment he checked the loads and shoved the gun away behind the waistband of his trousers, dropped the skirt of his coat in front of it.

He said, "Good evening, ma'am," and went out closing the door behind him. A moment later he heard the hook slip into place.

CHAPTER 4

Downstairs, things were getting lively as night settled. In addition to its transient trade, this hotel and its bar evidently made a popular hangout for the locals—petty businessmen of the town, farmers in from the dugouts and soddies of homestead claims around Ellsworth. They were a noisy lot; and among them Adams saw Frank Keyhoe, looking as much at home in this place, and this company, as he had in more elegant surroundings back in Kansas City.

Rim Adams, working without enthusiasm on a meal of leathery buffalo steak and rank-flavored coffee, watched him use his cue with the same spare, unhurried grace that marked all his movements. Keyhoe was obviously enjoying himself, and the young fellow wondered again if he would ever really begin to know this man.

Finished eating, Adams went forward to the cheap plank bar and ordered a drink; it was poured out for him in a tumbler that didn't look as though it had been washed lately. A single taste of the terrible whiskey was enough—he might have got it down but he saw no point in risking it. While he was debating whether he was tired enough to try one of those cots in the loft, the street door opened on new arrivals, and Rim Adams stiffened at the sound of a voice he knew.

He didn't look around. Instead, with a cautious movement, he brought out the pistol from behind his belt and laid it on the bar, folding his other arm atop the gun and the hand that held it. And he stood like that, tensed and waiting.

At his back the voice broke off suddenly. "By God!" the man exclaimed. "Here's the sonofabitch, thought he could get tough with Harry Dowler!"

Slowly Rim Adams turned his head.

The big fellow had been drinking—the whiskey shine was in his eyes, and even a few shots of this Ellsworth busthead should be enough to put the fight-mad into him after their encounter on the train. He stood on spread legs; behind him, other men waited, grinning, to see what he would do to this stranger in the battered derby.

When the latter only stared at him, Harry

32

Dowler's face began to color, his eyes narrowed. "I'm talkin' to you, you sonofabitch!"

Adams said coldly, "I figure it's whatever you've drunk, that's doing the talking."

The heavy shoulders rolled forward; even under the coat and the thick wool shirt, you could almost see the muscles bulge and knot smoothly. "What you do with the little gal? Got her stashed away someplace, waiting for you?"

For the first time, Rim Adams felt a real sting of anger. "Keep your filth to yourself!"

"Why, I'll break your neck!" the big man roared, And he lunged forward.

Rim Adams, who hadn't moved up to now, simply dropped his free arm to his side and wheeled away, revealing his hand and wrist propped on the bar with the revolver centered on the redhead's thick chest. Dowler saw it and hauled up in midstride; behind him there was a yell and a scramble, and the big man was left to face the steady muzzle of the gun, alone.

All at once there was quiet in the room.

The click of billiard cues was the last sound to die—Adams' searching glance found Frank Keyhoe with stick in hand, watching, his hawklike features composed and showing nothing at all. In this heavy silence, Dowler looked into the unwavering bore of the six-shooter and his florid features lost a little of their color. A muscle twitched a time or two, in one cheek. He spoke a little thickly. "I ain't wearing my gun."

"That's good," Rim Adams said. "Because if you'd tried to touch it, I'd have killed you!"

He plainly meant just what he said. Harry Dowler's chest swelled and slowly his expression changed. The features turned sullen; the fury in his

33

stare seemed to withdraw behind a cautious film. "Shee-it!" he growled obscenely, and with a shake of his whole heavy torso wheeled about and elbowed a way through the crowd. The street door crashed shut behind him; the room began to come to life again.

But Rim Adams, taking his gun off-cock and shoving it behind his belt again, was shaking with anger and with tension. He thought he saw Frank Keyhoe's nod of approval for his manner of handling himself, but it failed to help; for his own part, he was far from happy at getting entangled with the big redhead. He had a dismal feeling he hadn't heard the last of this....

He lay wide awake on one of the bank of army cots, underneath the low loft roof, feeling the rickety building sway to the pummeling of a plains wind. It was a real wonder he, or the others he heard snoring in the darkness around him, should have been able to sleep at all with the racket from the barroom, that went on unabated though it must be close to midnight. Yet he knew he had been dozing when something roused him, something more than the hubbub of voices and trample of boots, below stairs.

Rim Adams lifted his head from the pillow he'd made for himself by wadding up his coat—the only part of his clothing he'd removed, except for his boots and his derby. Frowning, he sorted through the medley of sounds and tried to decide just what, in all that hubbub, could have waked him. Inevitably, then, he thought of the young woman in her cubbyhole beyond the thin partition; he sat up for a look in that direction. And had his answer.

Enough light filtered up the stairwell to show him the figure silhouetted there. He judged that the sound of someone climbing those steps must have failed to register at all on his half sleeping, half waking mind until the footsteps halted at a spot where no man had any business—in front of the girl's door, somehow, that had alerted him. Now, distinctly, he heard the knob squeak, turning under stealthy fingers. Cloth brushed wood as the man put his weight against the panel. When the door failed to open Adams heard a muffled curse.

His hand was shoved beneath his coat, hunting the gun he'd placed there. He touched the smooth wood of its handle but in trying to snatch it up he gave the weapon a push, instead, and it went over the edge of the cot and he heard it strike the floor.

Suddenly the man yonder was rattling the doorknob, lifting an angry voice that was thickened by the liquor he'd drunk: "All right, you yella-haired bitch! I know you're in there. You gonna open this, or do I got to take it off the hinges?" Rim Adams threw himself across the cot, groping over the dark floor and sweating when he failed to locate the gun. Around him, sleeping men were stirring and mouthing incoherent protests. And the drunk, getting no answer, cursed again and hurled himself bodily against the door.

It gave, with a rending sprig as it slammed wide he caught at the jamb on either side, to keep from being thrown off his feet. There was a single muffled scream of fright from the room beyond. But by this time Rim Adams, no longer bothering with the gun, was on his feet and charging weaponless across the low-roofed space, kicking empty cots aside when they got in his way. He reached the man in the doorway, grabbed him by a shoulder of his coat, and yanked him about with all the strength that fury could give to his arm.

35

Though drunk and unsteady on his feet, it still took that much to haul the bulk of the man out of the doorway. Adams knew already that the face he saw revealed in the faint wash of light up the stairway would belong to Harry Dowler. The redhead knew him in the same instant, and he wasn't too drunk to relish this chance at Adams. A roar of pleasure broke from him.

Rim Adams knew he had to get in the first blows. He set himself and put his whole weight into them, aimed directly at the man's jaw. Dowler's head rocked on his shoulders, and Adams stepped back and sledged him just above the belt buckle, trying for his wind. It felt like hitting a plank. He doubted he could last any time in a real fight with this man, yet at whatever cost he had to be kept out of that room. A smaller opponent could only try to stay out of his reach and keep him off balance, and hurt him if he could.

Circling away, stockinged feet sliding over splintered boards, he felt Dowler's hand descend on his arm and clamp there. He pulled free, to the sound of the shirtsleeve ripping, but his arm felt numb halfway to the shoulder.

All the sleepers in the loft were on their feet by now, insanely yelling, and the uproar spread quickly as rumor of the fight reached the floor below. Rim Adams, risking a glance toward the broken door, thought he saw the woman's face palely watching in the shadows beyond it. The look was a costly one because, while his head was turned, a fist came and took him on the ear and set his whole head ringing. He felt the stiffness start to go out of his knees. Shaking his head, he discovered that Dowler had kept pivoting to face him, and now the crouching hulk of the man was poised at the very top of the stairwell.

Scarcely thinking, Adams launched himself straight at the other with head lowered for a battering ram. He caught Harry Dowler squarely in the chest; Dowler's boot, reaching for purchase found only the breakoff of the top step and a shout came from him as he felt himself start to go. Adams, trying to catch his own balance; was helpless; Dowler grabbed for something to save himself, and his big hands clutched at his opponent. Thus when the redhead went tumbling backward down the stairs he carried Adams with him.

They hit hard and rolled to the bottom in a tangle. Rim Adams took a battering, and when they ended up found himself underneath, with the room and the wall lamps and the circle of yelling faces appearing to spin slowly around him. But if he was stunned, his adversary seemed for the moment at least as badly off. Moving with what seemed like infinite slowness, he disengaged himself and pulled free of the inert weight on top of him. This appeared to rouse Dowler and brought him struggling to his knees, as Adams got his feet under him.

Dowler took an erratic swipe which Adams easily backed away from. Groggy, the young fellow steadied himself against the wall a moment; then he waded forward and drove a bent knee squarely into Dowler's face. The redhead was thrown backward and went rolling, as the yelling crowd scattered. Rim Adams stalked after him. He watched the big man get his hands under him and push himself up on all fours, head hanging, blood dripping from his face.

And feeling no compassion at all Rim Adams clubbed him with both fists, as hard as he was able, across the exposed base of the skull. Harry Dowler collapsed full upon his face, and this time he did not move.

Breathing hard, Adams pushed hair back from his sweating forehead as the landlord came bursting through the crowd. "What the hell you trying to do—bust up my establishment?"

"Talk to *him*!" Adams retorted, pointing to the unconscious man sprawled at his feet. "He's the one kicked in the door, upstairs. How about it—you tell him the lady was in there?" The man turned redder, unable to deny it. Adams nodded grimly and blew on torn knuckles. "If he comes up those steps again I'll kill him. Or anyone else that gets the same idea!"

He glared around at them, too furious to care about the figure he made—in his sockfeet, the shirt half ripped off him. But he was just as pleased not to see Frank Keyhoe anywhere in the room. Somehow he had an idea his new boss disapproved of his involvement with the blond woman.

Leaving Harry Dowler for someone else to bother with, he turned and mounted the stairs again, shoving through the clot of men who had come crowding down them to see the end of the fight. He was short-tempered, sore and bruised from the fight and his tumble down the steps. The door at the top was closed, but a pencil line of light shone beneath. He made his way to his cot and this time hunted until he found the six-shooter; returning with it, he knocked lightly on the door casing.

The woman must have been listening just on the other side of it. He heard a sharp intake of breath and then she said, "Yes?" When he identified himself, she moved something she had propped against the broken door and opened it enough to let him slip through.

She was wearing a long nightdress and wrapper, and her hair was done in a single golden braid that lay across her breast. The lamp on the washstand showed the frightened pallor of her face; it laid both their shadows, grotesquely, across one wall and an angle of the slanted ceiling. Rim Adams saw the question in her eyes and spoke first, to reassure her.

"It's all right. I don't think he'll be bothering you again, but just to play safe I want you to keep this for tonight."

She looked at the gun but made no move to touch it. With a trace of impatience he indicated the hook-and-eye catch that had been ripped loose. "There's no way at all now for you to lock this door," he pointed out. "I'll rest better if I know you're able to protect yourself."

At that, she nodded and took the heavy gun, holding it in both her hands. Her eyes sought his face, that was bleeding a little where a cheek had been scraped raw. "You're hurt!"

"No, ma'am. It wasn't anything. Don't worry about it."

"I don't know how to thank you. I don't even know your name!"

"It's Adams. Rim Adams."

"Thank you, Mr. Adams." She put out her hand. "I'm Caroline Sutter."

Adams showed his surprise. "Any relation to the colonel?"

"Only by marriage. His brother, Captain Tom Sutter, is my husband. I've been visiting relatives in Abilene; now I'm on my way to join the regiment at Fort Chase. I'd never been so far West before," she added, smiling a little wanly. "I'm afraid it shows...."

"Yes, ma'am...No, ma'am!" Dismayed, he heard himself stammering helplessly; her hand felt firm and strong in his own, but suddenly all he could see was the thing he had somehow missed before—the plain gold band, glinting on the hand that held the Smith & Wesson.

He could only hope he kept the shock from showing. He dropped her hand and reached for the door, saying gruffly, "Keep something propped against this, and I don't think you'll be bothered any more. I hope you'll get some rest. I understand the train pulls out early."

"Thank you," she said. "Thank you for everything, Mister Adams."

The door closed. He stood alone in the dark, feeling the Kansas wind pummel the creaking building, and numb with the knowledge he had let himself fall in love without bothering to learn that the woman happened to be the wife of another man!

CHAPTER 5

Caroline Sutter had thought Abilene bleak enough, and Ellsworth had seemed the very end of everything; but from her first disheartening glimpse through the coach window Chase Center seemed certain to pass them both. In the harsh and pitiless glare of prairie sunlight, there was no disguising its awful bleakness—no sign of a tree to soften it, no hint of green. She could only stare in dismay at a shapeless sprawl of raw, unpainted buildings, of tents and mud houses the color of the bare earth they'd been hewn from.

Then, a bleak clapboard station slid up alongside the halting train. She saw her tall husband and her sister-in-law waving from the platform, and she almost trembled with relief.

Which was probably foolish. After all, there'd been no more trouble after the nightmare scene in the hotel. When Rim Adams came to her room this morning to help her back aboard the train, she had been relieved to learn the redheaded man wouldn't be going on with them—she understood he was still laid up at Ellsworth, with a broken rib if nothing worse. And she had to admit, no one else had made any slightest move to bother her.

As for her champion—Rim Adams himself, that rather strange young man—he had had very little to say, after depositing her things and making certain she was comfortable. She was sure he'd avoided her—he'd sat beside Frank Keyhoe and hardly once taken his brooding stare from the landscape flowing past the window. And though she was probably naive, too recently married to have any real knowledge of men, some woman's instinct told her his attitude had changed in the moment she happened to mention the fact she had a husband.

Caroline didn't know whether to be angry, or embarrassed, or amused. Probably she ought to have told him sooner, but the thought had never occurred to her. Well, it didn't matter. She knew she could never be anything but grateful, for what he did that night in Ellsworth.

The train had lurched to a stop, now, and all thought of the stranger was forgotten as Tom Sutter came pushing his way along the crowded aisle. She saw his eager grin, the clean white of his teeth against the tanned and healthy face, and she lost something of the shyness that had all at once overwhelmed her. "My God, let me see you!" He seized her hands and swept her to her feet, and stood laughing down at her, admiring her with his eyes.

41

"Why you're prettier than the last time! A good sight prettier than that tintype you sent me away with!" He bent and kissed her, swiftly.

She flushed with pleasure. "You look awfully well yourself, Tom. Winter campaigning must have agreed with you."

"It was a picnic," he said, dismissing five months in the field with a shrug of his shoulders, that bore his silver captain's straps as only a Sutter could. "Is this all you have?" he added, turning to gather up her belongings. "Then let's get you off of here. Someone's waiting on the platform to see you."

Burdened with luggage he cleared a path for her, sharply ordering a pair of enlisted men out of the way. Stepping down to the platform Tom dropped her suitcase and gave her a hand off the iron step. And then Olivia Sutter was hurrying to embrace her and this time there was no awkwardness; for the two of them had been close, for years—whereas, when you thought about it, Caroline had only known her husband a little less than a month, altogether.

Goodness knew she had had plenty of chances to think about it lately, especially since starting the long trip West to join him. Theirs had been, she supposed, a whirlwind romance. Certainly it was romantic enough, the way it had happened—brother Tom accompanying Livy and the colonel on their visit to her family in Philadelphia, and the ball where Livy had introduced him to her oldest and dearest friend, Miss Caroline McCloud. She and Tom had made such handsome dancing partners, everyone said; and how really wonderful if two chums like Olivia and Caroline should find themselves married to brothers, with Tom an officer in the colonel's own cavalry regiment! The affair had developed so quickly—it had seemed so exactly the right thing, and her whole family had favored the match. Yet now she realized the man at her side was nothing but a handsome stranger, whose letters from the field during this past winter had been able to tell her scarcely anything about him....

The two girls hugged and kissed amid the bustle and noise of the station platform Livy, who was a little the taller, and dark where Caroline was fair, had wintered in Denver while the regiment was in the field; and so they, too, would have a great deal of news to catch up with. Just now there was time for no more than the most ordinary exchange—Livy saying, "Did you have a nice stay in Abilene?" and her friend countering, "It was so nice of you to meet the train. I was beginning to be afraid I wouldn't find anybody at the station."

"No danger of that," Tom Sutter answered quickly. "I wouldn't let any woman—any decent woman—show up alone in a burg like Chase Center! I'm afraid you have no notion what some of these Western towns can be like, my dear."

She thought of what had happened at Ellsworth, but said only, "I think perhaps I'm getting an idea...."

Tom signaled to a trooper who lounged against the station, nearby. He explained, "I've brought an ambulance from the fort. We'll get you there in grand style. But I'll tell you now—and I'm not joking about this, my dear: I want you to keep the curtains closed till we're through town."

Caroline looked at him. "What on earth for?"

"I'm serious! Chase Center's a good-enough place for a bunch of troopers to come in and blow off a little steam; but the less you see of it—and the less it sees of *you* the better I'll feel."

"It's a precaution we always take," Livy Sutter

43

put in quickly. "The officers' wives, I mean. We stay clear away unless it just can't be avoided."

"But aren't there any women in town at all?"

"Oh, yes. A few of the tradespeople have their wives here. Poor creatures, I feel sorry for them! As for the rest, those are all—well, you know— *women!*"

Caroline got her meaning and felt her whole face go warm. Livy rattled on irrepressibly: "Oh, it's really a terrible place. To make it worse, the people here seem to have it in for soldiers, and so when our boys come into town there's almost certain to be trouble. Colonel Mackey, the fort commander, would like to bring in his troops and enforce law and order, but though it's only two miles from the post he has no authority. Nor has anyone else."

Caroline's attention had been drawn, just then, to three men who stood some distance along the platform: Frank Keyhoe, talking to a man she didn't know, while the young man who called himself Rim Adams stood silently listening. She remembered now something Adams had told her last evening, without its quite registering at the time; it made her exclaim, "I think perhaps you're wrong. This is the last town along the railroad line?" When Livy nodded she went on, "Then, from what I heard, they're going to have a town marshal. And if I'm not mistaken, that's the man."

They both turned to look as she pointed. She heard a muttered exclamation from her husband. "Keyhoe!"

Livy said, "Why, it is, isn't it!"

"Do you know him?"

"I suppose everyone's at least heard of Frank Keyhoe. But as a matter of fact, I do know him. He's scouted for my husband, in the field. I've heard

44

Jeff speak very well of his services."

"He did his job." Tom Sutter was frowning, sounding less than enthusiastic. "But the man's a braggart and a headline seeker. I don't look forward to dealing with him as the town law."

Livy asked, "You knew he was coming here?"

"I knew he'd been asked. And that's Timberlake he's talking to—one of the local bigwigs, runs a warehouse and a freighting outfit. So, I guess we've got him, all right. I don't know the other man."

"The young man's name is Adams," Caroline said. "He told me, on the train, he'd be working for Mister Keyhoe. Tom, I'd like you to meet him. He did me a real kindness, when I needed help."

"Good for him!" her husband said. "But if he's studying to be another Frank Keyhoe, I can wait for an introduction!" He turned away, then, abruptly dismissing the subject. "I see Corporal Agard has the ambulance waiting. Let's be getting along...."

Caroline had never seen an army ambulance and felt a little strange at being asked to ride in one; she was reassured when it turned out to be simply a four-wheeled carriage, with canvas sides and a couple of mules between the shafts. Tom helped her and Livy in through the rear of the vehicle, piled her luggage after her, pulled the end canvas down and lashed it, and took his own place on the driver's seat beside the corporal. As the latter yelled his team into the harness, Livy caught her friend's hand and squeezed it.

"It will be *so* good having you here!" she whispered, almost fiercely, in a way that made Caroline turn to look at her in the stuffy darkness of the canvas siding. "For a woman, I mean," she added, laughing a little, "life in camp can be lonely sometimes. There's just one other officer's wife with

45

the regiment, and only a few more stationed at the fort. But, you wait and see—we'll have great fun, the two of us."

Caroline squeezed her hand in answer. "I'm sure of it. Haven't we always?" She added, "How far to where we're going?"

"The camp? Only a couple of miles. We'll be there in no time at all."

Apparently they had to go through town to reach it, and despite her husband's warning Caroline could not resist drawing back a section of the rolled-down canvas, for a glimpse of this Chase Center. She surely knew what to expect, after all, with Abilene and Ellsworth behind her.

It was worse than either.

Aside from the depot, and some big warehouses near the tracks, she saw hardly any solid buildings. Mostly they were tents, and crazy, patched-together structures of slab and canvas—mere shanties, with roofs that looked as though they had been made of flattened tin cans. Here and there the roofs were so near the ground she guessed they must have been set over dugouts scooped right out of the prairie hardpan; where stovepipes stuck through, it looked as though the earth itself were smoking. Half the buildings she was able to identify looked like saloons, and everything seemed to be scattered antigodlin fashion, with here and there a brief stretch of plank sidewalk crookedly flanking the wide and shapeless street.

But what really astonished Caroline was the numbers of men. They were everywhere—moving aimlessly about the street and in and out of buildings, or merely standing on sidewalk or stoop to watch as the ambulance rolled past. Every few yards, it seemed, her ears were assaulted by a fresh

46

wave of raucous sound pouring from the wide-open doors of a saloon, on one side of the street or the other. She saw a number of uniforms, but the men from the army post seemed to go always at least in pairs here—never alone.

She thought she didn't blame them. This was the toughest-looking assortment of humanity she had ever laid eyes on. She exclaimed, "Who *are* all these men?"

Her friend huddled nearer. "Isn't it frightening? Jeff says most are simply criminals, and army deserters and such, who follow the railroad and stop here because, for now, it's the end of the line—and then they simply stand around as though they were waiting for something to happen."

"But how do they live? What do they *do*?"

"Who knows! Steal from the teamsters and the buffalo hunters, I suppose; if nothing else, then from each other. You might not think so, but really, quite a lot of money goes through this place the railroad, you know, and the wagon outfits to Santa Fe. Then of course, there's the army post that helps keep the tradespeople going." She made a face, adding: "*And* the saloons, and the gambling halls, and—and, you know—the *houses!*"

As Caroline was trying to frame another question, a sudden commotion broke loose. She didn't actually see the fight start; there was a burst of yelling voices, and a clot of men split apart and revealed, briefly, the pair who rolled and grappled desperately in the dirt of the street. She caught a flash of sun on metal and knew it was a knifeblade, and felt the clogging of her breath.

Then the scene was lost and left behind. She had almost thought for a moment Tom would get down to stop the fighting, and was both relieved and then somehow just a little ashamed that he didn't. He was, after all, an officer. *Someone* in authority should step in to prevent such outrages, even if Chase Center wasn't Philadelphia!

The irrepressible Livy was saying, "By day it's usually fairly quiet. But hardly a night goes by without gunplay of some sort, and then we can hear it clear at camp. And our enlisted men *will* sneak past the sentries, after taps, and hike into town and get mixed up in the drinking, and the fighting. And sometimes, I'm afraid, even the killings...."

Listening to her friend rattle on, Caroline suddenly remembered that there was, in fact, authority here—that this was the inferno into which Frank Keyhoe was scheduled to descend, and try to bring about some kind of order. And then she thought of that young man, Rim Adams, following his chief into it; and all at once the picture gave her distress and made her shudder.

She was relieved when the last ramshackle building finally dropped away, and they were clear of the place.

Presently she saw a spread of low, fiat buildings ahead and decided that this must be the army post; she asked her friend and Livy nodded. "That's Fort Chase, all right; but we aren't stopping there. The 11th is camped along the creek, a little farther north. We're really much better off. The post is a miserable place—not a sign of shade, and even the married officers' quarters are most terribly cramped and uncomfortable. I've been inside them. I'll take my tent, any day."

"Will I be living in a tent?"

Livy smiled at her indulgently. "My dear, you're a soldier's wife now. There are some things you'll just have to learn about!"

In good time, then, the camp came in sight. The first thing Caroline noticed was a welcome contrast of cottonwoods in full leaf, breaking the monotonous, never-ending stretch of flat prairie; those trees, she assumed, marked the course of the creek. A moment later the road took a dip and showed her a whole little city of white canvas. The side curtains of the ambulance had been rolled up as soon as town was left behind, and she had an unobstructed view that, for a moment, left her a little breathless with the stir and novelty of it.

She looked at A-frame tents in neat rows, with men in blue uniforms moving through the company streets and smoke rising from the cook tents, and yonder the dust of mounted troops wheeling and turning in formation—at the walk, at the trot and the canter. The bawling commands of drill officers drifted faintly above the ruffle of shod hoofs on prairie sod. Tom had twisted about on the forward seat and he pointed out to her the corrals, the blacksmith tent where some of the fine, solid-colored cavalry mounts were being shod, the company commander's quarters facing the end of each street, the sutler's. A few more minutes brought them finally to a bend in the creek; and there, a little apart from the bustle of the camp itself, a separate cluster of canvas structures sat beneath tall cottonwoods, whose foliage flickered light and dark in the unceasing wash of the wind.

They drove past a tent of double size, formed of two fastened together with a tarpaulin over the entrance for a sort of porch, and halted a few yards farther on where an officer's wall tent stood alone. Livy spoke quickly, to forestall whatever comment her friend might have made. "This is yours. You can see it isn't as large as ours—after all, there has to be

49

some sort of protocol wherever the army is concerned, even when it's all in the family. But I saw to furnishing it myself, and I just know you and Tom will be perfectly comfortable."

"I'm sure we will," Caroline answered gamely. Then Tom was helping them both down, while the corporal saw to her luggage. Livy, still chattering brightly, raised the tent flap and ushered her friend inside.

The tent could not have measured more than ten by a dozen feet. A floor had been laid under it, of cottonwood boards that were already beginning to warp. There was a crude frame bunk that took up most of the room, a table that looked as though it had been knocked together by the same inexpert hand, a couple of camp chairs, a bench holding a tin washbasin and a bucket of water. "So it's a little cramped, and a little primitive," Livy Sutter said airily. "But, that's half the fun of camping. We'll all take our meals together, in the mess tent. I'll have Jeff see that a good, gentle horse is cut out for you, and the two of us will spend the summer riding. Oh, we're going to have great times!"

Such rattle-brained enthusiasm was infectious, and Caroline could only smile agreement even while she scanned the sloping roof and ridgepole, and with half her mind wondered if some way could be managed for her to hang her things. Livy gave her a quick hug, and whirled to go. "Right now you'll want to get settled in—and get acquainted all over again with that husband of yours! I'll see you at dinner..."

Alone, Caroline dropped her reticule upon the table. The murmur of the creek came quite clearly, and the whisper of wind in cottonwood branches. A heavier gust struck the tent, shook the ridgepole faintly and sent a slapping ripple through the length of one canvas wall. Somehow, not until this moment—not during the long train ride West, not at Abilene, not even in that cubbyhole room in Ellsworth with the drunken teamster smashing his shoulder against a flimsy door—did she really feel the distance that separated her from the safe world of her upbringing, and all that had ever been familiar.

Slowly Caroline unpinned her hat and laid it aside. She was making half conscious motions toward tidying her hair when Tom ducked in beneath the entrance flap, carrying her bags. She let her arms fall; she stood there in the half light of the tent, with constantly moving tree shadows sliding over the canvas so close above her head, and looked at this stranger who was her husband.

If he felt any reticence it failed to show. At once her bags were on the floor and a stride carried him to her. He looked hungrily down into her face; his arms swept her up and his kiss was on her mouth, swift and demanding. Afterward he drew back a trifle so his sharp blue eyes could look into hers. "God!" he exclaimed, his voice gruff with feeling. "I've been wanting that!" And when she opened her lips, trying to find the words to answer, his mouth came on hers again.

With his arms tight about her and her breasts crushed against his tunic, she felt the stirring of her own response. But abruptly he released her, a flush spreading through her throat and cheeks, and her mouth feeling almost bruised, she looked at him and saw he was frowning.

"What—what is it?"

"This damned place." A lift of his shoulder, with the silver captain's bars, indicated the tent and its haphazard contents. "It's not exactly what I'd pictured as a setting for my wife!"

That he should feel this way, dispelled in a breath her own momentary disappointment. "Oh, don't think of that, Tom. We're young. Any place will do, for a start. The good things will seem even better, some day, simply because we can look back to our tent on a Kansas creekbank!"

"Maybe." She hadn't realized he was a man who could be thrown into so dark a mood, so quickly. "Sometimes I just think it's a damned poor and thankless business—soldiering. In the war, there was a chance of promotions; now, everybody's downgraded and stuck where he is. Unless you're lucky enough to have your staff job, or even a decent garrison post—worse yet, if you've got enemies, like Jeff has—then you see where you wind up: Shipped out to the back of nowhere, to be left there till you rot!"

"Tom!" She could only stare, shaking her head a little in bewilderment. Now that she thought of it, there had been hints of discontentment to darken the letters she'd had from him, during his winter in the field, but they had not prepared her for this. She felt suddenly inadequate. A wife was supposed to be able to say the things that bolstered her husband's spirit, when they were needed.

But then a wry smile broke across his face and he said, "Don't mind me! I'm just tired. And the sight of you, in this filthy camp and this dingy tent.... I promise to behave." He touched her cheek, and she tilted her head against his hand, returning his smile a bit uncertainly. After that they both turned, hearing someone approaching, and Colonel Jeff Sutter's cheerful call from outside the tent: "Hello! Anyone home?"

At Tom's answer, the flaps parted and his brother Jeff ducked inside. Seeing Caroline, he spoke her name and walked over and dropped both hands upon her shoulders. He had come directly from the field, this tall, soldierly figure who wore a colonel's insignia, yet he might have just dressed for parade: His tunic sat that squarely on his broad shoulders, with the fringes yellow buckskin gloves tucked behind the belt, and his broad campaign hat placed precisely atop the sweep of yellow hair that fell to his shoulders. When he bent to brush her cheek with the silky fullness of his mustache, a strong odor of horse overlay the other male smells—pipe tobacco and, perhaps, a touch of brandy.

Much as Caroline admired her brother-in-law, something about him made her uncomfortable. Partly of course it was the awe that she shared with everyone else, for this hero of the late terrible war— one of the youngest men ever to earn the rank of general, Grant's right arm who had stood at his side for the surrender of Appomattox. But there was more: a feeling, at times, that he never really showed himself but was off somewhere behind his eyes, hidden and secretly observing. The smile he gave her now did not really touch the cool blue stare that accompanied it.

But why would he not remain aloof—a man in his position, with so many lives dependent on him? A man, too, who had been so much the target of jealousy, of petty vindictiveness and treachery from those in high places: enemies in the War Department, enemies in the Indian Bureau, selfseekers who would lose no opportunity to bring down a better man if they were able....You couldn't look at him, so proud and erect and superior, without feeling respect for what he was and what he had done, even in moments when his manner perhaps put you off a little.

He turned from her now, dismissing some small remark of hers as though he never heard it. He told his brother, "I hate to drag you away at such a time, but this army still survives on paperwork. I need you at my tent. I promise not to keep you longer than half an hour."

Tom looked at his wife, with a helpless lift of a shoulder. She smiled and placed a hand on the arm of each man, saying lightly, "I really do want to clean up a bit, and put some of my things away—if I can find a place for them. So, don't let me interfere with the duties of the service."

"Spoken like a real army wife," the colonel said, with that smile that deepened a dimple in one dark cheek but failed somehow to touch his eyes. "You can have him back directly." He touched a finger to his hatbrim and abruptly turned to leave.

In the entrance she watched them stride away, talking, under the dappled shadows of the creekbank trees—these two brothers, so much alike in appearance, so different in personality. And then a troubling thought came to her, as she looked at Jeff Sutter's tall shape and the sweep of yellow mustache, and of unshorn curls that reached to the collar of his tunic. Why, yes, it was true! Allow for the uniform, and there was a superficial likeness to the man Rim Adams had pointed out to her in the railroad coach: Frank Keyhoe—the gunman.

Immediately she felt the disloyalty of it, and was ashamed. You could not possibly liken Colonel Jeff Sutter to some cold-eyed killer, even if there were writers for the lurid popular press who might be willing to make a hero out of Keyhoe. The two had nothing at all in common—not really. One was a dashing hero; the other, only a flamboyant, publicity-seeking killer. Surely that was plain to anyone.

She regretted terribly she'd even for a moment let the notion strike her...

CHAPTER 6

Asa Timberlake was not a big man—on the short side, actually; perhaps forty-five, with receding dark hair and a restless manner, and a trader's shrewd, quick glance. Rim Adams, at this first meeting, was not sure he was going to like him. But then, hard experience tended to make Adams more or less hostile to strangers.

When Keyhoe introduced his deputy, Timberlake gave him a probing stare to which he replied with a curt bob of the head. Adams was more interested, just then, in the sight of Caroline Sutter getting off the train; covertly he took a hard look at the tall fellow beside her, handsome in his blue tunic with the captain's shoulderstraps. It must be her husband. He found himself resenting the too-good looking and too-ready smile, and the hand that held the girl's arm too possessively. He watched them as long as he dared, knowing his emotion was plain and simple jealousy, and that he was letting himself act like a damn fool.

Pulling his attention back to things that concerned him, he heard Keyhoe answering a question from Timberlake: "Plenty of time later to see what the town looks like. First, I'd rather hear a few more details about this job—and I'd rather eat than do either. It was an early breakfast."

The trader nodded. "We'll go to my place. I can have something brought in...."

Timberlake had his headquarters near the depot, in one end of a rambling, unpainted slab warehouse, surrounded by stock pens and a wagon yard that was no more than an expanse of beaten dirt. So far Rim Adams had had scarcely more than a glimpse of Chase Center itself, and even that much was hardly encouraging. What buildings he saw looked no more substantial than some of the shebangs that the men of Grant's command used to throw together, for temporary shelters, on the long road to Richmond.

The smell of mule pens came through an open window into Timberlake's office, but he seemed used to it. The room contained only a battered rolltop desk, a few straight chairs, a set of wooden file cabinets, a bookkeeper's desk with a high stool in front of it. Here, a nearsighted clerk sat at the unending job of keeping his employer's accounts in order. This colorless man, with the colorless name of Jones, was ordered off his stool and sent for food; he went out staring over a shoulder at Frank Keyhoe, his eyes wide behind their thick lenses. As the door closed Timberlake laughed shortly.

"You can count on it now," he said, "it won't take more than ten minutes for the whole town to know Frank Keyhoe has arrived. I doubt anything else much has been talked about, around the bars and the dives, since the news got out we'd sent for you."

Keyhoe said dryly, "I suppose I'll be lucky, if they haven't cooked up some unpleasant kind of reception!"

At this Timberlake merely smiled, a brief tilted quirking of his lips. "If they have, I reckon you can handle it."

56

Keyhoe shrugged aside the compliment, if that was what it was. Freed from the confinement of the day coach, he seemed possessed of energy. Rim Adams stood by the door and watched him prowl the office, restlessly, one of those thin cheroots slanted between his jaws.

The freighter had taken an envelope from his pocket. "Your first month's pay."

Keyhoe took the envelope, glanced into it; Adams saw a flash of greenbacks. "No quibble at the price, you notice," the freighter continued. "The responsible citizens among us got together and pledged ourselves to meet your salary. We all know there has got to be some kind of order here, if anybody hopes to stay in business. That's understood by everybody—George Youngman of the mercantile, and Lew McCord who runs the Kansas House...."

The tall man gave Timberlake a sharp look. "McCord? Is he in town?"

"You know him?"

"He just had one of the wildest resort tents in Cheyenne, last year when it was end of track for the U.P.! Are you telling me *his* money's in this envelope? And he knows what it's for?"

"He was at the meeting when we voted hiring you. He offered no objection. And he chipped in with the rest."

Frank Keyhoe shrugged. "Interesting," he said with mild irony. "It happens I had something to do with his taking leave of Cheyenne, before he was really ready to. What's more, I'd have thought Chase Center must please him just about the way it is."

"He's doing well enough." The freighter didn't sound too pleased. "He's got the biggest layout in

57

town. He cuts his whiskey and I've heard his games are rigged. But he has a crew of bouncers who keep order, at least most of the time; and if my teamsters want to go in there and let McCord's housemen pick their pockets—they're grown men."

"Sounds like Lew McCord." Keyhoe slipped the money into a pocket. "I'm curious to know what he'll have to say to me, after nearly a year...." Looking at the man, Rim Adams couldn't tell if this turn of affairs might have bothered him a little.

A mule brayed raucously in one of the pens outside. A sound of hammering had been drifting through the window and now Asa Timberlake said, "Step over here, if you want to see whether we mean business."

In a vacant lot beyond the freight yard, a tiny, solid-looking building was going up amid a litter of sawdust and unused timbers. The hammering came from there. Rim Adams saw the bars set into the one visible opening, the heavy plank shutter hinged to fasten over it. "You see what we've been doing?" Timberlake said.

Keyhoe said, "Looks like you're building a jail."

It looked hardly adequate; Rim Adams had seen larger outhouses. As though he read the same thought in Keyhoe's eye, the freighter hastened to admit, "It ain't too big—but when it's done, there won't be a stouter lockup in the State of Kansas. See those timbers? Railroad ties! The Kansas Pacific agent gave us a rate—that was *his* contribution."

Frank Keyhoe pursed his lips, the cheroot rolling from one side of his mouth to the other; it left a faint stain of blue smoke which he batted away from his face, with a stroke of a hand. "All right," he said noncommittally. "We'll look at it later."

He turned from the window. "What about an

office for me?"

The other hesitated, rubbing a palm across cleanshaven jaws. "That's sort of a problem," he admitted. "Around here, anything you'd call office space is pretty much at a premium. As it happens, though, I've got considerable extra room. I was thinking we'd bring in a desk for you, put it in that corner by the window. And if there's anything else you need—"

"No." Frank Keyhoe chopped him off in midsentence. "I work out of your headquarters and it makes me your man—at least your enemies, and mine, are going to think so." He shook his head. "Either I have my own place, or this deal is off!"

Rim Adams saw the freighter's mouth tighten and his sallow cheeks take on spots of color. But he shrugged and said, "Very well. Something will be arranged...."

The clerk returned then, bearing a tray of food covered by a towel, and Keyhoe and Adams pulled up chairs to take their improvised meal off a corner of Timberlake's desk.

The restaurant food was poor enough, but Rim Adams was too hungry to notice. While they were eating, a stream of men began to pour through the office, come for a look at the notorious Frank Keyhoe. Word had been spreading, as the freighter predicted; in the next hour Rim Adams saw too many faces, and heard too many names that he quickly forgot but knew he would have to sort out and remember eventually. For among these were the important men of Chase Center, the men whose businesses and property it was going to be his job to help protect.

He noticed how Frank Keyhoe unobtrusively studied each one in turn. Keyhoe, he felt sure, would be tagging and filing every name and face away for reference, in some handy region of his mind. Yet, outwardly, he seemed hardly conscious of the stir he created, just by being there. He interrupted his eating only once—when someone suggested, "I guess we all know of one man you're looking forward to seeing again."

At this Keyhoe slowly lifted his head, perhaps thinking it was meant in reference to Lew McCord—by now it was clear that, whatever happened in Cheyenne, McCord intended making himself no part of any welcoming committee for the new marshal. But the speaker went on to explain: "Chase Center should figure it an honor, bein' host at the same time to two such famous men as Keyhoe and Colonel Jeff Sutter..."

Keyhoe looked into the china coffee cup he was stirring with a circular swirling motion. Only Rim Adams, seated next to him, could have caught the faint tightening at the corners of his mouth; but for Adams it wasn't the first hint that he really disliked hearing mention of the legendary colonel. Now, after the barest of hesitations, Frank Keyhoe said casually, "I suppose we'll be seeing something of each other." And he raised the cup and drank.

There was one narrow-shouldered, surly looking man called Bert Weld—owner, apparently, of the town's livery barn and feed business—who seemed to take exception to Rim Adams from the moment of hearing him introduced as Keyhoe's choice of a deputy. Mouth drawn down sourly beneath the horns of an untrimmed black mustache, he kept watching Adams, eyeing this unshaven young fellow in the crumpled suit; all at once the hostility came spilling out: "Deputy, huh? By God, I could hire a dozen like him—cheap—hanging onto the bar at

60

McCord's!"

In a sudden embarrassed silence, Rim Adams stiffened as the fork clattered to his plate. But Keyhoe answered, in a level and unemotional voice: "Let's have one thing straight. The terms I gave for coming here included a free hand in hiring whatever deputies I need. To do this job I'll hire them out of McCord's, if necessary!"

The livery owner turned pale. He was struggling for speech when another person—a quiet-mannered fellow whose trimmed brown beard was shot with gray—said mildly, "It seems to me, Bert, we have to have faith in the man we've hired. Unless we're ready to give him our confidence, there's not too much even Frank Keyhoe can do for us. You can see that."

Weld turned on him. "What I can see," he cried, and his voice shook, "is that we've already got killers swaggering around this town, acting like they own it. Does it make sense to go pinning badges on them?"

"That ain't what we're doing," someone protested.

Weld overrode him. "You like to bet? One of these days, you may remember who it was tried to warn you!" Words failed the man. He stood glaring about him, breathing shallowly; then bootleather squealed as he turned and strode out of there, the door slamming and trembling in its frame.

His going left a painful silence, broken only as the one with the graying whiskers—he was a storekeeper, named George Youngman—spoke in a low voice: "I'll have to apologize for Bert, Mister Keyhoe. He's kind of rabid where those saloon toughs are concerned; and it's understandable, seeing that a couple of them murdered his boy.

61

Happened just a month ago, on the street in front of his place of business, and he hasn't rightly got over it yet. The lad was only twelve years old...."

Despite his resentment, Rim Adams could only exclaim, "Hey—that's too damned bad!"

"It brought things to a head, at least. It was then we finally decided we'd have to take some kind of action."

A sulfur match snapped and sputtered as Asa Timberlake lit up a cigar. Through puffs of smoke the trader said gruffly, "The fool had himself to blame. He knew this town was no place to bring a family."

"An easy thing for you to say," Youngman snapped, turning on him, "since any town to you is nothing more than a place to do business; when the profits look better somewhere else, you'll move on. But to some of us, this is our town. We think there's a future here; we believe in it strong enough that we *have* brought our families. What's more, we're ready to fight for them both!"

Timberlake shrugged and shook out the match and dropped it into a wastebasket. "All right," he said calmly. "I never pretended to be anything but a businessman. And it looks to me our deal with Keyhoe is a business proposition. We agreed to his terms; now we stay out of his way and give him a chance to deliver. Your understanding, Mister Keyhoe?"

"Good as any," the latter said, laying down knife and fork and pushing aside his empty plate. "I'm ready to be sworn in."

There was a silence. The men of Chase Center looked at one another, almost as though the idea had never occurred to anyone. Finally Timberlake made answer, with a hint of wry humor pulling at a corner of his mouth. "That could be just a little problem," he admitted. "Seeing that we've got no mayor, and no other town officers, looks like there might not be anybody to administer an oath. No reason to let it bother us, though." He opened a drawer of his desk. "I ordered this from Kansas City. You may as well pin it on."

Metal winked brightly, and Frank Keyhoe caught it from the air—Rim Adams saw the shape of the brand new, nickeled badge. Keyhoe held it in his palm, as though weighing it. When at last he lifted his eyes they were completely cold.

"I've been waiting for someone to say it. The fact is, neither the badge nor the job mean anything, do they? This town of yours isn't even a town. And it isn't any law I've been asked to serve, but only the personal interests of a few men who can afford to pay my salary. Now, isn't that the real truth?"

They looked as though he had struck them. Asa Timberlake took the cigar from his mouth, fumbled for speech, and could only shake his head. The shifting of somebody's boots sounded very loud in the quiet.

Then, passing a hand over his neat, graying beard, George Youngman tried to give an answer. "It may look like the truth, Keyhoe, but it isn't—not quite. The men in this room would like nothing better than to see a legal government organized, with elected officers and a town council and a regular police force; but for now we can't hope to get them. The townsite's never even been plotted or filed: We haven't had the nerve to try it."

"We're opposed by the lawless element—and the people like Lew McCord who profit from it. And on the other hand there's the military, out at the fort, who'd like nothing better than to take over here and run the place under strict martial law. We have too much pride in our community to allow that. But as it is we're trapped in the middle of chaos. Something has to be done!"

"And I'm to do it?"

"We're hoping you'll try. One thing must be understood, though. The fact that we pay your salary, doesn't mean anyone in this room expects special favors."

Another man took it up. "There's settlers pushing out into this part of Kansas. We'd like them to settle here. We'd like to see homesteaders bringing their wives and kids in, of a Saturday, to do their shopping. But unless the town is somehow brought to heel, it will never happen that way. We'll die on the vine, waiting."

"Not asking much, are you?" Frank Keyhoe said dryly.

"We're asking what we think you can offer," George Youngman replied. "Including a reputation that should make some of the wild ones stop and think twice. I promise you, if we hadn't felt certain you were the man, we'd never have put our money on you!"

Keyhoe tilted his chair back and looked at the lot of them; and Rim Adams found himself thinking, *After an appeal like that, surely pride and vanity will force him to agree!*

For himself he was wishing suddenly, and mightily, the tall man would simply tell them no! There was every excuse: The job had been misrepresented; it was turning out a far different matter from anything they had understood. A badge with no organized town government and no real authority behind it could be even worse than meaningless—it could be a handy target, for

64

anybody with a gun in his hand.

Surely Keyhoe would be justified to throw it back in Asa Timberlake's face and walk out. Yet even as Adams watched him and waited, hopefully, he knew that if Frank Keyhoe stayed then he would have no choice, either, but to try and see it to a finish....

Deliberately Keyhoe flipped the bit of metal into the air, caught it again. Then, all in the same movement, he dropped it into a pocket of his waistcoat as the front legs of his chair came down and he eased, with effortless motion, to his feet. He looked at these people and he said, "Gentlemen, I'll have to look around, and get the size of things. I'll give you my answer by morning."

They would have to be satisfied with that. And so, for now, would Adams.

CHAPTER 7

Seated on the bet in George Youngman's spare room, Rim Adams watched Keyhoe make his preparations.

Youngman had turned this room over for the new marshal's use, there being nothing in Chase Center fit to be called a hotel; and Adams would have to double up with his chief until an office could be constructed, over by the jail—after which, he would have a cot and do his sleeping there. His own efforts at cleaning up from the train trip had been simple enough: a quick washup and a scraping of beard bristles, a clean shirt from his bundle. Since then he had been waiting, in growing ill-humor, as Keyhoe went through an elaborate ritual.

First, the soft, high-topped boots needed blacking. These finished and set aside, the man had washed and shaved and then dressed in fresh clothing from the skin out, including an embroidered waistcoat and a white linen shirt with frilled bosom and blood-red stones at the cuffs and down the front. Now he stood before the high bureau, working with a pair of stiff military brushes.

He seemed unable somehow to achieve the exact effect he wanted; he craned his head from side to side, lips pursed beneath the flowing mustache as he deliberated over each brush stroke. In anyone else, such pure vanity would have roused Adams' scorn; but in a way he sensed there was something more involved here. A man like Frank Keyhoe must feel he had to be concerned with impressions.

Keyhoe's eyes caught the other's, then, in the glass. He said coldly, "Something bothering you?"

"I guess I ain't any too happy," Adams conceded, "after that business at Timberlake's. What we're getting into here looks a little different, now we're on the ground."

"Perhaps you want to back out."

"Give the word and I'll back out in a minute! But I ain't going to quit on you."

Keyhoe continued for a long moment to study his reflected image. Finally, laying the brushes aside, he said briefly, "For the moment, we're only looking over the proposition. I told you."

"Yeah, you told me."

Beyond the window that was propped open on a stick, Chase Center lay quiet in the late warmth of afternoon; the steady plains wind that fingered the sleazy curtains brought with it a dry tang of dust, but no sound more ominous than the barking of a dog, the rhythmic creaking of a pump handle

66

somewhere. It might have been any small prairie town.

In silence Rim Adams watched Keyhoe open his bag and take from it a pair of leather scabbards, each wrapped in its own pliant belt, and containing a pearl-handled six-shooter with a barrel so long it extended below the holster's open end. With practiced movements Keyhoe slipped the belts about his waist and buckled them. Absorbed and deliberate of manner, he slid each gun in and out of its holster a time or two and spun the cylinder, worked the action of the hammer under a hard thumb.

This done, from the corner where it stood he took a bundle wrapped in oilcloth, which had been strapped to the side of his leather bag. Dropping this on the bed Keyhoe unrolled it to reveal an ugly-looking, double-barreled shotgun. He broke it, found a box of paper shells in the bag and slipped a couple beneath the hammer. He laid the weapon across Rim Adams' knees.

"You'll carry this," he said. "You'll walk on my left, a couple of paces to the rear so we neither one interfere with the other's line of vision. You'll listen for my orders and you'll obey them, absolutely and without question. That clear?"

Adams picked up the shotgun, handled it and sighted down the barrels. Lowering it again to his knees he nodded.

"Let's go, then."

Keyhoe took his coat from the back of a chair and slipped into it. His flatbrimmed hat went on, set just so and carefully adjusted; a last inspection in the speckled mirror seemed to satisfy him.

Adams, for his part, had his derby on his head and his coat buttoned over the Smith & Wesson thrust behind his waistband. Shotgun hung in the crook of an arm, he stood and waited until Keyhoe was quite ready and then, without a word, followed his chief from the room and down the stairs. In a dazzle of nearing sunset they emerged for their first real look at Chase Center.

George Youngman's steep-roofed, clapboard-sided box of a house, standing off by itself, was plainly a mansion by the town's standards. The place had no clear design to it. Aside from a tangle of foot paths and a few straggling wheel tracks, the only real street was the road leading northward from the railroad to the fort, a couple of miles away. Alongside this road—itself hardly more than an expanse of barren dirt wide enough that one of Asa Timberlake's freight rigs could have turned right around in the center of it—Chase Center had simply mushroomed into being. In wet weather, Adams judged that the street and the weedgrown spaces between buildings would be one huge, bottomless quagmire.

And it was here Frank Keyhoe made his way now with an easy, toed-in prowl, the swing of his hands just clearing the smooth leather of the two holsters, his stare constantly alert. From his own assigned place, at the tall man's left and a step behind him, Rim Adams had a clear sweep for the muzzle of the shotgun. The first five minutes he had felt just a trifle foolish, carrying it; but when he took a good look around him he was suddenly glad for the weapon he held slanted across his middle.

He could feel his nerves begin to stretch and tighten as their progress was marked by suspicious eyes, in a blank and hostile silence. Almost as though a signal preceded them, men came out of deadfall and gambling joint and dugout to stand and watch them pass. There were no women, and no children. Any businessman who had brought his family here—like George Youngman, and the unfortunate Bert Weld—probably laid down hard rules against their setting foot on this wild street unaccompanied. As for the kind of women you naturally might have expected to see, it was probably too early in the day for them.

It might be imagination, but in this hour of sunset Chase Center seemed to him almost to be holding its breath—waiting perhaps for Frank Keyhoe to make some move and show his hand, or merely for night to settle and the lid to blow off.

But Keyhoe never once hastened or slowed his steady pacing. His hawkish face was too disciplined to reveal any uneasiness; watching the lean profile, Adams saw only the firm tautness at the corner of the mouth, the passive line of the dark cheek, the restless eye. By the time he finished his tour, Adams was sure the man would know this street well enough that he could draw a map. And not only that, but label every deadfall and tent and dugout and shanty, northward from the railroad to a last low cluster of hovels—the town's cribs, likely enough, vying for a soldier's first attention as he arrived fresh from camp.

Four mounted troopers came jogging in now, horses' hooves raising a quick screen of dust that the ground wind scattered. Its gritty breath against Rim Adams' face made him squint and briefly duck his head, as he watched the blue clad men rein in before a broad, low-roofed sod building on the far side of the street. This was one of the few more or less substantial buildings that made up the heart of the town—if the town could be said to have one. Adams saw George Youngman's name on the sign above the warped wooden awning, probably the store did a fair business, selling supplies to the military and the freight outfits and the buffalo hunters.

He spat a few grains of dirt from between his teeth, and then turned, startled, as he heard Frank Keyhoe's name spoken in a tone that sounded like a challenge.

Watching the arriving troopers, Adams hadn't noticed the man who emerged from a nearby doorway, to stand with boots spread and hands in pockets and the blood-red glow of sunset striking squarely across his stocky, bareheaded figure. Frank Keyhoe, though, sounded not at all surprised. He said calmly, "Hello, McCord. I heard you were in town."

"Did you?"

Lew McCord nodded pleasantly. He looked about fifty. Perhaps he was one of those men who seem unable to wear clothes well, and so don't make the effort, for his boots were unpolished, his coat rough and worn, with leather patches at the elbow. His string tie hung askew. His face, with its carelessly trimmed fringe of beard, had a swarthy look to it that made the coal-black eyes look even darker.

There was no gun in evidence, but Adams thought a shiny place on the right leg of his trousers showed considerable wear.

McCord's place was big but it looked temporary, something like a long, unpainted shed with a high false front and a double glass door, both wings standing wide open. "How's business?" Frank Keyhoe asked.

The other lifted a shoulder. "I get my share."

"I'm sure you do."

McCord's dead stare touched Adams briefly and

dismissed him leaving him with a cold thrill of dislike as it returned again to the tall man. "Maybe you'd care to step inside for a look around?"

"Are you inviting me?" Keyhoe asked, in evident surprise. The other man, smirking, stood back to make room and Adams followed them both inside, but he kept a nervous grip on the shotgun.

He could find little resemblance to that other gambling hall, in Kansas City. Here there was no crystal, no carpeting, no red velvet—nothing except a cheap-looking bar against one wall and of course the usual equipment for winning and losing money: ranks of card tables, dice and roulette, and at the back a gaudily painted wheel-of-fortune. The bare floorboards were covered with sand; the chandeliers consisted of a couple of wagon wheels with coal oil lamps, as yet unlighted, set around the rims. The sinking sun's level rays, reaching through the street door and almost to the back wall, filled the place with a ruddy glow laced with blue drifts of tobacco smoke.

Among the customers scattered through the long room, Adams saw a sprinkling of soldiers, and others he judged to be teamsters off the Santa Fe road with pay in their pockets, buffalo hunters and perhaps a hide buyer or two, and a few who had the cool efficient smoothness of professionals. Probably you had a good stake in your pocket, to begin with, or you knew better than to buck the games in Lew McCord's Kansas House.

Its owner said, "I figure things should pick up, in a week or two. Construction's bogged down on the Kansas Pacific, somewhere near the Colorado line; but once they get rolling again, we'll have the gandy dancers in from end of track again on payday."

"Still a far cry from Cheyenne," Keyhoe observed

71

pleasantly.

McCord's expression changed subtly, became ugly. "There'll never be another Cheyenne—or another operation the likes of the U.P.! A whole army of track-laying Irish rolling through that camp, night after night, with more money than they'd any of them ever had in their jeans before! No—that was the chance for a man to make a killing...."

He lifted his shoulders in a shrug; but Rim Adams, knowing the story—knowing it was Keyhoe who had run this man out of Cheyenne, and prevented him making the killing he had wanted—could feel the discord here. Between these two, the air almost vibrated with McCord's sour and rankling dislike.

The man went on, "I figure this town will do for a year or so—probably no longer."

Keyhoe said, "There's some wouldn't agree with you."

"You've been talking to Youngman." The resort owner let a sneer spread his upper lip. "The man's a fool! He thinks the farmers are going to come in and save his town for him. Farm this prairie hardpan? They'll starve trying it! There's talk," he added, "of a new line to be built south of us, from the river clear to Santa Fe. That should kill the place dead."

"It's possible," Keyhoe admitted. A solid-looking roulette table stood prominently at the front of the room, not in play at the moment. As he spoke he sauntered over and idly took the ball from the wheel. He said, "Meanwhile, I guess you can be counted on to do your bit to help."

"Me! Help this town?"

"Help kill it, I meant," Frank Keyhoe corrected him.

The other's dark look narrowed. Keyhoe flipped

72

the ball in his palm and caught it again; but when he reached as though to give the wheel a spin, a sharp word from McCord stopped him: "Keep your hands off, Keyhoe! I have a rule, nobody but the houseman touches that wheel!"

Deliberately Keyhoe looked at him. "What are you afraid of—that I'm looking for a brake? Or, that I might find one?"

The blood pulsed into McCord's face. Into the breathless stillness that held the room he said, in a voice that shook slightly, "You're pressing pretty hard!"

Keyhoe regarded him for a moment. Then, tossing the ball again onto the slotted wheel where he had found it, he gave Rim Adams a summoning nod.

They had started for the door when a word from the resort owner stopped them. "Not yet, Keyhoe!" Plainly on his guard, the latter turned back. A trace of anger still showed in Lew McCord's face, but his voice was back under control. "I really can't have you walking out, before the house has had time to set up drinks for the new marshal and his deputy."

Rim Adams stared. If Keyhoe was puzzled he let nothing of it show; after a moment he shrugged slightly and said, "All right." In dead silence he walked across the rough and sanded floor, to pick up the glass the bartender filled for him. Uneasily, Rim Adams followed him over.

It was fine whiskey, obviously McCord's private stock. McCord watched while his guests drank. "What do you think of it?"

"Very good," Keyhoe said, setting down his glass.

"Glad you approve." And then McCord looked at the bartender and suddenly the iron was back in his voice. "From this moment, Frank Keyhoe is not to be served here! You understand, Keyhoe?" he went

73

on, bearing down. "This *ain't* Cheyenne—and what happened there won't happen a second time!

"I went along with sending for you, because the town can use some kind of civilian law as a counterweight to the pressure from the military. But your authority doesn't extend to Lew McCord's place. *I* keep order here, and I need no outside help!" A nod of his head pointed out something Rim Adams had already noticed—a pair of restless-eyed men who leaned against the wall on opposite sides of the long room, another man on a high lookout's stool with a shotgun resting across his knees. "From now on, Keyhoe, you stay out of my place of business!"

His declaration of war left McCord a trifle breathless, his eyes glittering, a faint moisture shining in the creases of his cheeks. Keyhoe took time answering; then he said, quietly enough, "You're wrong, Lew. I haven't said I'm going to take this job—but if I do, there'll be no exceptions made. None at all!"

And turning again to the bar he took the bottle from the staring house man's fingers and poured himself a second, forbidden shot of McCord's private whiskey. He tilted the bottle in invitation to Rim Adams, who hastily shook his head. Under McCord's baleful eye, Frank Keyhoe calmly lifted the glass to drink.

It was in that tense moment that the first, startling gunshot let loose on the street outside.

CHAPTER 8

Adams felt his own taut nerves bunch and leap, but Frank Keyhoe's control was admirable. With every eye on him, he showed no reaction as he brought the glass to his lips. Out in the street, where sunset hung like a red curtain, a voice cried thinly through the stillness: *"Keyhoe!"*

Head thrown back, the tall man took his drink deliberately, unhurrying. Adams searched the fine, hawkish profile but could read nothing in it.

The voice called again: *"Keyhoe, you dirty dog! You hear me?"*

As if for emphasis the gun fired twice more, the sounds of the shots mingling and dissipating, sopped up by the flat prairie that embraced the town. *"You heard that, I guess! Come out here and let's see if you're really ten foot tall!"*

The tall man set down his glass, brushed a knuckle across the full flow of his mustache. He turned his head and looked directly at the resort owner. "Some friend of yours, McCord?"

"None of my doing," the other answered quickly. "Sounds to me like someone who wants to take your measure. You could have expected that."

With the slightest of shrugs to settle the hang of the long-skirted coat, Keyhoe stepped away from the bar and now Rim Adams saw the look in the amber-colored eyes. It was an expression unlike any he had seen on the man before. The young fellow blurted, "You aren't figuring to—?"

"Stay on your toes," Frank Keyhoe ordered. "But if this is what it appears to be, I want you to keep out of it!"

The protest dying in his mouth, Adams dumbly nodded. Keyhoe, not waiting for an answer, had swung immediately toward the door; Rim Adams stirred himself to follow. During that moment there was no sound in the long room. But as they stepped outside, a racket of voices and scraping chairlegs and trampling rush of boots broke out in the room behind them.

Here on the street, too, there were plenty of witnesses. They seemed to cluster at every doorway and building corner, in an area flanking the stretch of roadway before the gambling hall, and there was a waiting eagerness about them. As for Keyhoe's challenger, however, it was hard at first to pick him out in the glare from the sinking sun that rested now, like a swollen drop of blood, on the very edge of the horizon.

Just opposite McCord's, a two storied building with a high false front blocked off the angry red glow—painted lettering identified this as the NOVELTY THEATER, but from the beer shields on either side of the door Adams suspected it was really some sort of dance hall and saloon. Now, in the shadow of this building, Adams saw the figure standing alone in the center of the street. "There he is!"

Keyhoe didn't act as if he heard. Adams nudged his elbow, pointing, and this time Keyhoe turned his head and nodded as he saw. Without haste, he touched the lapels of his coat and then ran his fingers downward, deftly flipping the skirts up and out of the way behind the jutting gun handles. That done, he let his hands fall easily to arm's length.

"I heard my name," he said, in a tone that carried without effort or emphasis. "I'm Keyhoe."

Having called him out, the challenger stood

76

frozen as though he could neither speak nor move. He stayed just as he was, even when Frank Keyhoe began walking toward him. Almost from habit, Rim Adams started to follow. At once, without looking at him, Keyhoe made a gesture of his left hand that reminded him of his orders. The young fellow held where he was, clutching the shotgun as he watched his chief move out into the street.

The other man stood waiting. With each step that brought Keyhoe nearer, he seemed to draw in a little on himself, his head to settle further between his shoulders, his knees to lose a little more of their stiffening. Actually he did not look like very much—in pants and jackboots, without hat or shirt, the sleeves of filthy longjohns rolled to his elbows. Once he turned his head, a jerky movement, as though looking for an escape. But he held his ground; and a half dozen paces away, Keyhoe halted.

"Well?" he demanded harshly. "How about it? Would you say I was tall enough?"

Still no answer. As though impatient of waiting, Frank Keyhoe began rapidly now to close the distance, deliberately giving his opponent a choice of using that gun, or backing away, or being brushed aside. And Rim Adams, his own view partly blocked by Keyhoe's back, never knew for certain what happened next.

He thought the other man panicked and tried to raise the gun. In a stride Keyhoe was upon him and with amazing quickness his own right-hand weapon left the holster. He didn't fire. His arm simply lifted and swung—a short and chopping motion; the thud of the gunbarrel connecting with the man's skull sounded distinctly. The challenger crumpled.

Everything seemed to happen in one instant then.

A small murmur of shocked sound broke from the bystanders. Against this, Rim Adams heard his own voice shouting, in quick alarm: *"Keyhoe! Watch out!"*

The shotgun leaped in his hands but with Keyhoe in the way he could not hope to use it; instead he ran out into the street, swinging wide in a frantic effort to get a clear shot at the figure he had glimpsed at a corner of the Novelty Theater. He felt his legs pumping, but everything seemed somehow frozen—his own futile lunge, and Keyhoe down on one knee now, and two pistol shots that mingled almost into one.

Yonder, at the corner of the big dance hall, a man slowly bent double and toppled to the ground; it seemed to take him forever to fall.

After that, time resumed its normal flow, and the street again took on sound and movement. Adams had no mind for any of it. Clutching his shotgun by the action, he reached Keyhoe who still knelt in the dust with forearm on bent knee, and smoke dribbling from the mouth of one of those silvered guns. Keyhoe ignored his stammered question. "Watch this one," he said crisply, indicating the man he had clubbed into unconsciousness.

The challenger was stirring, making feeble motions. Adams nodded and pointed the shotgun at the man's head; Keyhoe, rising to his feet, walked over for a look at the one his bullet had felled.

With the street beginning to come to life around them, Adams watched his chief use a boot toe to stir the limp body. Leaning, he picked up a gun and tossed it aside, afterward dropping his own gun into the scabbard as he turned and ordered, "Bring the other one over here."

Adams simply got a handful of the stinking,

78

sweat-rimed undershirt and hauled the prisoner to his feet, starting him toward the building corner where Keyhoe stood waiting. As he neared he became aware of a touch of color against the drabness of unpainted wood; what caused it, he saw now, were the bright dresses of some half dozen women who had come out of the dance hall and were lined along the porch, watching. Adams paid them little attention for he had just caught sight of the look on Frank Keyhoe's face. He caught his breath.

It was the face of a devil. The skin appeared as though stretched tight across the bones and there was a dead pallor beneath the weathered toughness, a cruelty in the eyes as Keyhoe took the prisoner and slammed his shoulders hard against the wall, letting his head snap back against the wood in a way that made Rim Adams wince.

"Look at your partner!" His voice held an edge of steel. "Go ahead—*look at him!*" Keyhoe's bullet had struck his victim squarely in the chest. The dead man's shirtfront was a mass of blood. His eyes were wide but they stared at nothing; his mouth, under a ragged mustache, gaped open, as in a soundless shout.

A moan broke from Keyhoe's prisoner and he started to double forward, a man about to be sick; but the tall man slammed his head back again, and terror must have jarred the sickness out of him. He faced his persecutor, and now he started to shake until his shoulders heaved, and the hands at the ends of his arms jerked like broken things.

"Do you know him?" Rim Adams asked.

Keyhoe's voice dripped with scorn. "Know him? I've known a thousand of him! Nobodies—all wanting to be killers if they could only find guts enough!" The grip on the prisoner's shoulder tightened until his face twisted with pain "What was the deal? You set me up, was that it? And then he shoots me when I'm not looking for it—and you both share the glory? Too bad. It's been tried on me before. It's never worked yet!"

The prisoners lips writhed, wordlessly. In utter contempt Keyhoe flung him aside, a thrust of his arm driving him stumbling to his knees. "Get away from me," he said. "Don't ever let me see you again!"

Breathing hoarsely, the would-be killer scrambled up and went running, to shoulder blindly against someone and then lose himself in the crowd. His gun lay forgotten in the dust where he had dropped it.

That crowd bothered Adams. Even now hardly a sound came from them, and he didn't know how to read their mood. Looking at them nervously, while the bloody glow of sunset died and the sky grew blank, he noticed Lew McCord. It seemed to him the resort owner appeared disappointed. Now McCord turned abruptly and strode back into his place of business, elbowing through the men who filled the doorway, and Adams forgot him as he heard Keyhoe speak.

The tall man was regarding him with something he could read only as cautious approval. "You did well," Frank Keyhoe said briefly. "I should have recognized the trick, and known there had to be a second one somewhere. I'm glad to see you kept your eyes open."

This, Adams suspected, was warm praise from a man like Keyhoe, and he felt a flush of pleasure begin to spread into his cheeks. But then he saw, for the first time, the ripped sleeve of Keyhoe's coat, and a smear of blood. "You've been hit!"

The other men nodded briefly. "So it would appear," he agreed, as though it were a matter of slight importance.

"You better have that looked at! Do you suppose there's anything like a doctor in this town? At least they'd have one at the fort...."

Someone said, "Nothing that boozer at the post could do for him, that can't be done here just as well.... Hello, Frank Keyhoe!"

They both turned, their eyes lifting. The woman coolly regarding them from the steps of the Novelty would have been worth looking at, almost anywhere; against this drab setting, she was a surprise to stop a man's breath. Her lowcut gown, of the same shade as her intricately piled, auburn hair, set off the flashing whiteness of bosom and bare arms, the striking contrast of bold black eyes and curved lips. She made the girls crowded behind her on the porch look like very little.

When Keyhoe made no answer she remarked, half smiling, "I guess I've been forgotten!"

The tall man, his eyes on her, answered with a hint of amusement in his tone. "Hardly forgotten, Belle. I'm just surprised. It's been a long time since Denver—and I had no idea you were even in town. You working here?"

"In this dive?" She indicated the dance hall with a scornful toss of her head. "You expect to find Belle Wadsworth working in a place like this? Hell, no—I just own it!"

"Congratulations," he remarked dryly.

"You'd better come in here and let me do something about that arm."

"I've got to dispose of this, first."

Belle Wadsworth looked at the body sprawled in

81

the weeds. "That's not your concern. Let the town bury him—the town's had lots of practice. You come along—your friend, too."

With the going of the sun, a swift prairie dusk was already beginning to creep across this flat land, and along the street the shadows were thickening; here and there a lamp already glowed behind an oiled paper window, or laid its smear of light across the canvas wall of a tent. By now the crowd in the street had broken up and was drifting away. With a nod for Adams to follow, Keyhoe walked around and up the broad steps where Belle Wadsworth and her girls waited for them.

Despite its name, the Novelty Theater was as Adams had guessed—a saloon and dance hall. It was a good deal more ornate layout than McCord's gambling dive, across the street. Here there were mirrors, and scrollwork on the backbar, and crimson window drapes. Booths and tables about the rim of the big hall were for private drinking. All that made the place a theater was a low platform at the far end, equipped with reflected candle footlights, a sketchy proscenium, a wrinkled canvas curtain with a forest scene and a waterfall crudely painted on it. Here too was a battered piano without a front, so he judged that must be where the musicians did their work.

At the moment the evening's business had not yet begun, but the bartender was at his place. The lamps in their wall sconces were already lighted and a crippled old man, snuffling with a cold, was working his way painfully around the dance floor scattering handfuls of powdered wax from a pail. Belle Wadsworth gave the swamper orders that sent him back to the kitchen, looking for hot water to be brought to her rooms. Afterward, singling out one of her troupe of girls she gave her a shove toward

82

Keyhoe's companion, saying, "Ruby, see that this young fellow gets a drink—I think he could use one. And be nice to him."

"Sure." Impudent and knowing eyes looked up at Adams, from a rather pinched but not unattractive little face. A gust of cheap perfume assailed him as a tiny paw of a hand slipped possessively into the crook of his elbow. "You just sit over here at the table, mister, and tell me about yourself; I'll fetch the drinks. I know we're going to get along!"

A trifle reluctant, Adams let himself be propelled where the girl wanted him to go. Once he shot a look of appeal at Keyhoe, but the latter appeared to have forgotten him; he was already following Belle up the stairway. Across the back of his left hand, trailing the banister, was a crimson trickle of blood from below his coatsleeve.

CHAPTER 9

The old swamper knocked at Belle Wadsworth's door, with the things she had ordered. She took them from him, and they talked for a moment, and he went snuffling away carrying Frank Keyhoe's coat. As she closed the door Keyhoe demanded, "Where's he taking that?"

"One of my girls is handy with needle and thread. She'll sponge out the bloodstains and fix that rip in the sleeve, so's you'd never know anything had happened."

To this he merely nodded, turning the glass of amber whiskey in his hand. Belle went on, "Jerry was telling me, somebody's already picked up that man you killed and carted him away. They told Jerry his name was Hopkins or Hoskins—something like that. I'll have him find out for sure."

"Don't bother."

"You don't even care enough to want to get their names straight?"

That got her an angry look. "Lay off, Belle!"

She went through a door into the bedroom adjoining, came back with a pair of scissors. To make room to work she moved aside the pitcher and basin and other things she had set upon the center table, and turned up the flame in the lamp. Its glow touched upon the polished surfaces of a room whose furnishings probably had no match in Chase Center—the clawfooted table, the comfortable chairs, the drop-leaf writing desk that held her business records. There was a carpet on the floor, drapes at the windows; the walls even had flowered paper, and there were cheap color prints in frames. Belle, seeing Keyhoe's appraising glance, had said simply, "I had it all hauled from Kansas City. I'm particular what I have around me to look at—even living in a hole like this one!"

Now, with scissors poised, she told him, "I'm sorry to have to do this to your shirt."

"Forget the shirt," he answered shortly, and deftly she clipped away the bloodsoaked sleeve at the shoulder. Some of its material had been driven into the wound by the bullet's force and was stuck in clotting blood, and her lips drew out thinly as she pulled the threads free. Keyhoe, for his part, gave no show of pain but, with his good elbow resting on the table, calmly lifted his glass and drank.

He sat patiently silent as she carefully washed the wound—the water in the basin quickly turning pink, pale but never flinching even when she treated it

84

with liniment, lacking better antiseptic, and bound it with clean white cloth she tore from what looked like an old bedsheet. The job done, Keyhoe stretched the arm out before him and flexed the fingers, and the woman said, "I wouldn't say it was serious at all. *That* time you were lucky!"

He watched her move about, clearing away. He poured another drink for himself from the decanter, then let it sit while he took out one of his cheroots and bit off an end. Belle returned in time to light a match and get the cigar going for him. She regarded him critically.

She said abruptly, "You've changed."

"How do you mean?"

"That, for one thing." She indicated the filled glass. "It'll be your third drink while you've been sitting there."

He looked at the glass, almost as though in surprise; but then he shrugged. "Man who's been shot in the arm deserves *some privileges.*"

"You had already been drinking before that happened—I could smell it on your breath. Yet in Denver, I never knew you to take anything more than a nightcap. Don't tell me you finally formed a taste for the stuff." Her eyes narrowed slightly. "Or—has it become something you need?"

Keyhoe raised his head and his stare rested on her, and at the ferocity she saw in it Belle Wadsworth closed her rouged lips firmly upon a sudden indrawn breath. She turned abruptly away, the full skirt whispering, and walked over to a side table where she opened a hinged wooden box and took out a tailor-made cigarette. She lit it for herself, and leaned her hips against the table while she looked at Keyhoe through the first drift of smoke.

He seemed to have got over his momentary flash

of anger. Changing the subject he commenced, "Looks as though business here was good enough."

"I make money," she answered shortly, a careless gesture of the cigarette drawing a blue line of smoke. "If I didn't there would be no excuse for staying in a place like this!"

"There are other places—real towns. You should be able to do as well in any of them."

"You think so? Take another look, Frank!"

She lifted her face into the full glare of the wall lamp, letting it fall pitilessly across the slight sagging of her cheek, and the lines at her throat and the corners of her mouth. "The best years are back there somewhere," she said, with a toss of her chin over one bare shoulder. "God knows I'd give nearly anything to see Chicago again—but, what would Chicago want with me? At best I'd be running some cheap house or other—and I haven't come to *that* yet! The Novelty is poor enough!"

Keyhoe suggested, "Ever thought of marriage?"

A stiffness went into her shoulders, a frigid coldness into her voice. "I've thought of it," she answered, her eyes squarely on his. "But the man I had in mind never asked me, and he never will. And that's spoiled the whole idea for me...."

He was the one to break gaze. He looked at the glass in his hand, lifted it to his lips and drained off what was left of his drink and set the glass aside. Down below, on the main floor of the building, the thump of a banjo and squeal of a concertina struck up suddenly. Belle Wadsworth seemed to shake herself free of a mood that had settled upon her; she stubbed out her cigarette and turned irritably away from Keyhoe, looked toward the window where dusk was thickening into full night.

"No—this is my world," she said. "Yours, too.

86

We're alike, the two of us. If we're lucky we both have some good years left, but there's no use fooling ourselves: We're going to spend them in towns just about like this one!"

"I don't admit that," Keyhoe said, and swung restlessly to his feet. "Chase Center is all right to make a stake—but I promise it won't be the end of the road for me!"

"No?" She turned back to him, her eyes flashing angry scorn. "And what about the stake you had a year ago—when you quit the railroad? Where did that go? Cards? Horses?"

"A man can have a setback," he retorted stiffly. "The next hand can bring it all to his side of the table again!"

"I see.... And meanwhile, you're back where you started! You'll pin on that cheap piece of metal the boys bought for you, and you'll go down there on the street and lay your life on the line against men like the pair who nearly did for you tonight!

"Don't look for any help from the men who brought you here," she added warning. "Youngman and Weld have no more guts than any other businessman. As for Asa Timberlake, his own yard boss is one of the leaders of the rough element—a redheaded tough named Harry Dowler."

"Ah!" Keyhoe murmured, one eyebrow lifting. "That name's familiar!" He went on coolly, "But it's too soon to start worrying. I haven't even said yet I'm taking the job."

"Don't lie to me! You're broke. You've got no choice but take it!"

"That would be my affair." But a subtle change came into the hawkish features. Keyhoe took the cheroot from his mouth, looked at it and laid it on the edge of the table. Then, deliberately, he walked

87

over to the woman. Looking boldly into her eyes he said, "I grant you there are things I didn't know about this town an hour ago, that make it suddenly a good deal more attractive."

His hands went to her shoulders and drew her to him, and his mouth came down on hers. She let him have his kiss, not really responding, her eyes open and completely without warmth. When he drew back, his hands still upon the soft flesh of her arms, she slowly shook her head.

"Damn you, Frank Keyhoe!" she said bitterly. "All you ever wanted from me was to use me and then walk out of my life again. I don't know why I have no more pride than to let you do it."

He made no attempt to answer; but when he drew her to him again she melted against him and her own hands came up and clutched, hard, at the wide shelf of his shoulders. As they kissed the sound of the instruments, and the tromp of feet on the waxed floor of the dance hall below, came to them through the flimsy building's timbers.

Rim Adams, seated in a booth with the girl called Ruby, was getting vaguely drunk. He knew he was, and knew he shouldn't; but the whiskey was good and he was in a poor mood after that scene at McCord's, and the killing in the street. When the girl tried to fill his glass still again, however, he put his hand over it and said gruffly, "I better quit now!"

His derby had fallen to the floor. He groped for it and laid it on the table, and ran the fingers of both hands through his stiff and tangled hair. The noisy voices and discordant music and thump of feet added to the confusion in his head. Ruby said hopefully, "You want to dance? Belle will get mad at me if I ain't doing my job."

88

"Belle said for you to be nice to me," Adams reminded her, speaking carefully because his tongue gave him some trouble. "I want you to sit here and keep my company. I don't suppose you really feel much like dancing."

"Oh, God, no!" she breathed. "Us girls are always dead on our feet by time the joint closes."

Adams looked at her more closely. She had tiny breasts and thin arms and a face of a gamin. "How old would you be, Ruby? Sixteen?"

It put her immediately on the defensive. "I'm old enough! Nobody's asking you to pry into my affairs, Mister Adams!"

"Never meant to," he answered, a little stiffly. "I was only trying to make talk."

"You know, it's kind of nice at that—havin' somebody want to talk to me," she admitted, her defenses dropping slightly. There was even a trace of wistfulness in her that she hadn't let show till then. "The men that come in here don't waste much time on talking. But, you just ain't too much like any of them!"

He let that go. "How does *she* treat you?"

"Belle? Oh, she's all right. She can be mean as hell sometimes; but then, she's got a lot on her mind, running a joint like this."

Adams started to ask how long the girl had been working here but decided against it. There was something appealing about this waif, but he didn't want to know any more about her than he already did.

The atmosphere of the big room was all at once thick and turgid with the trapped, daylong heat, and the increasing racket assaulting his ears made his head ache. A woman cried out sharply and something struck the end of their booth, hard enough to dislodge the shotgun he'd leaned there and send it sliding to the floor. Adams grabbed it up and piled to his feet, but whatever the trouble was it had already subsided. The walls seemed to reel slightly and he clutched at the table's edge.

Ruby said, "You going someplace?"

"Air's bad in here," he mumbled. "If Keyhoe comes looking for me, tell him—" He broke off, for he saw the gunfighter descending the steps from the upper story.

Keyhoe had on his mended coat and there was no sign of blood; one would scarcely have guessed he had taken a slice from a bullet, less than an hour ago. When he spotted Adams and came walking toward him, the latter saw what was pinned to the front of his coat. The sight was enough to sober him instantly.

He said, "So I guess you've made up your mind? We're taking this job?"

Keyhoe glanced down at the nickeled badge. His cold stare probed the younger man's. "I asked you once before: Do you want out of it?"

"And I told you before—it's your decision."

Keyhoe nodded shortly. "Then I'll tell Youngman and his friends we start work in the morning." His stare settled on the girl, Ruby; when it swung back to Adams it held an edge of speculation. "I'm turning in early. I suggest you do the same. It may be the last good night's sleep you'll be getting for a while."

Adams was already reaching for his derby and his shotgun. "Wait for me," he grunted. "I've seen enough of this town for one day." They were outside in starry darkness before he remembered, with a twinge of guilt at his rudeness, that he had not bothered to say goodnight to the girl.

CHAPTER 10

For a day and a night, Chase Center had lain strangely quiet under Frank Keyhoe's brand of personal rule. To Rim Adams—carrying the shotgun at the marshal's elbow as they made their regular tour of the long street—the strain of waiting for things to erupt seemed hardly bearable; but so far he could only describe the atmosphere of the place as a kind of armed truce. It must have been the killing, that first evening in front of the Novelty, that did it. The town hadn't yet thrown off the shock of seeing Keyhoe stand up to two would-be murderers and put them down. Like Adams himself, it seemed to hold its breath.

On that first day, the only threat of open violence came in late afternoon when an outfit of buffalo hunters—in to pick up supplies at Youngman's—ran afoul of some Santa Fe teamsters and instantly squared away for trouble. At the crucial moment, Frank Keyhoe appeared as though from nowhere and, shouldering into the knot of angry men, simply broke it apart. Rim Adams, with shotgun clutched in sweaty palms, thought that time the explosion had really come; but the magic of Keyhoe had its effect—though perhaps the ugly warning of the shotgun's double snout had some share in it, too. In any case the explosion didn't quite take spark; the crowd that had been a threat of danger sullenly let itself be split and scattered.

Afterward, walking away from the scene, Rim Adams managed to comment around the dryness in his throat: "Until they get the jail built so we can make arrests, our hands are pretty much tied."

The other man looked at him. "When they finish that jail," he retorted coldly, "is when our problems really begin."

"I don't see how you figure."

"Why, the minute we make our first arrest, we'll be proving we actually mean business. They'll be waiting for that. It will be the signal!"

Adams hadn't thought of this, and it sobered him.

The interminable day ended. Dusk fell again, the steady plains wind fanning up the stars as the bowl of sky darkened, and Chase Center came alive; once more lamplight flared behind oiled paper windows, sounds poured from every open door along the shadowed street with its smell of dust and horses. But the night was as ominously quiet as the day had been.

The whole length of the street, from the K.P. tracks north to where the lights of Fort Chase glimmered faintly, there was only one real disturbance—toward midnight a fistfight broke out in one of the cribs, but was quickly settled. As yet, not a gun had been fired since Frank Keyhoe pinned on the marshal's badge....

In noontime stillness, Rim Adams had walked over for a look at the completed jail. It stood, boxlike, on its barren square of Kansas earth, the ground about littered with sawdust and wood chips and discarded scraps of timber. Nearby, new milled lumber stood in a pile, and the foundations and framework of the marshal's office was already going up.

In Asa Timberlake's freight yard yonder he could hear men talking and swearing as they manhandled

92

crates into the big wagons—evidently Timberlake was getting ready to send off another of his bull trains, for Santa Fe. The single daily string of cars from the east had just pulled in to the depot and gone again, taking with it the pulse of drivers and the fading, lonely voice of its whistle.

Adams walked into the jail and looked around. It was a stuffy and airless space, low roofed and hardly ten feet square; despite ventilation by a pair of high, barred windows, it stank of the creosoting of the railroad ties it had been built from. When he struck a wall with the flat of a hand, it seemed solid enough. Only one detail was lacking: the heavy door had no lock.

Frank Keyhoe had rejected the padlock Timberlake supplied, claiming it was not stout enough. None to be had in town satisfied him, and at his insistence an order had gone to Kansas City for the particular type he wanted—a delaying movement, Rim Adams suspected. For his own reasons, Keyhoe wasn't ready yet to put the jail to actual use.

A shadow fell across the open doorway. When he turned and saw the man who stood looking in at him, Adams thought he could feel the short hairs stir and rise at the back of his neck.

Harry Dowler showed all his teeth in a hungry grin. "Well!" he grunted. "So *you're* Keyhoe's boy! It never occurred to me the two of us had already met!"

Slowly and carefully, Adams walked into the open, the two men eyeing one another like cur dogs edging around a fight. Dowler seemed to be unarmed, and Rim Adams had left his shotgun leaning against the door frame.

He noticed a slight swelling under one eye that

93

made the redhead's craggy face appear lopsided—a memento, he wondered, of the fight in the hotel at Ellsworth? From the time he learned Harry Dowler was yard boss for Timberlake, Adams had known this moment was coming. He'd dreaded it, but he would not walk away from it either.

He said bluntly, "How's that rib?"

Reminded of it, the big fellow's eyes took on a wicked shine. "Bothers a little, now and then," he admitted, touching a palm against his shirt. "But not enough to slow me down any. Don't let it stop you."

"I'm not looking for more trouble with you," Adams told him. "Far as I'm concerned that's all settled. You stepped out of line and somebody had to call you on it."

The redhead snorted, and spat. "You and that little blond bitch!"

In spite of himself Rim Adams felt his hands pull up into fists. "Is there only one way," he gritted, "to keep that sort of filth off of your tongue?"

Dowler was grinning as he saw he had stung a rise out of the other. But in the next breath his glance shifted and suddenly his grin lost its shape; uncertainty replaced it. Adams, wheeling aside, looked to find Frank Keyhoe standing motionless in the white sun blast.

Keyhoe said, "Dowler, you've got just half a minute to walk away from here."

Rim Adams burst out in protest: "Frank! *No!*"

But the marshal ignored him. He calmly regarded big Harry Dowler, and all at once the redhead's heavy features flooded with color, clear to the roots of his rusty hair. His thick chest lifted; he said hoarsely, "So that's the way it is?"

"That's the way it is," Keyhoe answered crisply. "This man is my deputy; I need him. I won't tell you

94

again that you're to walk wide of him, as long as the two of you are in this town!"

Dowler's mouth worked. Finally a single ugly word broke from him and he ground the heel of one cowhide boot into the sawdust litter, turning heavily. The man's high shoulders swung as he headed at a long stride toward the activity of Asa Timberlake's wagon yard.

Outraged pride made Rim Adams cry out, "Did you have to do that? You've only made a fool of me! I can fight my own battles!"

Keyhoe let him have the same look he had shown the redhead. "No, you can't!" he said flatly. "Not while you work for me. I won't be hampered with any personal feuds. Do you understand?"

Adams rubbed a palm across his jaw and found the hand was trembling. But when Keyhoe repeated the question, in the same harsh tone, he settled his breathing with an effort and answered gruffly, "I suppose so...."

The marshal appeared satisfied. "Good!" he said, and dismissed the matter. "I was looking for you." He indicated the shotgun leaning against the door frame. "You'd better bring that, and come along."

"There's trouble?" Adams demanded quickly.

"Could be."

Keyhoe would offer nothing further. But a sudden urgency crowded out all thought of the redhead, as Rim Adams hastily snatched up the weapon and fell into step with his chief.

That same waiting quiet lay upon the town. The long street was nearly empty, excepting only a quartet of horses tied at the hitching rail in front of the Kansas House, and carrying the army's familiar McClellan saddles; yet, as always, there was an uneasy sensation—for Adams at least—of being

95

followed by hostile eyes. When Keyhoe turned in at the entrance of Lew McCord's deadfall, the deputy couldn't hold back his astonishment.

"We ain't going *here?* I thought McCord invited us to stay out of his place!"

"It would appear," the marshal answered in a voice as dry as the dust underfoot, "He's seen fit to change his mind...."

A quarrelsome sound of drunken voices came to them as they approached the propped-open door. Inside it was no cooler, and it was breathless; the sharp contrast with the dazzle of the street blinded Adams a moment but his eyes adjusted enough that he could see the big room was something less than half full. A clot of activity near the roulette table resolved itself into the blue clad shapes of a group of horse soldiers; that was where the noise came from—the belligerent voices and unsteady jostling of men who had taken on more liquor than they could comfortably handle. From the edge of anger in their voices Adams judged that luck, and the wheel, weren't going in their favor.

Lew McCord, wearing a candy-striped shirt minus a collar and bringing with him the smell of stale sweat and of cigar smoke, materialized at Keyhoe's elbow. "You took your time," he said.

The marshal looked at him. "Is *this* the trouble? Appears to me you've got housemen enough to manage a handful of drunks."

McCord answered coolly, "It's supposed to be your job to keep peace with the military—and I won't have my place wrecked."

"And you're afraid you might, if they lose a few too many times on your wheel?" McCord didn't answer that; he scowled and his lips worried the cigar and rolled it, sodden and fuming, into a corner of his mouth.

The ball dropped into the slot. The croupier droned his call, and one of the troopers at the table swore savagely. "What the hell kind of luck am I supposed to call that?" He made a staggering circle, and as he came around Rim Adams saw it was the captain who'd been to meet the train, the day they arrived: Caroline Sutter's husband.

Tom Sutter's tunic was unbuttoned and awry, his face flushed from the heat and the whiskey he'd been drinking; sweat ran down his cheeks and shone beneath the brim of his pushed-back campaign hat. Now his stare had touched upon the newcomers, and his head jerked sharply. "It's Keyhoe, by God!"

"Hello, Tom," the marshal said.

An utter stillness settled as the captain left the table and walked over. Swaying, slightly, he lifted a finger and pointed at the piece of metal pinned to the tall man's coat. "I'd heard you let the town hang that damn thing on you. A civilian lawman! Guess that puts us on different sides of the street."

"In a way," Keyhoe agreed, "I suppose it does."

"I figured as much! Never saw an army town yet, wasn't bound to keep the boys from enjoying themselves when they came in out of the field!" That drew a mutter of agreement from his friends at the roulette table. Adams could see now that they were enlisted men—a sergeant and a pair of privates, all seemingly drunk as the captain himself.

The latter pushed a fist loosely across his mouth; his badly focused stare found Rim Adams. "And this is your deputy? Yeah, I heard of him, too. Young fellow seems to have made a hell of a big impression on my wife!"

Keyhoe said, "I didn't know you'd been married, Tom, till we saw her on the train coming out here. A

97

fine looking woman."

"You don't even know!" Sutter told him, with a grin of such lewdness that Adams all at once felt a kind of sick mortification.

But Sutter's wavering attention had returned to the badge. "Does this thing mean the 11th is going to have trouble with you, Keyhoe? Or, are you going to mind your own business?"

"You and your friends will *be* my business, any time you step across the line."

The captain's lip curled. "You always were an arrogant bastard, even as a scout: now I guess all those magazine articles must have gone to your head. Well, the boys in the 11th don't have much time for reading. We just aren't too impressed with you, Keyhoe. Maybe you better watch that line, yourself!"

Abruptly he swung away and headed back to the table. "Come on, damn it!" he shouted, pulling what looked to be the last of his money from his pocket. "Spin that wheel! Black has got to come up *some* time!"

Adams saw the croupier's questioning glance and McCord's brief nod. As the wheel was put into blurred motion, Sutter flung his money onto the table and, plucking a half-drained whiskey bottle from one of his friends, draped an arm across the sergeant's shoulders as he put the neck of the bottle to his mouth and tilted it at the ceiling. Rim Adams watched in dismay.

Whatever might be his own dislike of the army he had been in long enough, and been well enough indoctrinated, to find something distasteful in an officer with no more dignity than to choose enlisted men for his drinking companions. But even worse was the knowledge that this was the husband of that

98

soft, bright-haired lady who had filled his thoughts since the time at Ellsworth. He wondered if she had learned about this side of the man she was married to, and found himself fervently hoping she didn't know.

He heard McCord saying to Keyhoe in smug satisfaction, "He'll leave as soon as he's cleaned."

The marshal's eye held a hard glint. "But you expect me to see to it he and his friends go peaceably!"

"Your job," the resort owner reminded him, pleasantly.

The ball clicked into its slot. The wheel slowed. The croupier called: "Six, red, even...."

Tom Sutter cursed in petulant fury as he flung the empty bottle from him. It struck a table where there was a poker game going and smashed there, scattering cards and chips and sending angry players scrambling to their feet. The captain, unheeding, was already making for the door. He reeled unsteadily and one shoulder struck the edge of the frame; he corrected his course and plunged outside with his friends trooping noisily after him.

Lew McCord, hands shoved deep into his pockets, grinned at Keyhoe around the soggy cigar butt. "No trouble after all, then," he murmured.

Keyhoe only looked at him. The marshal was feeling in a pocket of his coat; failing to find what he was looking for, he heeled about and walked over to the bar where he asked the counterman, "You have any cigars? Other than those horrors your boss smokes?" Expressionless, the man fished a box from under the bar for his inspection. As the room returned to normal, Frank Keyhoe selected a handful.

There was a sudden commotion in the doorway.

Tom Sutter was back. He came leading a saddled horse—dragging it by the reins, his trooper friends laughing and yelling and slapping its flanks with their hats when the terrified animal tried to balk. They got it inside somehow as Keyhoe turned from the bar, holding his cigars, and Lew McCord angrily yelled something no one heard. Yonder, McCord's housemen broke from their stations against the wall, looking uncertainly at their chief for orders.

Sutter's voice rose above the hubbub, aided by years of drill field and parade ground training: "By God, I'm not cleaned while I own a horse and a McClellan saddle! Rim Adams, gawking like the rest of the room, had no idea as yet what the captain could have got into his head. Tom Sutter had circled an end of the roulette table, now, while his companions continued to worry the animal and it rolled liquid eyes in terror at the clatter of its own hooves against the wooden floor. "On the black, damn it!" yelled Sutter, sweating and hauling. "I'm putting him on the black!"

At length the horse actually heaved itself up and got its forefeet planted on the tabletop, but no amount of tugging and pushing by its tormentors could make it go any farther. With drunken suddenness, Tom Sutter lost his temper. He cursed and tossed aside the reins, as one hand reached for the revolver in his military holster. Before anybody could have stopped him, the pistol rose and he shot the beast between the eyes.

To the thunderous crash of the gunshot the horse jerked convulsively; forelegs buckling, it bowed its head and rolled slowly sideward off the table's edge and collapsed, shaking the building. One shod hoof struck out feebly against a timber of the heavy table. Then it went still, with Tom, Sutter left holding the smoking pistol and staring foolishly at the thing he had done.

CHAPTER 11

Shocked, and numbed by concussion, no one in that room seemed able to react or to move at first. Then Rim Adams let out trapped breath, and lifted his head to see Frank Keyhoe striding purposefully across the room from the bar.

The marshal's face looked white and terrible; he still clutched the handful of cigars, as though he had completely forgotten them. He came right at Tom Sutter and the latter, jarred into movement by the sight of him, fell back a step and lifted the smoking gun.

"Stay away!" he cried thickly.

"You damn fool!" The hand that held the cigars hit him in the face. Sutter fell back against the end of the table; flinging aside the shredded ruins of tobacco, Keyhoe seized his arm and with a punishing twist grabbed the pistol from his fingers. One of the enlisted men—the sergeant, a tough, sunburned man with a jaw like a shovel—reached for the marshal. Almost without a break in his movement, Keyhoe swung the gun around and rammed its barrel into the man's swelling paunch, deep, and the noncom grunted and doubled forward.

By that time Rim Adams came up, bringing the shotgun; but though all the enlisted men were wearing sidearms, the marshal's quick move seemed to have jarred any fight out of them. The sergeant, sick and retching, was holding his middle with both arms. Tom Sutter, on the other hand, seemed to have had some of the whiskey knocked out of him. He raised a trembling hand and touched his face, where Keyhoe's knuckles had broken the skin.

"Proud of yourself?" the marshal asked.

Sutter didn't answer; his stare moved on to the slaughtered horse and suddenly he looked very sick. When Keyhoe reversed the pistol and offered it the captain seemed not even to see it at first. But finally he took the weapon and dropped it into its holster, and without saying a word moved for the door on uncertain legs. The sergeant still leaned against the table, bowed over the arms that clutched his belly; the remaining pair of enlisted men, chastened and leaderless, started to follow Tom Sutter outside.

Lew McCord found his voice. "What about that damn thing?" he demanded harshly. He shoved a thumb toward the dead horse. Already flies were beginning to collect and buzz about the spill of sticky blood. "I want it out of here, Keyhoe!"

The marshal, not bothering to look at him, was already speaking to the sergeant; slowly the latter brought his head wavering up. His face looked positively green. It was a sundarkened face, knobby as a walnut, with a tremendous drooping mustache and a bad cast in one eye. Keyhoe said, "I think I remember you. You were a corporal when I scouted with the 11th. The name's Mannion, isn't it?"

It took an effort but the words came out, half whispered, through bitterly writhing lips. "I'm never gonna let you forget it! I think you busted something inside there, damn you!"

"You'll live," Keyhoe said with scant sympathy. "You and your men, go get your horses and some rope, and drag that carcass out. My deputy will keep an eye on you till it's done. Move!"

Mannion looked at him, with sick and hating eyes, and then he looked at Rim Adams and the ready shotgun. He cursed and lurched toward the door. Adams held back a moment, watching as Lew McCord walked over to the marshal with a cool grin on his face. "That could have been worse," the resort owner said.

Keyhoe said, "You, McCord, will either take the brake off your wheel, or I'm closing it down."

The man's face changed in a flash. The mouth tightened on the cigar stub; the eyes narrowed to a glitter. "I don't know what you're talking about!"

"Your man was careless," Keyhoe retorted. "They couldn't even see it—but I'm no drunken soldier! I'll give you twenty-four hours, no more. You take off that brake, or I'll be coming in here with an axe to knock the thing to pieces. You know I mean it!"

McCord's face changed color, he seemed about to argue, but something in Keyhoe's look and tone of voice must have decided him to hold his tongue. Fury was in the stare that followed Keyhoe as he turned abruptly, nodding for Adams to follow him from the gambling hall.

In the high sunlight, the men of the 11th had gathered in a knot at the hitching pole where only three horses were left, now, under their McClellans. Sergeant Mannion seemed to have recovered from the blow to his belly, but Tom Sutter stood with both hands resting on the pole, his shoulders bowed, his head hanging. Frank Keyhoe glanced at Adams.

"Well, now you've met one of the family—you've met the one she married. Pretty hard to take?"

Adams felt the warmth flood into his face. "Am I that easy to read?"

"It's a hard world," Keyhoe said. "Your woman is married to that clown—and now he's cost me a

103

fistful of ruined forty-cent cigars." He looked down at his palm, with a grimace wiped it against a trouser leg. "I should send McCord a bill!

"Well, let's put them to work...."

Rim Adams roused from a troubled, jealous dream of Caroline Sutter. He saw her looking on in horror as the drunken man in the captain's shoulderstraps shot the horse and it slowly, almost lazily, toppled; but after that the dream changed and became confused. Tom Sutter turned to stare at his wife. Adams saw the lewd possessiveness in the sweating face, knew suddenly he meant to kill her as well. He tried to interfere but was powerless to move. He saw the smoking gun turn deliberately on its target, and with all his strength cried out—and woke on the hard bed in Youngman's spare room, shaking, his throat distended and in his own ears the hoarse shout that must have broken from him. Adams lay there, drenched in sweat, as his racing heartbeat gradually slowed and the easing of nightmare panic returned him to a sense of reality.

He knew it must be the dead middle of the night. It had been close to that when he turned in, soon after he and Keyhoe returned from being called out to look at a body someone found in the weeds behind one of the town's deadfalls. The man had been one of the floating population, his name uncertain. Reluctant answers to the marshal's questioning had brought out that he'd been the heavy winner in a two-day poker game—hence, the waylaying and the slugging and the silent blade shoved between his ribs. His pockets were turned wrong side out, and empty. Even his boots were gone. There was nothing in the world to be done about him....

A gleam of lamplight turned his head toward the deal table by the open window; there, in shirtsleeves, with the lamp's shade tilted to spill its light directly on what he was doing, Frank Keyhoe sat working over one of his pair of pearl-handled guns. A pungent smell of gunoil overlaid the scent of the warm night breeze that stirred the curtains. Keyhoe seemed too engrossed in his task to hear any sound Adams might have made.

The latter watched for a moment as he finished polishing the gleaming gunbarrel, then took new brass shells from a box, examining each carefully before slipping it into the chamber. Apparently satisfied, Keyhoe rocked the cylinder home and sighted down the barrel. He laid the gun down and picked up a half-empty tumbler of whiskey and drained it off, afterward refilling the glass from an opened bottle.

Aware suddenly of the ache in his own dry throat, Rim Adams levered himself up onto an elbow, bedsprings squealing faintly under him, and said, "I could use a shot of that."

The other gave him not so much as a look as he set down the bottle and reached again for the cleaning rag. Adams frowned, and swung his legs over the edge of the bed. He'd slept in nothing but his trousers. Still confused and in a daze from the nightmare, he sat a moment rubbing a palm across his scalp and down to scratch at the sparse matting of dark hair on his chest; afterward he got up and, on bare feet, crossed the room to the table where he reached over Keyhoe's shoulder for the bottle. He froze like that.

Keyhoe, with a single smooth motion, had snatched up the weapon he had finished loading and its muzzle was trained squarely at Adams, the bore

105

nearly touching his ribs. Startled, he sucked in his belly, his wild stare meeting the look in Keyhoe's amber eyes; all at once he was more scared than he had ever been, for he knew he had never stood closer to death.

"My God!" he breathed hoarsely.

Slowly the gun lowered; he looked at Keyhoe's scowling face, and saw the whiskey shine in the man's stare. Suddenly he was shaking so he had to back away, to steady himself against the edge of the washstand. "What was the idea of that?" he cried.

"You took me by surprise," Keyhoe said roughly. "I thought you were asleep." Adams watched him put the gun aside and, as though without thinking about it, pick up the filled whiskey glass and carry it to his lips.

The young fellow swallowed past the dryness in his own throat, slowly regaining control. He said, "But—I spoke, and you acted like you never heard. You know, I think maybe you didn't! This has happened before now—more than once: I'd say something to you and it's as though I wasn't even there!"

He thought the other man was not going to answer. Keyhoe put down the glass, his head tipped forward until the strong brow shadowed his eyes, and the lamp's glow failed to pick out any expression about the mouth with its strangely short upper lip. But now he spread both palms flat upon the table top and his head came up, and a breath swelled his chest. "I thought I covered up well," he said heavily. "But if *you've* found me out, I wonder how many others there are that know?"

"Know what? That you're going deaf?"

The marshal only looked at him a moment. Then: "It was during the war—in Arkansas, at Pea Ridge

106

Battle. I stood too close to the big guns. I lost the left ear, then; the other didn't begin to bother too much, until about six months ago."

Adams said, "And that's the real reason you hired me, I suppose. The reason you insist that I'm always there to protect your bad side...."

"You literally have my life in your hands," Frank Keyhoe pointed out, "every minute we're patrolling that street!"

"Don't you think you might at least have told me?"

"It wasn't a matter of vanity, Adams, whatever you might think." The amber eyes regarded him. "I suppose you realize I have personal enemies who'd be glad to pay for what you're in a position to tell them, now."

The younger man drew back. "Are you saying I'd sell you out?"

"No. No, Adams, I'm not saying that. In fact, I guess I trust you—even if I don't exactly know why."

Rim Adams swore. "If *that's* your best answer, it don't sound to me like you trust me at all! Maybe we ought to call this quits—right now!" He swung away, mad clear through; he plucked his shirt off the washstand where he'd flung it last night and shrugged into it. At the bed he seated himself and began to pull on his socks.

Frank Keyhoe, watching him, said finally, "So you're really walking out...."

Adams picked up a shoe, flung it down hard in exasperation. "By God, I just don't know what you expect of me!"

Instead of answering, Keyhoe gave the bottle a shove. "Have that drink and simmer down."

"I changed my mind. I don't want it." Sulkily

107

Adams fumbled at the buttons of his shirt as he watched Keyhoe address himself again to the water glass of whiskey. "*You* seem able to put it away, all right!"

The other swirled the amber liquid, staring into the glass. "Wait till the first time you have to walk up to a man with a gun in his hand, and take it away from him. Perhaps then you'll see the value of something to help settle your nerves for you, afterward!"

"Nerves?" It was a new idea for Rim Adams. "I didn't know you had any!"

Keyhoe drank and set the glass down, and rubbed the ball of a thumb across his mustache. "I'll tell you this, Adams: A man has no trouble with his nerves as long as he can thrust his luck. But you can go to that well, once too often. Constantly laying your life on the line is a game for fools!"

"Then maybe it's time you got out of it, while you're still ahead!" This was a new experience for Rim Adams, who had never heard this man speak his mind so directly on anything touching his own affairs. Shaking his head he exclaimed, "With your name, and your reputation—there's no sense in you waiting to kick out your life in some dusty street, in a place like Chase Center. Why, man, you're a *legend!*"

"So I'm told...."

In the stillness that lay about them, the sawing of insects outside the window seemed very loud. A moth had found its way in and was circling the lamp and knocking itself crazy against the shade. Frank Keyhoe scraped back his chair, leaving his matched guns upon the table, and went to the washstand, where he filled the basin from the pitcher. Watching him, Rim Adams said, "Most men I know would

108

give anything to be looked up to, the way you are—to have done all the things you've crowded into a single lifetime." Something prompted him to add: "I'm wondering. Of it all, what part would you say was the best?"

"The best?" With his face lowered above the bowl, Keyhoe paused as though considering. "That's not too hard to answer. There's nothing like scouting, really." And he splashed and blew.

"Scouting?" the other repeated. "For the military, you mean? With Colonel Sutter?"

Keyhoe shot him a look, across one bent shoulder. "Oh, yes," he said dryly. "Yes, I've been out with Jeff, and with that worthless brother of his, too. Only, I'm talking about the old days—and better officers than either of them!" Straightening, he wiped a palm across his face, whipped the water from aquiline features and tawny, drooping mustache. But then he went motionless. He seemed to look at a corner of the ceiling—or at something far beyond it.

"You never saw a plains sunrise, boy, with the smell of the dawn wind and bacon on the fire, and the sound of the men stirring and the horses jingling on the picketline. You never traveled across a land without a fence or a building to scar the view. You never rode into a Sioux village, the poles of the tipis notched against the sunset and that strange, musical language in your ears—and you, equally ready to receive a friendly welcome or fight for your life, not knowing which…. A good life, Adams."

"Couldn't you always go back to it?"

The question broke whatever spell of reminiscence had held the tall man rooted. He stirred, and shook his head, and reached for the towel on its hook at the side of the washstand.

"That's a youngster's sport. A man reaches an age when a night spent in a set of soaked buckskins leaves him aching and half crippled. From there it's only a step to being one more of those used-up, time-rotted scarecrows you see hanging around every army post, still trying to tough it out somehow until the fever or a Sioux arrow finally does for them. Anybody that's not a fool knows enough to get into another line, while he's still of some use to himself."

Through with the towel, Keyhoe tossed it aside. "Back to what we were talking about: Now you know about me—and by this time you know something about the business you're involved in. I suppose I should have been honest with you, but anyway I'll put it to you straight: Will you stay on— be my ears? If you want out, I won't hold you."

It was his chance, and only a minute ago Rim Adams would likely have seized on it; now, for some reason, he stood mute. He looked at Frank Keyhoe, and behind the glitter of whiskey in his eyes could read a poorly concealed anxiety, waiting upon the answer. Suddenly he understood that this man of legend was altogether human, and in need.

He took a breath. "I never did like to throw in my cards before the hand was finished," he said gruffly. "So I guess I'll stick." Afterward he could only hope he wouldn't live to regret what he had so glibly promised.

CHAPTER 12

After the heat and stinging dust of the parade

110

ground, the colonel's guests were glad enough to take refuge on the wooden platform before his tent; here the tarpaulin gave a pleasant shade and the tall cottonwoods, rocking overhead, helped filter the force of the prairie wind, so that some of the creek's coolness could reach them. And here, as soon as Livy Sutter had everyone settled on the army's uncomfortable folding chairs, she busied herself pouring ice tea for the ladies while her husband handed out something stronger to the men.

In contrast with his visitors, who were beginning to look a little wilted, the colonel's uniform was flawless and his boots showed not a speck of dust; to watch him move among the group on his veranda, tossing his head as he laughed politely at some remark or passed a compliment, one would scarcely have guessed that this immaculate, white-gloved figure had just sat the saddle for three quarters of an hour in the blistering sun, reviewing his regiment in full dress parade, while his guests watched from the comparative comfort of a buggy.

"This wind!" the senator's corpulent wife complained to Olivia. "Does it never stop blowing? How do you keep from going insane?"

"Oh, you get used to it," she answered gaily and slipped a hand into the crook of her husband's arm. "It's just one of the little inconveniences of living in the field. A body would feel cheated, without it."

Jeff Sutter squeezed her hand gallantly. "Don't you believe her! The fact is, she's one of the best troopers in my command. She makes light of every hardship. I've yet to hear her complain."

The senator, rather more corpulent even than his wife, mopped sweat from his florid cheeks. "After all," he pointed out, "it's a privilege for a woman to take her place at her husband's side. Especially when the man she's married to happens to be a national hero!"

Livy bobbed her head and the colonel made a deprecating gesture with one gloved hand. "Now, that's just a little strong, don't you think, Henry?"

"Your big problem, Jeff—you're too modest." The senator waggled a finger at him sternly. "Never pays to hide your light under a bushel, I always say. Do you agree, Livy?"

She smiled, and fondly patted her husband's arm. "He never has been one to blow his own trumpet."

A man who sat alone on the edge of the platform, a notebook open on his knee, made a wry face at that that none of the others noticed. Discovering he had snapped his pencil, he dug a silver penknife from his waistcoat pocket, opened it on a thumbnail and began to shape up a new point.

The senator's personal secretary, a soft-looking fellow with thinning blond hair and bespectacled blue eyes, spoke up. "I hope you hadn't forgotten, Colonel—you promised we'd have an opportunity to meet this Frank Keyhoe chap. I think Miss Jenny is going to be very put out if you fail us. She's been talking of nothing else." The rather vapid young lady beside him blushed and tried to look embarrassed, but the senator quickly took it up.

"That's the truth, Jeff!" He nodded at his wife. "You can ask Sarah if she ain't been pestering me, too, ever since you mentioned that man was in the neighborhood! Don't know why it is the ladies, in particular, want to meet Frank Keyhoe; but he's become a famous man, back East—and after all, there ain't much for the womenfolk in going out with us while we get us our buffalo or two apiece. If you want to keep peace in my family you'll trot him out!"

112

Sutter reassured his guests "I haven't forgotten. Keyhoe had word to be here this afternoon, after parade. He should be along any time."

"Good—good!" The senator wagged his massive head and attacked his whiskey glass.

Olivia Sutter said brightly, "Jeff, honey, can I see you a minute? About the refreshments...." He excused himself and followed her into the tent, to face her suddenly angry frown. "You *didn't*!" Livy whispered tensely. "You didn't really invite that—that—!"

The colonel spread his hands. "You heard them—it was practically an order. I can't make Henry angry. If his wife, and that silly girl of Belton's, are going to make such a fuss, what can I do but produce him?"

"But he's nothing more than a murderer, in spite of the magazine articles! Don't those females out there realize—?"

"Hush! They'll hear you! Besides," her husband said, smiling a little in the face of her anger, "Frank's really not as bad as that, you know. I've always rather liked him."

"That's your privilege!" Though she had lowered her voice, her ripe lower lip thrust forward. "But you have no right expecting me to entertain him. Besides the killing and the gunplay, he has no more morals than an alley cat! Tom says he's openly consorting with some woman, right in front of the whole town!"

"Belle Wadsworth, I suppose he means. Yes, they're old friends. And my brother Tom sometimes talks too much!" He touched her shoulder, smiling fondly at her. "We really must get back to our guests."

She caught at his sleeve as he started to turn from her. She said fiercely, "And so he'll come here, and those people will make over him, and lionize him—when it's *you* they should be paying attention to! How is any wife supposed to like that?"

His smile took on am edge of steel. "Don't worry!" he promised. "Henry Lang may think that he's out here to make a royal tour of the prairie and bag himself a buffalo; but he's not leaving again for Washington before he's had an earful. He's too big a man in the Senate and with the War Department, for me to miss this opportunity—believe me!

"We're on our way, my dear—you wait and see. I'm going to get an important command, out of this—and one of these days, my brevet and my brigadier's star back again. Do you trust me?"

She clasped her hands before her like a little girl, her eyes shining. "But of course I do! They must know, sooner or later, that they can't do anything without my strong, handsome husband!"

"Good girl!" He bent swiftly and his silky mustache brushed her cheek. "So do as you're told, and entertain the senator for me and when Frank Keyhoe comes, treat him as though he were a gentleman." Straightening, he nodded past her toward the tent opening. "You've no choice, anyway. I see he's already arrived."

Livy turned quickly; when she saw the two horsemen just dismounting before the tent platform, her mouth drew long with dislike. "And who is the person with him?"

It was the colonel's turn to frown. "Apparently he's chosen to bring along his deputy. I never told him he could do that! Well, we shan't put up with either of them any longer than necessary. Come along, my dear—you know you at least have to say hello...."

As they tied their livery stable horses to a cottonwood, Frank Keyhoe must have seen Rim Adams anxiously roving glance; he said, in a gruff aside, "I think I know why you wanted me to bring you. But you needn't be so damned obvious!"

Adams flushed but did not trouble to answer; for at that moment his search was rewarded, and his heart seemed to lurch in his ribcage. She had come out of the second, smaller tent, a little distance along the creekbank, and she stood for a moment motionless against a background of grass and tree heads turned golden in the afternoon light. She was dressed all in white, and even at this distance her blond loveliness turned his mouth dry and his palms wet with perspiration.

Then Tom Sutter followed her out, bending to clear the low tent flap. With an ache of jealousy Adams saw her turn and speak to him, saw the captain make some answer and then, taking his wife's arm, lead her toward the colonel's tent, the shadow of leaves overhead sliding across them both.

A word from Keyhoe reminded Adams of where he was. He took his eyes from Caroline and her husband, and stepping up onto the wooden platform found himself, for the first time, confronting Jefferson Sutter—Abe Lincoln's famous boy general.

In published pictures, the man had rather resembled Frank Keyhoe; seen together like this, their differences were more striking. Adams couldn't help thinking that his chief came off a shade the better. Lacking his flowing mustache, the colonel would have been slightly dish-faced, with a weak chin and faintly bulging eyes. It was the soldier's bearing, Adams thought, that did the trick for him and lent him an aura. Like Keyhoe, this man

115

wore the mantle of a legend in a way that no one was apt to miss.

His manner was reserved as he offered a gauntleted hand and met Adams with a brisk, curt shake, immediately dropping it. "And here's Livy," he said, bringing forward a dark-haired young woman. "My dear, of course you remember Frank Keyhoe. This young man is his deputy. Mister—I'm sorry, what name was that again?"

Adams repeated it, fumbling off his derby. The woman scarcely nodded; her face, that might have been pretty when she smiled, held a displeasure now that she made no effort to conceal. Adams found himself thinking, At least we know we aren't here on her invitation!

He had no time to develop the thought, because there were other people to be introduced, in quick and confusing succession. He shook hands with a portly and sweating person who, he gathered, was the guest of honor, a senator from some Eastern state—which one, he didn't quite catch. There was his secretary, a young man with a limp handshake. Of the two women, the older was the senator's wife and the younger, vaguely pretty one, his secretary's fiancée.

Adams received a perfunctory greeting from each and returned it in kind, well aware that no one was interested in him. Frank Keyhoe, on the other hand, was at once surrounded by Sutter's guests. A babble of eager talk began to grow there in the shadows of the creekbank trees.

Then, in the background, Adams glimpsed the colonel's brother. Tom Sutter was watching Keyhoe, and the malice in his stare was as ugly as any Rim Adams had ever surprised on a human face. He guessed that Tom had not forgotten what happened

116

two days ago, in McCord's deadfall. He thought, Having made a damned fool of himself over the shooting of the horse, he'll never forgive Keyhoe, or me, or anyone else that might be able to remind him of it!

When the captain turned and strode away in the direction of his own tent, Adams was just as pleased to see him go. Someone had shoved a glass of whiskey into the young man's fist; with Keyhoe and Jeff Sutter monopolizing all attention, he found himself standing awkward and forgotten on a corner of the shadowed platform. He tried the whiskey, found it was excellent stock.

A step sounded beside him; a voice said pleasantly, "Hello." Hastily he turned and found himself face to face with Caroline Sutter.

Now that she was real again, and actually standing before him he seemed unable to speak. She looked cool, untouched by the warm day or by the prairie wind that swayed the cottonwoods and worried the ropes and canvas of the nearby tent. There was just a touch of blue, he saw, at the high throat of her white dress—a ribbon that matched and brought out the color of her eyes. She said, "Don't you remember me?"

That brought words from him, but they seemed to Adams a confused and hopeless stammer: "Of course. Sure, I remember. How in the world could I—? I mean—how are you?"

"Just fine. And you?"

Adams nodded. He would not have imagined that any one person could be at the same time so happy and so miserable. He managed to get out: "You look as though army life agrees with you. It seems to suit you real well."

"Why, thank you," she said, smiling. At once she

117

sobered, looking at him with a frown of serious intensity puckering her brow. "I've thought of you often, Mister Adams. I keep hearing such dreadful things about that town—and I know, whatever goes on there, you and Mister Keyhoe must be right in the midst of it. I've been afraid, any minute, I'd learn something awful had happened to you."

Such obvious sincerity and concern turned him warm inside. "It hasn't been too bad," he assured her quickly. "Those people knew what they were doing, when they sent for Frank Keyhoe. His name alone is enough to keep the tough element careful, and make them walk easy. So far they do, at least."

"Even so it must be dangerous! Last night, when everything was quiet, I could have sworn I heard shooting—as though the wind carried it."

"I suppose you may have. It wasn't anything much. A muleskinner got fired up over the bad liquor they tried to serve him in one of those dugout saloons, and set out to take the place apart. He was easy to settle." He didn't know whether she was convinced by his way of making light of the matter, but he passed over it determinedly, adding, "I appreciate your feeling concerned, but I wish you wouldn't. We're only doing a job, the best we can."

"I know all that. But I also know what you did for me, on the way out here. I could never feel quite"— she groped for a word—"impersonal, about someone to whom I owe so much."

That left him stammering, and it was almost a relief when Livy Sutter came up, all smiles and apologies, to take her sister-in-law by the arm and lead her away toward the tent—"to help with arrangements." But though she smiled, the look the colonel's wife gave Rim Adams was coldly disapproving. He had an impression she had decided

118

Caroline had been talking to him long enough. Caroline excused herself and Adams, instantly lonely again, stood and followed with his eyes until she was gone from sight.

He turned abruptly then, in irritation, as a newcomer came sidling up and dispelled his mood. This was someone he had hardly noticed before, remembering him now as hovering in the background but missed somewhere in the general flurry of introductions. "Brinegar," the stranger said, seeing his puzzlement. "Merl Brinegar." And he murmured the name of a Washington newspaper. He offered a pale and narrow hand, that had a wiry strength when Adams took it briefly.

"A reporter," the young fellow grunted without real interest.

"That's right, Mister Adams. Covering the senator's little jaunt into the wild frontier. He laid wagers with his colleagues as to whether he can actually hit the broad side of a buffalo, even with Jeff Sutter to steady his hand. I'm supposed to be along to see he stays honest."

Adams gave the man a closer look. He was small and birdlike, well enough dressed except that his clothing was rumpled and smelled strongly of the pipe he clamped in one fist. He had an intelligent, fox face, bracketed in brown sideburns. He looked about forty, but would be one of those men about whom it was hard to be definite. Adams said, "You know this country?"

"Never been west of Chicago before," the newspaperman admitted promptly. "Which makes me ideal for the assignment. My readers know exactly what they want, and I don't disappoint them by putting in irrelevancies, such as facts. I could just as well have filed my copy from a hotel bar in St.

Louis."

"Maybe you should have! A deal more comfortable than what you'll run into out here—not to mention safer."

"Oh, I don't know." The newspaperman shrugged narrow shoulders. "Two days now in the wilds of western Kansas, and I've yet to see the elephant—as I believe your expression has it. Or even anything resembling a trunk or a tail."

Dryly, Adams suggested, "You haven't taken a good look at Chase Center, then."

"Well, that's true. Things get interesting there, I've heard—something about Keyhoe bluffing a gambling hall owner into closing down a crooked wheel. In fact, I heard Tom Sutter and the marshal had a little trouble in connection with it."

Adams' jaw tightened. "You're apt to hear almost anything."

"Perhaps, if I were to come into town one of these evenings you'd like to show me around so I can see for myself what goes on."

"No, thanks!" Adams shook his head firmly. "My job is tough enough without riding herd on newspaper reporters...."

Brinegar seemed to take no offense. He puffed smoke from his pipe and gazed off toward the scene at the other end of Jeff Sutter's crude veranda. There, the colonel's guests had formed a circle around Frank Keyhoe. The younger woman seemed fascinated by the pair of pearl-handled guns and he had obligingly brought one out to show her; she took it in both hands and squealed with astonishment at the weight of it.

Smiling indulgently, Keyhoe reclaimed the weapon and demonstrated its action, and pointed out his initials worked into the silver chasing on the sides of the butt. Adams heard the senator ask him, "And you've killed men with that gun, Mister Keyhoe?"

The tall man made a slight gesture. "A man does what he must, to stay alive," he replied, as the women looked at him with expressions of mingled admiration and fear.

The newspaperman commented, with wry amusement, "Your friend is really enjoying this."

"He's only being polite," Adams said.

"You think you're fooling me any?" Brinegar snorted in derision. "Or are you really that naïve, yourself, that you don't know a colossal vanity when you see it? Look close, then, because you're looking at three of the biggest—right here on this platform!" And his nod indicated them—Keyhoe, the colonel, and the senator. "Nothing in the world counts with any one of them, next to his own public picture! Take my word for it, friend—a man in my profession can always spot them, because we're the fellows they depend on to make or break them. Without the press, who'd remember any of them from one day to the next?"

Rim Adams, who was himself sometimes critical of his chief, all at once found himself defending him. "Frank Keyhoe," he exclaimed, "has been shot at least four times, by bullets any one of which could have killed him. I know because I've seen some of the scars. Do you think a man would put himself through all that just out of vanity?"

"You don't?" Merl Brinegar retorted, with a sideward and faintly sneering look. "Why, he's such a victim of vanity, he doesn't even realize he's let himself be trotted out like a trained bear, as entertainment for Sutter's company!" At what he saw in Adams' stare, his grin widened and the

121

narrow face broke into a mass of wrinkles.

"No, I see you don't believe me. Then let me give you a clue: Tomorrow, this party leaves for its privately conducted tour of the prairie, and a shot or two at a buffalo. After we come back, I'm informed there are plans afoot for a military ball to be held at the fort, in honor of the colonel and his guests. It'll be Jeff Sutter's big day. So, you wait and see if Keyhoe is invited—and when he isn't asked notice how he takes it. You just might have your eyes opened."

Adams started a retort but the other, with that same knowing smile, simply turned and walked away, and left him seething.

Despite all his flaws Frank Keyhoe was still about twice as much man as anyone he could remember knowing; after some fashion Adams had even come to look upon the tall gunfighter as a friend. He certainly wasn't ready to listen to some cynical newspaper reporter make small of him.

Overhead the cottonwoods rustled. It was cool and pleasant enough here beside the creek, but Rim Adams scarcely noticed. He finished the drink in his hand almost without tasting it. Caroline Sutter, an achingly lovely vision in her bright white dress, had returned to join the group on the other end of the platform, but now gave no sign of being so much as aware of him.

Coming here this afternoon, he told himself with acid bitterness, had surely been the act of a damned fool....

CHAPTER 13

Burke Roan floundered up the steps of the Novelty Theater and tried the door, when he found it locked, he swore in sick ferocity and began to pummel it with a fist that could rip hide from a mule's spine, in the flick of a bullwhip. Finally the latch was thrown and the angry bartender thrust his head out. "Get the hell away from here. We're closed."

"So's every damn place along the street," Roan said. "All I want's a drink. I need it!"

"This ain't no saloon," the man retorted. "If it was I wouldn't let you in. You not only look like a pig— you smell like one! Now, beat it!"

The door slammed in Roan's face. Turning away with a curse, and squinting directly into the morning sun, he missed his footing and stumbled down the steps to land on hands and knees in the dirt.

Burke Roan wasn't drunk; quite the opposite. He'd awakened in the weeds of a vacant lot, sober and sick with hangover. His clothing stunk of vomit and spilled liquor and stale sweat. Jesus! He must really have got ahold of some lousy booze last night! He remembered vaguely something about losing too much at coon-can in one of the dives he favored, and there'd been that little whore who took his money and then kicked him out of her crib because he was too drunk to protest. Well, early as it was, by God he was going to find somebody to sell him a drink, or somebody would be sorry....

He lurched to his feet. Staggering as far as to the wooden arcade in front of Youngman's store, he clung to a post while he searched the street. Some place had to be open and doing business. Not Youngman's—though the double doors were opened and hooked back against the wall, the merchant didn't deal in what he wanted.

Roan shoved away just as someone came out of the store carrying a sack under each arm. A heavy shoulder sent the man reeling back against the edge of the doorway.

He wasn't more than a boy, actually—about thirty pounds lighter than the muleskinner and thin to the point of boniness, though hard work had strung good muscles on his frame. The beginnings of a yellow mustache, so pale as to be hardly visible, bracketed the corners of his mouth; a thatch of hair to match it showed beneath the brim of a battered straw hat.

He managed to hang onto his sacks of flour and dried beans, clutching them against him as he braced against the doorframe and stared at the bigger man, with mild brown eyes. He exclaimed, "Do you own the street, maybe?"

"Far as you're concerned I do!" Burke Roan answered.

Too late the other seemed to read the danger in him; it made his voice a trifle shaky as he said, "I have an idea you're looking for a fight!" The words were scarcely out before Roan, grinning, hit him full across the face.

It was a contemptuous blow, open-palmed; it spun the smaller man half around and this time he dropped the sacks he was carrying. One split open to let white, dried beans spatter across the sidewalk. And in trying to keep his balance, the young fellow tripped and went sprawling.

For Burke Roan the morning was suddenly more tolerable—this felt as good as a double shot of rye.

124

And now somebody new was entering the scene. This one had been working at the tailgate of a wagon that stood in the sun, its team tied to one of the arcade pillars. He came hurrying up to demand, "What's going on here?"

George Youngman, in the doorway, said indignantly, "The big fellow hauled off and knocked your brother down, Hawkins. From what I seen he had no reason."

"Stay out of this, Youngman!" Roan warned, and saw him change color.

The new man gave Roan a single look, and then turned to lean and hook his victim under one arm and help him to a stand. These were brothers, all right, and neither appeared to be armed. While the younger one stood as though dazed, exploring the cut lip with the tip of his tongue, the other picked up his hat for him and put it on his head, then stooped again for the sack of flour. The beans were a loss, strewn all over the plankings from the burst sack. He scowled reproachfully at the waste, and scattered them with a kick of his heavy work shoe.

The younger one said, his voice trembling with fury, "He done it all, Dave! He rammed me and then he knocked me down. He wants a fight."

"And you'd be fool enough to oblige him, wouldn't you? You better learn to save your fighting for times when there's sense to it!" Dave Hawkins shoved the sack of flour into his brother's hands. "Now, go put this in the wagon." With an angry shrug the other turned to obey.

Both the rig and the horses gave evidence of having traveled a considerable distance. The canvas, sagging on its bows, was deeply stained by mud and streaked by rain. Roped securely to the side of the box was a sturdy-looking plow.

The muleskinner's lip drew back. "Immigrants!" he sneered. "Appleknockers from the sticks! You better move on out of this town, mister," he told the elder Hawkins. "We eat your kind. We serve 'em up with dandelion greens!"

The warning got him a long, hard look. Youngman fidgeted nervously in the doorway, with beads of sweat shining on his cheeks. Roan knew what was chewing him. The old fool liked sod-busters. He wanted Chase Center turned into a farming town, with church on Sunday and maybe even a school. He was one of those who had sent for that gunman, Keyhoe, and brought him here to tame the place for them.

Keyhoe.... At the thought, caution entered Burke Roan's soul and sobered him just a moment. But the marshal wasn't in evidence; and meanwhile here was this farmer, this Dave Hawkins, turning away as though no insult Roan could think up was worth noticing. Furious, Roan lifted his voice and hurled a vicious obscenity after him.

The fellow paused in the doorway, shoulders stiffening. Deliberately he came about and then, without hesitation, walked straight at Burke Roan, as the latter fell into a crouch with fists cocked and ready. At the last moment Hawkins' firmly muscled arm absorbed and deflected the blow Roan threw at him, and the farmer's own rock-hard knuckles struck in past Roan's guard and took him on his blunt jaw.

It jerked his head around in a way that seemed enough to tear it from his neck; Roan felt his legs buckle and the ground came up, slow, to meet him. He wasn't seriously hurt, but surprise and rage blinded him like a suddenly drawn red veil. As though satisfied, Hawkins was already turning away

126

again. An oath tore from Burke Roan and sprawling on his back he dragged out his gun, as someone shouted warning. Roan leveled the Colt's long barrel, fired and missed. He fired again into the echoes of the first shot, and saw his victim flung violently against the sod wall, to crumple there.

When he pulled himself to his feet, with the smoking gun ready, there seemed no further need for it. It was almost as though no one knew he existed: Both the storekeeper, and the other Hawkins brother, were too busy fussing over the crumpled body of the one he had shot.

The farmer wasn't dead. George Youngman, with clucking tongue, pulled aside the bloody shirt to reveal that Roan's bullet had punched a hole clean through, just below the ribs, from which the red blood welled freely. Without a word he rushed into his store and returned immediately bringing a towel and a handful of flour from the barrel. He plastered the flour thickly into both mouths of the wound, and slowly the bleeding let up and finally quit. With young Hawkins' fumbling aid the storekeeper managed to make a pad of the towel and use the hurt man's belt to fasten it in place.

Roan had watched all this with an open sneer. Now, standing over the wounded man, he waggled the gunbarrel and said contemptuously, "I could put him out of his misery with less bother!"

The younger brother's ashen face lifted. Before he could say anything Dave Hawkins groped and caught at his sleeve, and from somewhere the wounded man dug up the strength to exclaim faintly, "Billy—no! Don't rise to his baiting! Just get me out of this damn town...."

The hand fell again, but young Billy Hawkins heeded his brother's urging though he was trembling

127

as he glared at the muleskinner. Burke Roan grinned down into his face. Then the grin froze as a new voice said, "If you don't drop that gun you're holding, this thing can drop *you!*"

Convulsively he twisted about and saw the one who stood behind him, out in the sunbright street. He knew this blackheaded young man with the pale eyes and oddly slanting cheekbones, and the ill-fitting derby that he stubbornly wore almost as though daring someone to knock it off for him. He had become a familiar and much discussed sight here in Chase Center, and so had the ugly-looking shotgun he always carried in the wake of Marshal Keyhoe. But now he stood alone, and the shotgun was pointed squarely at Burke Roan's thick chest.

"I'm not going to wait forever!" Rim Adams said crisply.

With the sun's hot weight upon his shoulders, Adams faced the bigger man and tried to show him a stern and convincing scowl. Wait till the first time you walk up to a man with a gun in his hand and take it away from him, Frank Keyhoe had said once. This looked like the moment, for something had to be done and there was no one else in sight to do it.

Where the hell is Keyhoe? he thought, and believed he knew the answer. In recent days he had seen little of his chief during off-duty hours; it was his strong impression that Keyhoe's nights were being spent at the Novelty, in those upstairs regions where Belle Wadsworth had her rooms.

Something broke in the face of the other man, suddenly. He lowered his arm and let his gun fall to the sidewalk. "Kick it over here to me," Adams ordered. A swipe of a cowhide boot sent the gun skittering across the dust, and he leaned carefully and came up with it, considerably relieved when he had shoved the gun behind his belt. Still, his legs seemed to lack stiffening as they carried him toward the store, conscious of eyes that watched him from many points along this no-man's-land that was the town's street.

The young fellow on his knees with his arms about the wounded man was eyeing him, too. "Who the hell are you?" he demanded belligerently.

"Town marshal's deputy." Adams looked at the storekeeper. "How bad is this man hurt?"

Youngman shook his head. "Hard to say. Not much I know to do, except maybe take him to my place and make him comfortable."

Billy Hawkins demanded, "Ain't you got a doctor in this town of yours?"

"There's one at the fort...."

"No, thanks!" Billy decided firmly. "Help me get him into the wagon and I'll take him back to camp with me. We can do as much for him as some damned army butcher!"

The storekeeper looked doubtful. "I ain't sure he can be moved that far."

"You heard what he said to me," young Billy retorted. "The last words he spoke was, 'Get me out of this damn town!'"

"Now, son, I don't want you getting the wrong idea about our town," Youngman began hurriedly.

But the young fellow wasn't listening. "One thing I'm sure," he said, his challenging stare pinned on Burke Roan's face, "anybody comes messing around our camp, is gonna find there's enough of us to drive them off quick enough!" He looked at Rim Adams, then. "What I want to know, is what happens to the bastard that shot Dave?"

Adams hesitated hardly at all, in making what he

129

knew was a momentous decision. "He's under arrest," he answered. "If your brother dies, he'll be sent to the nearest court and stand trial for murder."

He saw Burke Roan's head give a jerk. But young Hawkins was still unconvinced, still suspicious as he demanded, "How do I know this?"

"Because damn it, I'm telling you!" And Adams swung away to his prisoner and showed him the muzzle of the shotgun. "I reckon you know where the jail is."

"You ain't puttin' me, or nobody else, in that jail!" Burke Roan declared. But under the shotgun's threat he heeled around and started walking stiffly ahead of Adams, across the wide street. They left Youngman and the Hawkins boy preparing, between them, to maneuver the wounded man into the rear of the wagon.

Rim Adams had dynamite on his hands, and knew it. The very quiet of the street told him so; for all the sun's heat, his palms felt clammy on the shotgun. A dustdevil came bearing toward them, caught and surrounded them both for an instant in a tawny, stinging swirl. Rim Adams tried all at the same time to watch his prisoner and the windows and doors of the buildings opposite, and somehow see through the back of his head.

And then, as they gained the opposite side and turned toward the jail, Harry Dowler was suddenly before him. Burke Roan had looked big enough, but the yard boss was even bigger. He leaned his shoulders against a building's corner and Adams' nerves leaped as he saw that Dowler held a six-shooter dangling idly in one hand.

Roan had halted and half turned, an expectant grin on his face, evidently thinking the redhead would quickly change the shape of things. Adams, his mouth gone dry, kept the shotgun trained on his prisoner as he told Dowler, "Stay out of this! Don't give me any trouble!"

"You're only making trouble for yourself, kid," the redhead told him reasonably. "You're set to stir up something even Keyhoe can't settle. You don't really think the town's going to let you jail him?"

Rim Adams' knees were shaking and he knew his face must be as empty of color as dried bone, but he forced himself to meet the threat of the revolver that was trained, casually, at a spot just above his belt buckle. "To stop me," he said, "you'll have to kill me. With the charge this thing carries, I know I can get at least one and maybe both of you while you're doing it. You want to try?"

Slowly, Dowler's gun lowered. Roan, seeing this, cried sharply: "Harry!" but the redhead, who knew a standoff when he saw one, shook his head.

"That's how he wants it—let him play it out. This thing is a long way from finished." He drew aside, motioning with his shaggy head as he thrust the gun into its holster. "Go right ahead, Adams. Don't say you ain't been warned!"

Burke Roan was silent, angrily brooding, during the rest of the uneasy march to jail.

CHAPTER 14

When for the first time the plank door had been slammed on a prisoner and the padlock snapped in place, Adams crossed the twenty feet that separated the jail from the newly finished marshal's office. Inside, he racked his shotgun, laid the key and the

131

gun he'd taken off Burke Roan upon the desktop, and lowered himself into the barrel chair while he fought down a first gloomy surge of panic.

From the window beside him he could watch both the jail and a piece of lower Main Street stretching toward the railroad tracks. Asa Timberlake had wasted no material on this office Keyhoe insisted on. It was little more than a box, with barely space for the desk and chairs, the cheap file cabinet that as yet had nothing in it, the army cot in the corner where Rim Adams slept. Its unglazed windows were equipped with crude wooden shutters; no thought had been given to a way of heating either the office or the nearby jail.

Just now, winter seemed a long way off.

Gradually Adams felt his nerves settle. He listened to the drone of a trapped fly bouncing about the raw unpainted walls, the clank and rumble of a work train passing the depot with supplies for the construction crews at end-of-track. Presently he heard a light prowling footstep that he knew well. It turned him tense again and he was on his feet when Frank Keyhoe appeared in the doorway.

A single glance at the other's face told Adams his chief was aware of the news. The marshal returned his look a long moment before saying, with resignation, "All right—let's hear it it."

Adams hesitated. "I don't know what you've already heard…"

"Never mind what I've heard. I want your version." Keyhoe walked to the desk, dropped his hat on it and seated himself. Rim Adams drew a breath, and with his superior's eyes on him related, as exactly as he could, just what had happened in front of Youngman's.

As he talked he could see no change of

132

expression, nothing to tell him how the other took his story. He found himself sweating, and talking louder in his effort to justify himself. "If this fellow Hawkins should die," he concluded defiantly, "then according to my book Burke Roan is guilty of murder. It's as simple as that!"

Keyhoe had made a steeple of his lean and tapered hands he looked at them and murmured, "And so you threw him in jail..."

"I did what I thought had to be done!" Adams retorted. "You weren't there to tell me otherwise."

What Keyhoe might have said to that went unspoken; they were interrupted, as a newcomer entered the office.

It was Asa Timberlake. The trader was hatless and in his shirtsleeves, just as he had come from his own place at the wagon yard next door. His glance raked Rim Adams, settled on the man seated at the desk. He said petulantly, "I've been watching for you. I was beginning to wonder if you meant to come in, this morning!"

Keyhoe chose to ignore the thinly veiled criticism—the implication, if it was one, that he was spending too much time these days, and nights, in Belle Wadsworth's rooms on the second floor of the Novelty. He said calmly, "Something I can do for you?"

"You can do something for yourself," Timberlake answered curtly, and looked at Adams. "You can keep this deputy of yours from pulling any more boners, like the one he just did."

"Arresting a man for attempted murder?"

Timberlake made an impatient, slicing gesture with one soft palm. "The hell with that!" he snapped. "Burke Roan works for me, Keyhoe.

"So?"

133

"Damn it all, how do you expect me to make any money, if you've got my men cooling their heels in that jail of yours!"

Rim Adams broke in. "Maybe that's something you'd better take up with *them!*"

It got him another icy stare from the freighter. Pointedly not answering, the man turned back to Keyhoe. "It appears there's something we had better get straight, Keyhoe. My crews are to be let alone. That isn't what I hired you for!"

At his words, the iron entered the marshal's face. "You didn't hire me, Timberlake!" he snapped. "You were only one of a committee. I was asked to bring some kind of order into this place. If you don't like the results, you'll have to get the committee to vote me fired!"

The other's cheeks turned slowly mottled. "Don't think it can't be done! You may not have as firm a hold on this job as you think. In case you've forgotten, I have power in this town, and I can use it."

"Go right ahead." Keyhoe reached into a pocket of his coat, took out an envelope and tossed it on the desk. Adams had seen it before; it looked like one that had arrived in the mailbag on yesterday's westbound train.

"There are other jobs," Keyhoe said. He pointed at the envelope. "That happens to be an offer from Ellsworth. They're about to cut in on the Texas cattle trade and they want me to take the post of city marshal—at better money than *you* pay. So don't try to threaten me!"

"As for my deputy, he used his head and did the only thing he could do. Until we know whether Burke Roan has done murder or not, the man's going to stay right where he is!"

134

Timberlake's mouth pulled tight. Without a word he swung about and strode abruptly out of the office.

Rim Adams found his voice. "Thanks," he said gruffly. "For standing up for me...."

The marshal nodded. He picked up the envelope and returned it to his pocket. Adams said, "That's the very job you were talking about, on the train coming out—one you said you might like to tackle. You going to?"

"I've already got a job," Keyhoe said.

"I dunno. Timberlake sounds like be could mean business, about getting you fired. Do you think Youngman, and Weld, and the others will give in? Or will they stand up to him?"

Frank Keyhoe shrugged and, rising from the desk, went to the door and looked out upon the silent summer day. When he turned his head, his expression was somber. "Whatever the leaders do, there's one thing we can count on: The tough element has been waiting to see us try and use that jail for the first time. Now it's happened, they won't let it go without a challenge."

Rim Adams demanded anxiously, "What do you suppose will happen?"

"Who knows? They'll probably let us stew awhile, to begin with. When the real trouble breaks—" He turned again to contemplate the quiet, lazy morning. "We'll just hope we catch wind of it ahead of time...."

It had been a day of waiting. On Keyhoe's orders Adams scarcely stirred from the desk in the marshal's office, or from his constant watch over the jail. He'd had meals brought in for himself and for the prisoner, standing guard with shotgun ready as

135

the plank door was opened and Burke Roan's plate passed in to him. The teamster cursed him through the door's small barred window, making promises of what would happen to Adams when his friends made their play to take him out of there.

"Getting a little nervous?" he chided, his grin showing whitely in the shadows. "You better be! Harry Dowler won't be holding off much longer." He seemed confident and cocky, not at all abashed that a death sentence might hang over his head. Probably, Adams thought, he knew exactly what he was talking about. No doubt messages had been signaled to him, throughout the long day. He likely knew all about whatever was planned.

The deputy's own supper sank like lead, in a stomach turned queasy by prolonged anxiety. He ate it at the marshal's desk, an oil lamp lighted, shotgun leaning against the wall beside him. As he swallowed the final mouthful of coffee to wash down the last bit of meat and beans, he heard footsteps approach the open door and looked up, hoping it was Keyhoe; but it wasn't.

"Merl Brinegar," the man in the doorway reminded him helpfully. "We met at the colonel's tent, a week ago."

It took a moment of readjusting his thoughts, before Adams could place the newspaperman. "I remember," he said in some irritation.

"I thought you were supposed to be out covering a buffalo hunt, with Sutter and his senator friend."

"Correct! We got back this afternoon—I've just been to the depot, to put my copy aboard tomorrow's eastbound." Not waiting to be invited, the little man entered and helped himself to the extra chair, dropping his plug hat on the desk and taking out a briar pipe and a leather tobacco pouch. Adams saw now that his narrow fox face was sunburnt and peeling, his forthead white by contrast above the line made by the hatbrim.

The deputy asked dryly, "Did you enjoy yourself? How was the trip?"

Brinegar lifted a shoulder. "A bore. And a colossal waste of ammunition. The senator missed everything he shot at, including three antelope and a wolf; and no one else dared shoot any better— except the party scout, an old man in the smelliest set of buckskins I ever saw. He went out quietly on his own and brought in meat enough to keep us from starving to death."

"See any Indians?"

"Never a sign. But finally we did run across a stand of buffalo, about fifty head in a wallow. Somebody propped up a rifle for the senator and aimed it, and the big beasts stood quiet and let him shoot one of them though it took four bullets. After that we were able to call it quits and come in."

Brinegar had his pipe charged and the pouch stowed away in his rumpled clothing. As he sucked match flame into the bowl he peered at Adams through the quick spurt of tobacco smoke. "Changed your mind, about showing me around this community of yours?"

"I already told you I had too many other things on my hands," Adams said coldly. "Anyway, you picked a poor night. If you're really a newspaperman, you should have got wind that there's trouble in the air. This town's on the verge of erupting."

"Why, then," the other said blandly, as he shook out his match and dropped it on the floor, "for my purposes I couldn't have picked better. In my business, we thrive on other people's trouble. What

137

seems to be going on?"

Adams scowled at him, debating whether he was right to be telling the man anything at all. And then he stiffened, almost certain he heard a sound somewhere just outside the window.

Had someone spoken his name, or was it only nerves misreading the normal snapping and sawing of insects in the dry weeds? Brinegar had plainly heard nothing; he started to speak again but broke off as Adams lifted a warning hand. In the same moment something struck the window frame—a stone, that hit the wood and dropped away.

Instantly Adams was on his feet, with shoulders pressed against the wall out of range of the opening. He put his question into the darkness: "Is somebody out there?"

"Mister Adams?" It came so faintly, a mere whisper of sound, that he barely made it out. "This is Ruby Jerrod—you remember, I work for Belle Wadsworth?"

"Yes, Ruby?"

"Please I got to talk to you! I'm afraid for anyone to see—me...."

A moment only, he hesitated. "I'll come out."

He saw Brinegar's curious stare pinned on him. "For all you know, it may be a trap."

Adams thought of the girl with the gamin's face and somehow didn't believe it. But he picked up the shotgun and hung it across his arm as he stepped outside.

He moved quickly from the lighted doorway. A milky overcast shrouded the face of the moon, blurring the edges of the shadows. As he rounded the building corner, he found the girl standing in darkness that was made even deeper by contrast with the spill of lamplight from the window. Her

138

face showed as a pale oval.

When Adams came to her she clutched at his hand; though the night was warm, with the earth giving up the heat it had trapped during the long, sweltering day, her touch was cold. He made out the glitter of sequins on her brief skirt, caught a whiff of cheap perfume. Ruby spoke and her voice had a tremor of fear in it. "I wasn't sure you even heard me!"

Adams touched her shoulder and found she was shaking. He could hear the quickness of her breathing; he said, "What is it, Ruby? Quiet down and try to tell me what's got you so upset. Why were you looking for me?"

"I had to warn you!" she exclaimed, her words tumbling over one another. "You're in terrible danger—you and Mister Keyhoe! They're getting ready to attack the jail, and they'll kill you both if they can!"

It confirmed his own growing concern and he felt his mouth go dry. "Who are you talking about, Ruby? And how do you know?"

"Why, everybody knows! It's all the people here that want to get rid of you! They hate the lid you've put on the town—they hate the jail. They mean to tear it down and set your prisoner loose. They're just hoping you may try to stop them!"

Rim Adams stood silently absorbing what the girl had told him, while the night insects made their rhythmic sawing in the weeds and the warm smells of the prairie breathed upon the town. Finally he was able to say, "Did Belle send you to warn us?"

"I haven't seen Belle. I came on my own."

"That was a risky thing to do. But, I can imagine she'll be grateful."

The girl's reply was muffled. "I didn't do it for her, or for Frank Keyhoe either...."

He almost missed her meaning. "You did it for *me*?" he stammered, and felt his face grow warm with embarrassment.

"All right, I'm just a girl who works in a dance hall—but I can appreciate it when somebody treats me decent! Her fingers touched his wrist and fell away and she added quickly, "I got to go, now. But please look out for yourself, Mister Adams!"

"You sure you'll be safe?" he began, belatedly. "Nobody followed you?"

But she was gone already, and he heard her moving quickly away through the clotted shadows.

Someone came up on the blind side of him; he was starting to lift the shotgun when the glow from the window showed him Mel Brinegar's face. He said irritably, "That's a good way to get yourself killed!"

The newspaperman passed it off. His eyes, reflecting the light, held a glitter of anticipation. "What's going on here, Adams? That young woman came to warn you of trouble. What about it?"

"Nothing that concerns you, or the paper you write for," Rim Adams answered, and was cut short by a disturbance some dozen yards from where they stood.

Dimly filtered moonlight showed him the struggling figures. There were muttered curses—a blow—and then, unmistakably, a woman's scream that was broken off as though a hand had been clamped over her mouth. Rim Adams waited for no more, but started forward almost without thinking. At his shout the figures broke apart and he saw one crumple to the ground. And Adams whipped up the shotgun and let go with one barrel, aiming directly

140

above the heads of the pair who turned to see him coming.

The weapon's roar was tremendous in the stillness. Adams thought he heard a bleat of pain. Hurrying forward, he didn't know if some of the shot pattern might have found a target, didn't care if it had. He'd accomplished what he wanted which was to scatter those men and start them running; halting at Ruby's side, he listened a moment to the sound of her attackers making a hasty retreat.

He leaned over her. "Are you hurt?"

"No," she answered, in a muffled voice. When he helped her to her feet she clung to him, sobbing hysterically. "But you were right! They must have followed me from Belle's...."

Adams slipped an arm about her shoulders and held her close until her trembling subsided. The night had absorbed the blast of the shotgun. Nothing seemed disturbed by it except for a dog that barked a few times in the distance and then fell silent.

The girl pulled away now and he let her go. "I'm sorry," she exclaimed as she wiped her cheeks with both palms. "I'll be all right. They scared me pretty bad."

Dubiously he watched her push a hand into the tangle of her hair, try to smooth out her rumpled skirt. "Maybe I better walk back with you."

"No, no!" she said quickly. "I'll be more careful after this. They won't catch me again!"

He looked at her. Her makeup had run and smeared and her pinched little face looked ghastly in the thin light. Deeply touched, Adams could only say inadequately, "You're a good scout. Believe me, I'll never forget what you did tonight!"

It sounded lame enough, and he could only stand watching as she turned and walked away from him a second time. When at last the continuing silence satisfied him she hadn't run into further danger, Rim Adams drew a breath and turned back—and as he did so, glimpsed Frank Keyhoe approaching across the vacant lot. Quickly he moved to intercept his chief, shouldering impatiently past Merl Brinegar when the latter tried to catch at his sleeve and continue his questioning.

Marshal and deputy met in the office doorway. "I heard the shotgun," Keyhoe said crisply. "What's going on?" Having heard the young man out, he swung away without offering a reaction and walked inside the building, his deputy followed, still carrying the shotgun.

Merl Brinegar trailed after them, though he hadn't been invited. Seeing him, Keyhoe scowled and demanded, "Who the hell is this?" then answered his own question: "Oh, yes—the newspaperman. Stay around, friend, you may get yourself a real story!" He went to the desk and dropped into the chair behind it.

"What the girl told you," he informed Adams, "confirms what I've been able to learn. Looks as though we're in for it—sometime before midnight, if my guess is any good. It's your friend Harry Dowler. He's got the riffraff organized and they mean to have their showdown. Arresting Burke Roan is just the excuse." The gravity of the situation showed plainly enough in the marshal's pallor, and the look of strain about his eyes. The amber eyes themselves, in the glow of the lamp, seemed to Adams to have a reddish, slightly bloodshot cast; and from this Rim Adams knew suddenly the marshal had been drinking heavily. The knowledge filled him with a hollow misgiving.

Though the lean, strong hands lying on the desk
142

showed no unsteadiness, no hint of trembling, he sensed somehow that Frank Keyhoe was deathly afraid.

He cleared his throat. "I don't suppose there's any chance of getting help? The men who hired us should do something to back us up."

Keyhoe was shaking his head before his deputy finished speaking. "No chance at all. You might as well forget it."

"I suppose."

"But don't forget to reload that," the marshal added, indicating the shotgun. Adams nodded and went to the file case in the corner of the room where he broke out a box of paper cartridges and recharged the weapon, afterward dropping several spares into his pocket. He also got out his hand gun, the old Smith & Wesson converted to brass; when he had checked the loads and the action and shoved it behind his belt, he felt as nearly ready as he would ever be.

Mel Brinegar had been watching in silence. He said suddenly, "I don't suppose you have an extra one of those?"

The others looked at him. "Are you handy with a gun," Keyhoe asked, a dry edge of humor in his voice.

"Never fired one in my life. But you were saying a minute ago, you're short of help."

"Thanks all the same," the marshal told him. "You'd probably shoot off your foot. Besides, this is all the arsenal we have. No more weapons than we need for the two of us...."

As he spoke, somewhere in the night a man's voice lifted in a faint wordless shout. Hard of hearing or not, Frank Keyhoe heard that; as though at a signal he half rose from his chair, cupped a

143

hand behind the lip of the lamp's shade and blew the flame. Rim Adams felt the thudding of his heart as the room plunged into darkness.

CHAPTER 15

"When they come," Frank Keyhoe said, "it would help if we knew from what direction...."

The jail and this flimsy office were both badly exposed, standing well back from the street in an open space of weeds and trash, with the Timberlake wagon yard flanking it on the south and the nearest neighboring building on Main Street some fifty yards away. As they stood tensely waiting between the darkened buildings, Rim Adams saw that in fact an attack could hit them from almost any direction.

Though the shout had not been repeated, he wondered if the other two felt, as he did, a sense of restless and ill-defined movement. A wind had risen. It found a sheet of old newspaper and picked it up and scooted it a little distance across the bare ground before it caught up in the weeds, causing Adams' nerves to leap and pull the shotgun's tubes that way before he saw what had startled him.

He settled himself, and found his voice. "I'll take a look around."

Keyhoe answered shortly, "Go ahead. Only, don't stumble into anything. Be careful!"

"You don't have to tell me!"

He went at a quick prowl, carrying the shotgun at high port and searching out every sound and everything that moved. Alone, he felt at once more exposed but also less vulnerable. And, unable to discover anything that spelled clear danger, he turned toward Main Street where it seemed most likely to be signals would appear.

Gaining the dark wall of the nearest building he moved forward, where he could have a look into the street. To his left, beyond the jail and the bulk of Timberlake's warehouse and freight barns, a lamp burned above the empty platform of the Kansas Pacific depot; another glowed dimly inside. Everything appeared quiet enough at this lower end of town, but farther up there seemed to be a core of activity. He could hear a confused sound of voices, and thought he made out the shapes of men moving about in a streaky blur of dust and lampglow. After some debate he reluctantly decided this needed his attention.

He ventured nearer, advancing cautiously along the edge of the street and wherever he could keeping close to scattered building fronts. The noise strengthened, began to take on an angry overtone that was really frightening. It was the voice of a mob, he thought, and unlike anything he had ever heard before—though it did remind him a little of a sound he had heard a time or two on battlefields during the war: the sound of men working themselves up to killing.

Having come as close as he dared he halted, clutching the shotgun in sweating palms as he saw the street was filled with men. Some merely stayed on the edges, out of the way, curiously watching; but there was a constant milling and moving about and, always, that steady buzzing of sound, almost like a swarming of hornets. Torches flared, with a drip of burning oil and drift of smoke. Rim Adams, watching, had a dismal certainty that things were near a point when the pot would start to boil over.

And when the moment arrived this crowd would begin moving toward the jail.

Yonder rose the graceless clapboard box that housed the Novelty, its windows ablaze with light, and he felt a rush of guilt as he thought of Belle's girl Ruby. He ought to have made certain she got back safely; it had been wrong to let her try to pick her own way through this dangerous town tonight. Yet, he thought, as Keyhoe's deputy he was a marked man himself. Ruby was in less danger alone….

A shift in the crowd voice, then—it seemed to lift an octave, at a stroke. He would never know what had triggered it, but he saw that mass of men sway and bulge and suddenly they were a solid front, moving straight toward him along the street. The roaring swelled and as quickly ebbed again, as though action now took all their energy—fallen nearly silent except for the rhythmic, determined slog of boots and brush of clothing. Dust, stirring and lifting, welled up and the glow of torches and lighted windows turned it into a saffron fog that enveloped them.

Rim Adams stood obscurely near a building corner, and watched them come. Faces were mere shapeless blobs, but the glint of guns and rifle barrels showed plain enough, swinging to the massive and uneven rhythm. For just a moment he was swayed by an insane impulse to defy them all and turn them back under the muzzle of the shotgun. But there were too many. Not even a blast from both barrels, directly in their faces, could keep them from rolling right over him.

He could only draw back as the front wave came abreast and then swung by, close enough that he might almost have reached out and touched the

146

nearest fringe. He smelled dust and sweat and burning oil, and he switched the shotgun from one hand to the other while he wiped nervous palms dry upon his trouser legs.

Suddenly a voice with a crack in the center of it bawled right in his ear, "Hey! Ain't you—?" A bearded face thrust within inches of his own; a hand clutched at his clothing. *"Here's Keyhoe's deputy!"*

Almost without thinking Adams let the man have the shotgun's tubes across his chest, as hard as he could swing. He tore the fingers loose, sent the fellow staggering as the outcry died in his throat. And Rim Adams, completing his movement, wheeled and went at a running scramble between a pair of neighboring buildings as a yell arose behind him.

With the taste of fear in his mouth he reached a dark rear corner and swung sharply to his left. This building, hardly more than a shack, had a flimsy, openfronted leanto tacked to the end of it. On an inspiration Adams checked himself and plunged in here, pressing back into the deepest shadows where the walls met the shallow roof. He was barely in time. Running footsteps spurted and two vague figures went by, followed seconds later by a third and then two more, as he crouched with the shotgun ready and tried to control his own shallow breathing.

But those seemed to be all of them though he listened til the sounds faded. Afterward, knowing they would be doubling back if he waited and let them learn they had missed him, he emerged cautiously from his hiding place. No challenge met him. Quickly he began a long circle in the direction of the jail. As he went his legs felt mushy and uncertain under him—the sure measure of his anxiety.

147

He brought his goal in sight, and in the next instant saw the mob. They were halted out there in the street, as though not sure about the next step or about coming any closer. Adams, panting for breath, dropped to one knee in the high weeds where he could watch without himself being seen.

So far no sound, and no faintest glimmer of light, came from the two tiny structures huddled in the middle of the open lot. He listened to the shuffle of boots, the murmur of voices. Then Burke Roan's unmistakable voice cut through the night noises: "Who's out there? That you, Harry? You boys come to break me loose?"

Harry Dowler answered. "It's us, Burke. Where's Keyhoe?"

"Damn if I know! He was in his office, a minute ago. Harry, you got to get me out of this!"

Dowler sounded taut-nerved and impatient. "We ain't walking into no trap, to do it!"

Burke Roan cursed him—Adams could see the prisoner's face, palely, against the darker blackness of the window set into the jail's thick door. He could imagine him clinging to the sturdy bars.

A braver segment of the crowd had edged closer now and, in the forefront, Adams saw a figure that loomed bigger than the rest. Harry Dowler's light-colored shirt, dimly visible, was no target for the shotgun, but Adams found himself putting a hand in under his coat to finger the butt of his revolver. If there was even a chance of picking off the big redhead with a lucky bullet, he could almost have been tempted to try it. But he balked at shooting a man out of hand, and as he hesitated the figure moved and melted with the others and it was too late.

Then, from the darkness somewhere near the

148

office shack, a voice spoke with the sting of a whip: "Dowler? Frank Keyhoe! I'm giving you a chance to take that rabble with you and leave."

To Rim Adams it seemed as though the very night held its breath. Certainly there was a long moment, before Keyhoe's unexpected challenge received any answer, it came then in a bellow from the redhead. "You sonofabitch! You can't tree this town! I don't care who you are—you're only one man. Even if that chicken-livered deputy hasn't headed for a hole, there's still no more than two of you. We're taking Burke Roan from you, and then we're pulling that jail to pieces!"

"Try it...."

That raised a howl, and right then Adams was certain everything was about to smash wide open. But such was the respect they had for Frank Keyhoe that no one moved at all. And Adams, deciding he could do no good where he was, eased to his feet and began to fade back, with the aim of making a wide swing past the rear of the jail and so come in to join Keyhoe.

Suddenly there was a swell of sound from the crowd, and out of it came running footsteps. He halted, bringing up the shotgun, as he thought for an instant they were coming at *him*. But when he caught sight of the pair of scuttling figures, and saw that one had a torch, he all at once guessed what they were up to.

He saw the second man lift and swing something he carried, saw a glistening sheet of liquid splash and spread and heard the rattle of the empty tin as it was flung aside. The torch described a brief, bright circle. Dripping burning oil, it streaked over and struck the wall of the jail; kerosene caught and flared up and quickly an entire corner of the building was engulfed, as the mob's voice grew to a roar.

The firesetters turned and fled to safety; standing frozen and somehow unable to move, Rim Adams let them go. He could only watch the flames take hold as a rising wind whipped at them. And now Burke Roan was yelling again, with sudden terror in his voice. "Harry! What you trying to do, burn me to a crisp? God damn it, get me out of here! *Get me out!*"

Yonder, Harry Dowler raged and cursed the ones who had been in too great a hurry, and torched the jail before it was time. Adams could hear him bawling orders: "Who has that crowbar? Get over there and start working on them windows. The rest will cover you."

It took some urging. At last someone got up his nerve. Firelight picked out the metal rod he carried as he came scurrying across the open; and Rim Adams thought, with growing frustration, Where the hell is Keyhoe?

Except for that one warning, there had been nothing from the marshal at all—not even now as they set about burning and tearing apart his jail. Adams waited tensely for the bullet that would knock over the man with the crowbar, or drive him back; it never came, and now he had gained a side of the jail where he was beyond Keyhoe's reach. The window there was high, but large enough that even someone of Burke Roan's size should manage to squeeze through. Without hesitation the man thrust his iron between a couple of bars, set a boot against the wall and proceeded to put his weight against it.

A screech of protesting timbers sounded, above the crackling of the flames and the racket of the mob in the street.

150

It was up to Adams, apparently. Bestirring himself, he switched the shotgun to his left hand and brought the six-shooter from behind his belt. He had a good target, clearly illuminated; he could probably have killed the one with the crowbar, but as his finger was tightening on the trigger he dropped the muzzle slightly and shot him in the leg instead. The steel implement went flying as the man was knocked cleanly off his feet, screaming.

If no one had noticed Adams until now, what he had just done would change that fast enough. His nearest cover was some yards away, a small pile of timbers left over from building the jail; from there he could at least make an attempt at holding off the mob, if he had to. He ran forward and dropped behind it, aware from the momentary warmth of the fire against his face that those in the street must have had a good enough look to recognize him.

They respected Keyhoe, but they had no reason to fear his deputy. Rim Adams knew he was in for it. He laid the shotgun handy and with shaking fingers steadied his revolver across the top of the pile. The strong scent of creosote stung his nostrils, and then a gun barked spitefully and the first bullet drove into his scant barricade.

Merl Brinegar, watching from the rear corner of the jail building, was aware of the heavy slogging in his heartbeat. In a pleasurable mix of fear and excitement, such as he had seldom experienced, he saw Rim Adams take cover while the man the deputy had shot crawled painfully away by fits and starts through the weeds and litter, like a stepped-on bug. When the echo of Adams' shot mingled with the first angry gunfire from the mob, Brinegar waited for nothing more.

He turned and left that place at a dead run, tripping once in the darkness, to fall and scramble up again. He flanked the rear of the jail, crossed between it and the marshal's shack and so came up on the place where he had left Frank Keyhoe. The tall man had seemingly not moved at all. He was still at the forward corner, still watching the crowd, as though they had nothing to do with him. He seemed unaware of Brinegar until the latter seized him boldly by an arm, saying, "What's the matter with you? Can't you hear what's happening out there? They have your deputy pinned down. They'll kill him, if you don't stop them!"

Frank Keyhoe turned his head, expression unreadable in that poor light; to the other he looked almost like a man in a funk. When he got no answer Brinegar exclaimed in growing anger, "Perhaps it doesn't matter to you if they burn your jail to the ground. But damn it, that young fool is risking his neck just to save your job, and your reputation!"

A gust of wind brought oily smoke from the blazing jail swooping down, to engulf them both. When it swirled off Brinegar was left doubled over, coughing and retching. He was like that when, through streaming eyes, he saw the other man suddenly turn and walk away from him.

At the moment he couldn't guess what the marshal intended. Just before stepping into the open, Keyhoe paused as though to brace himself. Brinegar saw him slide both pearl-handled guns from their holsters. And then, deliberately, he moved out and the newspaperman stumbled after—but only as far as the corner of the shack. There, still fighting the smoke that filled his lungs, Merl Brinegar leaned a hand against the rough, unpainted wood while he watched what he knew was to be one of the big

152

events of his life.

He had heard of two-gun men, and had written his share of wild tales about them; *this* was the reality. Going into action, Frank Keyhoe kept his left hand and the gun it held out of action, low at his side—a reserve, strictly. The weapon in his right was leveled at the line of his chest, and as he moved without hurry into the full gleam of the fire, the wavering light gave Brinegar a moment's illusion that the very ground trembled beneath the man's slow stride.

Keyhoe offered no warning—he wouldn't have been heard if he tried. Instead, selecting a target among the guns that were probing for Rim Adams, he fired and that gun went silent. He fired again and a second man went down. Like a machine, Frank Keyhoe advanced upon the mob, methodically emptying his gun; then, seemingly without breaking the rhythm, he dropped it into its holster and caught its mate from the air as his left hand deftly performed the border shift. To Merl Brinegar, watching open-mouthed, it was almost as though the next shot came while the gun was still in midair.

It was a performance legends were born of; he recognized it as such and was awestruck. As for the mob, they appeared bewildered at first, then stunned. Keyhoe, never halting his slow and steady forward pacing, seemed invulnerable. He dropped two more of his enemies and the rest gave up. With one accord they broke and turned to flee, before this man whom Brinegar had nearly charged with cowardice.

Rim Adams, behind his barricade, found himself at a loss at first to know what was happening. One moment he had been fighting for his life, and then the furious voice of the crowd took on a note of panic and all at once no more bullets were seeking him out. When he risked a look above the pile of creosoted timbers, what he saw lifted him to his feet in pure astonishment. He had thought he was beginning to know this Frank Keyhoe; the killing machine he saw now, with the Chase Center rabble scattering like rabbits in front of him, was away beyond all his imaginings.

Then a voice shouted his name; he looked around to see the sweating and distorted face of Harry Dowler. The man bawled hoarsely, "I've got *you*, at least!" and in that instant the muzzle of the gun pointed at Rim Adams' head looked like the mouth of a tunnel. But someone, fleeing, stumbled into the big man and the gun exploded harmlessly into the dirt as Dowler went to his knees, putting out both hands. Belatedly Adams remembered he still held a weapon of his own. When Dowler's head lifted, the lank fall of hair across his forehead glimmering redly in the firelight, he was staring into the deputy's gunbarrel.

Adams could have killed him. Instead he ordered crisply, "Leave that lying where it is, and get up!" Dowler looked at the gun beneath his fingers, and the other could read the desperate impulses that worked across his face. But he rose with empty hands, and Adams jerked his head and said, "Now, get out of here!"

The big man's mouth worked, with ugly hatred. "Next time, Adams!" he promised. "There'll always be a next time!" Abruptly he swung and plunged off into the darkness. And it came to Rim Adams that all was quiet now except for the crackling of the flames, and the moaning that arose from one or two of the wounded lying in the weeds. The battle at the jail had ended.

The tally was three dead, all of them victims of Keyhoe's guns Four had wounds bad enough to leave them incapacitated; no one would ever know how many that fled had taken lesser hurts. Adams could scarcely believe he himself had come through without harm. When with Merl Brinegar's help he had hauled sufficient water from the freightyard pump to douse the fire, he discovered it had eaten into one corner and wall and a portion of the roof; but the sturdy jail building would still serve, with a certain amount of patching.

And now came the final irony: Opening the door with the key he had in his pocket, Rim Adams discovered why there had been no sound from the prisoner since the shooting ended. It was a wild bullet through the window that had done it, obviously fired by one of his own friends. Burke Roan, with half his face gone, would never stand trial, no matter if the farmer he had shot lived or died.

But—Frank Keyhoe?

The marshal had vanished, immediately the fight was over, neither Adams nor Brinegar saw him go, nor could they get any clue from the awed and curious townspeople who came clustering about the jail, to gape and stammer questions. But afterward Rim Adams was somehow not really too surprised, when the cleaning up had been done and he walked into the office shaking with letdown and nervous exhaustion, to light the damp and find a drawer of the desk standing open.

As he more than half expected, the whiskey bottle he knew Keyhoe stored there was missing.

CHAPTER 16

The second morning after the battle, Rim Adams entered Youngman's and found the storekeeper and the livery stable owner, Bert Weld. Here there was stillness, and the heavy weight of Kansas summer heat; outside, the street lay nearly empty and scoured by the constant prairie wind. Adams nodded and said good morning, and George Youngman placed both hands on the counter and wagged his head as he answered pleasantly, "It *is* a good morning! For Chase Center anyway. Bert and me were just talking about the difference in the town, this last couple of days!"

"I have to admit it," the livery owner said grudgingly. "The riffraff—the floaters and the tough element that have made it unlivable—they're still pouring out. A half dozen of the worst dives and deadfalls are closed already. I didn't really think it was possible, but it looks like you and Keyhoe have tamed this place. All in one night!"

Remembering the terrible figure of Frank Keyhoe, advancing on that crowd in the wavering light of the burning jail and methodically shooting them down, Rim Adams could almost believe it. Lately, on their patrols, the marshal and his deputy had found a subtle but definite change, an absence of the tension that had sung constantly along a man's nerves when he walked through the street, heretofore.

Honesty prompted him to say, "If the town's tamed, it was Keyhoe's doing. I was on hand, that night, but I didn't contribute much."

Silence met his statement. The two townsmen exchanged a look and then George Youngman, clearing his throat, said, "That's highly commendable, wanting to give the credit to your chief. Yes, I like to hear it."

"For my part," Bert Weld said heavily, "I been hearing and seeing things that make me wonder about Frank Keyhoe. When I ran into him yesterday afternoon the man acted as though he hardly knew me—he was positively gray. I can spot a bad hangover when I see one! It's all over town that he drinks more than he has any business doing, and spends more time than he should—openly—with a woman I don't think I have to name!"

Adams felt the sting of anger. "What Keyhoe or anyone else does on his own time is his own business, or ought to be! If he's done the job you hired him to—because you knew damned well no one else could do it for you!—then I reckon you've got no excuse to be poormouthing him now!" And as Weld's face swiftly colored, Adams turned abruptly to Youngman. "That fellow Burke Roan shot," he said. "The farmer. You heard anything from him?"

"Nothing, for a fact." The merchant seemed glad to change the subject. "Not since his brother hauled him away in the wagon."

"I been thinking maybe I ought to ride out to wherever their outfit is camped, and see about him. Can you tell me how to get there?"

"According to what Hawkins said, it's in a grove of cottonwoods in the creek bottom, some three miles east where the railroad crosses on a trestle. Just follow the tracks and you shouldn't miss them. I'm glad to have you do this," the merchant added quickly. "I'd ride out with you if I had the time. Those people are the kind we want to encourage. Maybe, when they learn what's happened here, they

157

just might feel a shade friendlier toward this town of ours."

Rim Adams looked at the liveryman. "You got a horse I can rent for an hour or two?"

Weld, still angry, nodded stiffly. "Come along. I'll fix you up." He asked Youngman, "You were about to tell me what time that thing starts, this evening."

"Supposed to be at eight," the merchant said. "It ain't my cup of tea, but Emma's looking forward to it; so I reckon we'll be there since we're invited." Seeing a puzzled look on Adams' face he said to the young-man, "You've heard about the doings at the fort, I reckon? They're throwing some kind of a shindig for the colonel, and his company from Washington. A military ball, I guess they call it."

Rim Adams ironed the expression out of his face. "I heard about it," he said gruffly. He didn't say that he had heard it from Mel Brinegar, and that the newspaperman had hinted at the consequences if Frank Keyhoe learned he'd not been invited.

Rim Adams didn't pretend to know all of the marshal's affairs; but certainly his chief hadn't hinted at any knowledge of what would be going on at the army post tonight....

He found the wagon camp without difficulty, following the directions supplied by George Youngman. He rode up the creek-bank with the railroad trestle at his back and, almost as soon as he recognized the grove of cottonwoods, saw the wagons—eight of them—and the spiraling smoke from a couple of cookfires.

These people kept a tidy camp. The stock was rope-penned at a little distance, and there was no unsightly clutter. The women had taken advantage of the opportunity to do some washing; the hot wind

158

fluttered a dazzle of clean garments in and out of the tree shadows where their lines were stretched. Rim Adams could see people moving about, and kids weaving a pattern with their happy-go-lucky yelling and playing among the wagons.

Then someone saw the horseman approaching, and the word went out and in a trice the children disappeared. When Adams came up he was met by a pair of sunburnt, hardfaced men, one armed with an old cap-and-ball horse pistol and the other carrying a Civil War rifle. "If you're from Chase Center you don't need to come any closer," the newcomer was warned sharply. "We've already had our trouble with that place!"

Rim Adams reined in, holding his hands well in sight. He could see this same suspicious caution in all the faces; he could hardly blame them. He said, "I'm looking for some people named Hawkins. They here?"

"Maybe," the same man said curtly, not giving an inch. "And maybe not."

But now a new voice said, "Hey! I know this man. And the towhead, young Billy Hawkins, came trotting up. "Hell, yes! This here's the deputy marshal—the one I told you arrested the fellow who shot Dave, and likely saved his life."

"Hello, Billy. Rim Adams leaned to shake the rawknuckled hand the boy reached up. "I been wondering how you folks had made out. From what you say, sounds like your brother must be on the mend."

"He's doing all right, Mister Adams. You want to see him?"

"It's what I came for."

Adams dismounted and was introduced to the men with the guns, who had instantly shed all their

159

hostility. It seemed he had to meet every last person in the company, before he could be conducted at last to a wagon that had a tarp stretched from one side of the box to a pair of upright stakes, forming a shelter.

Under this, Dave Hawkins had been made as comfortable as was possible in spite of his wound, seated with his back propped against a wheel. Someone had done a good job of bandaging. His face showed something of his pain but his eyes were bright and steady; when Adams had tied his livery horse, and he and young Billy ducked under the tarp and squatted on their heels beside him, Hawkins gave the visitor a strong handclasp. "I'm glad of the chance to tell you," he said, "that I'm grateful for what Billy tells me you done."

Adams passed this off with an embarrassed shrug. Dave Hawkins' wife, a pleasant-faced young woman with a baby on her arm, brought over tin cups and filled them from a steaming, graniteware pot; Rim Adams thanked her and then, between swallows of the coffee, proceeded to tell these people the outcome of the affair with Burke Roan.

Billy sounded delighted to hear it—"So his own friends killed him! A fittin' end for a skunk like that!"—but his brother seemed distressed. He shook his head and told Adams, with a look of honest concern, "I don't like to think of it happening to anybody, skunk or not. After all, I'll soon be up walking around again But he won't, not ever!"

Adams made an indifferent gesture with the hand that held his coffee cup. "Don't waste your sympathy. The world will never miss a thing like Burke Roan." He changed the subject. "And so, the lot of you are here looking for free land?"

"Our bunch is from Indiana; we picked up the others on the way. We're hunting the right place.

Everywhere so far, the likeliest all seem to have been taken."

"You think you might want some of this?" Adams indicated the prairie stretching back from the shallow creek bottom. "I can't see it, myself. I like trees, and a little water. And I could soon get enough of this wind!"

"Oh, I don't know." Hawkins looked up into the branches that rose above their camp. "These cottonwoods grow fast. A man could set out a windbreak around his place, and it wouldn't be too long before they're working for him. Water's a problem, yes; but you can dig for it. Or, better yet, take out your land along a creek and irrigate." He dug blunt fingers into the dirt, turned up a handful and studied it thoughtfully as he crumbled it and let it sift from a palm that was toughened by plow and hoe handle. "I imagine I could get a crop out of that."

Adams didn't debate the point. Instead he said, "Youngman and some other people in town would be happy to hear you say so. They'll do anything to get people like you to settle. And of course there's a steady market at the fort, ready and waiting for the produce anyone might have to sell them...."

Time passed pleasantly as they talked. Other men drifted over to join the group under the shadow of the tarp, and the conversation went deeply into the problems and the promise of cultivating this Kansas prairie land. Once, at some comment from Adams, one of them burst in with an incredulous look at his clothing and the battered derby: "You surprise me, mister. You sound like you really know about these things. I wouldn't have expected it!"

Rim Adams grinned at him. "Don't let my getup fool you. Hell, I'm just a dirt farmer, my own self.

161

But, it's a while since I worked at it. Kind of fun to be talking again with people that speak my language." And though he hadn't really thought of it in quite that way, it was the truth.

He realized with a sudden start that hours had passed, and it was the light of late afternoon that shook gold from the cottonwood heads, while the creek bottom lay in shadow. Turning down a friendly invitation to stay for evening meal, he got his horse and mounted, insisting that he had been off the job long enough and really must get back to town. He could hardly explain, since he hardly understood himself, the vague sense of urgency that told him he should be away no longer.

With their farewells in his ears, he rode off as he had come. Once he paused to twist around in the saddle and look back, from a little distance, on the grove and the wagons and the activity around the fires, that sent sparks spiraling upward toward the treeheads and the paling sky. He was sorry to be going from here. It had been as congenial and pleasant a time as he could remember—a welcome interlude in a troubled period of his life.

Riding on, he wished these people well in the search for their land, and their dream.

The jeweled pendant Belle Wadsworth fastened in her ear, by the reflection of her dressing table mirror, exactly matched the deep green of the gown she was wearing for the first time. She knew the gown was striking, with its deepcut bodice and the sheen of the full skirt; but in her mood this evening she could see little except a certain roughness of the skin at the hollow of her throat, a slight sagging of the raised bare arms. Overwhelmed by what she read as the cruel signs of aging, she dropped her hands to

162

the table and for the moment could only stare with intense self dislike at her own image in the glass.

It did little good to tell herself the breasts were still firm enough, the corseted waist nearly as small as it had ever been.

The gloomy run of her thoughts broke, suddenly, as the door of her apartment above the Novelty was flung open without warning. Instinctively her hand groped for the light caliber revolver she always kept in a drawer of the dressing table. With a whisper of the still, full skirts she rose and hurried to the connecting doorway, and saw Frank Keyhoe standing in the center of her living room.

"Frank!" she exclaimed. She left her gun on the center table as she stepped past him to the door and, after a glance into the empty hallway, quickly closed it. She came back to Keyhoe and, laying a hand upon his arm, said his name again.

"Frank! Thank God you're all right! You are, aren't you?"

When he swung his head to look at her, she couldn't miss the unnatural pallor of his cheeks. "Why shouldn't I be?"

"After all that's happened? Don't forget, I had a box seat two nights ago." Belle flung a hand toward the window, and the street below where the last daylight lingered. "I saw the mob, and heard them. I watched them start for the jail; I heard the guns and saw the fire reflected in the sky. The man I sent to investigate told me, later, you scattered that mob and killed at least three of them—but no one could say where you'd gone to, or if you might have been badly wounded!"

"That rabble!" Keyhoe snorted, dismissing them with fine arrogance, and a toss of his leanly handsome head. "They're still running!"

163

"It's the truth," she had to admit. "The way this town's been emptying out, I'm afraid business will never be the same. But you're too reckless with your life, Frank! No one has a charmed existence, yet you act as though you did. The first time I brought you up to this room—remember?—you were bleeding where a bullet had struck you in the arm. Didn't that teach you anything? Perhaps the next bullet—"

She knew from the iron that came into his face that she had said the wrong thing. It occurred to her she had perhaps touched on a buried fear that he did not want to acknowledge, even to himself. The thought startled and silenced her for a moment; and Keyhoe, without answering, turned from her and, seeing the decanter on the sideboard, went over there and with the easy familiarity of someone accustomed to making himself at home here, uncapped and poured himself a strong drink.

"And why were you so long coming to see me?" she went on. "You surely must have known how anxious I'd be! I spent a whole night wondering if you might be lying wounded somewhere, or even dying. It was nearly noon yesterday before I heard you'd been seen around, apparently unhurt—and still you've kept me waiting. How could you do this to me?"

Keyhoe looked down into her face, and at the hand she'd laid upon his sleeve. "Perhaps," he told her heavily, "it was just because I didn't want this kind of a scene! I knew how it would be, and that it would be a nuisance. I'm not your property!"

"I know that, damn you!" she cried; she gave the sleeve an angry shake and then, her face breaking in bitter lines; laid her forehead against his arm. "I didn't want you in my life; but you came, and you took over. Now I think you owe me something—at

164

least, not to torture me deliberately! There's no need to be cruel...."

She raised her head; his face swam indistinctly in the blur of smarting tears that she instantly despised, hating any sign of weakness. But perhaps it was the tears that made him slip an arm about her waist and, still holding the half-emptied glass, bend his head and kiss her—but all too briefly. Even as her hands caught at the front of his coat he released her and stepped away, draining the glass and setting it down. Head a little on one side, he looked at her again, appraisingly.

"That dress you're wearing," he said, his eyes following the rich green fullness of the skirt to the floor. "That's really something. Don't think I ever saw it on you before."

"I've never worn it before."

He nodded, a quick movement. "Good— excellent! In fact, it couldn't be better!" He nodded again, and she saw the man's oddly pouting lips twist in a wicked smile. "I hadn't mentioned it, but I'm taking you out this evening."

"Taking me out?" she echoed, frowning. "I don't understand..."

"Never mind. I've rented a rig, and time is wasting." He saw a shawl draped across the back of a chair; he stepped and picked it up and put it around her shoulders, and said with approval, "That should do. Come along." Before she had time to think, his hand, taking her elbow firmly, swept her toward the door.

But there she pulled away, turning to face him. "What's got into you? I can't go anywhere, even supposing there was any place to go! Business will be getting under way in another hour. I'm needed downstairs, to run things."

"The business can run itself," he told her curtly, and his hand closed upon her elbow again. She braced against it, studying his face, and experiencing a cold premonition.

"There's a devil in you, Frank Keyhoe!" she cried. "You better tell me what it is you've gone and cooked up, or I won't take a step!"

And then his face changed, and she felt the first touch of terror. "Oh, I think you will," he assured her in such a tone that she could no longer defy him.

With this strange, driven man beside her, and his grip like a vise propelling her, she found herself swept along the hall and down the stairs and, without even time for a word of instruction to the man behind the counter, across the barroom and into the last fading light of the street. A top buggy— rented at Bert Weld's stable, no doubt—stood at the hitching rail with a horse waiting between its shafts.

Even now she had no idea what he had in mind. Perhaps the raw ugliness of the town had become too much for him and he wanted to get out of it for an hour or so, as she so often wished she could. Seated beside him as they rolled away up the street and the last tawdry buildings fell behind, she actually let herself believe for a moment that she was in for a pleasant outing. She drew close to him and tucked a hand into his elbow, acting out one of her thwarted fantasies of respectability—taking a drive in her own carriage in the cool of the summer evening, after a confining day in town. It helped to know she looked her best.

Keyhoe said little, aiding the illusion. In the west the sun had dropped from sight, leaving a lemon afterglow spread all along the flat horizon. The horse kept up its unbroken, easy trot and the first shadows stretched long across the prairie. And then

166

Belle saw a scatter of tents and sprawling buildings hugging the darkening earth, with lampglow showing already in windows and smearing taut canvas, and the first gnawing suspicion came to disrupt her playacting mood. She stiffened and turned to look at the impassive and inexpressive profile beside her.

"Why are you bringing me here?"

He neither looked at her nor gave any sign of hearing. The buildings of Fort Chase drew nearer and took on the pattern of an army post—the parade flanked by barracks and headquarters buildings, with corral and stables and bakery and supply at the lower end. Men in uniform moved about and voices carried in the early dusk; from the stables as they passed came the brief shrill trumpeting of a horse, a snatch of song in an improbable Irish tenor.

This faded and presently gave way to the thin sounds of trumpet and violin and guitar, emanating from a lighted building ahead. Trembling now, Belle turned to the man beside her and with horror in her voice exclaimed, "Frank! For God's sake, turn this thing around and take me home!"

When he turned his head, his face was blurred by the deepening dusk but she thought she could read the sardonic cruelty in it. "Ah, but this is the big event of the year."

"You know I'm not wanted!"

He said dryly, "I did notice they're a shade stingy with their invitations...."

The lighted building drew nearer; they could see a number of rigs and horses waiting, while through the open windows there were glimpses of people moving about inside. New arrivals entered, a lantern over the door showing officers and civilians and the women on their arms, chatting and laughing.

167

Belle clenched the fist in her lap to stop its trembling. "Don't do this to me, Frank!" she begged in a tense and shaking voice. *"Please!"*

She got no answer, and desperation drove her then. She grabbed the ironwork of the seat and would have leaped across the turning wheel, but Frank Keyhoe was too quick. His hand descended on her wrist, closed on it and hauled her back. His voice was suddenly as fierce and brutal as the bruising grip that numbed her fingers. "We're going in, all right. So, save your breath!"

He did not release her but kept that cruel grip on her arm as he maneuvered the buggy to a halt and wrapped the reins about the whipstock. Alighting, he hauled the woman after him and, still holding her, groped behind the seat for the weight on the leather strap, which he snapped in place on the horse's headstall to anchor it. Belle had given up pleading and protesting. She waited stoically, her face drained of emotion, her lips set.

Now Keyhoe transferred his grip to her elbow. He removed her shawl and tossed it onto the buggy seat, and nodded in approval as he looked at her by the light of the door lantern. "You'll be the handsomest woman here," he promised, but her eyes looked coldly past him at nothing unheeding. Even so, some feminine instinct made her touch her hair, to put it into place. She gathered the hem of her full skirt as Frank Keyhoe guided her toward the open door, through which light and color and sound poured out at them.

CHAPTER 17

The building was probably a mess hall, refurbished for the occasion. The plank flooring had been waxed, and oil lamps burned along the walls. A wooden table held a punch bowl and glasses; the musicians were three Fort Chase enlisted men, blowing and sawing and plucking away at their instruments with crude efficiency. Of the guests who had already arrived, a few couples were trying to waltz to the makeshift music but most stood chatting about the sides of the long room, evidently waiting.

Frank Keyhoe looked them over coolly while he adjusted the hang of his coat. Belle, for her part, steeled herself as heads turned to stare. As she had feared, she found that a good half of these men, both military and civilians, had been her customers— even the respectable businessmen of Chase Center sooner or later found their way, at least once, into the Novelty. Tonight they had their wives with them, however, and their disapproval couldn't have been more complete.

Belle at least knew she looked better than any of these dumpy, frowsy women who stared daggers at her; all the same, her daring gown was utterly out of place here. She was painfully conscious of that, whether Frank Keyhoe seemed to be or not.

Taking her in his arms, he looked down into her face as he said, "Smile and enjoy yourself. We'll show these clods what a waltz is for!" He swept her away, then, across the warped and poorly polished dance floor, moving with that lithe grace that invested everything he did. And when the piece ended he applauded as though the three-man orchestra had been anything but terrible.

Afterward he led Belle to the refreshment table where he dipped punch for them both. When he handed her the drink she said, for his ears alone, "You realize, I'll never forgive you!" If he heard he ignored it, and saluted her with his own lifted glass.

Full night settled. More people arrived but as yet there was no sign of the guests of honor, from out at the 11th Cavalry's encampment. Belle and Keyhoe danced some more, and later dropped out and stood against the wall, observing. As yet they had not spoken to another soul, and scarcely to each other. Belle, miserable and apprehensive, began to wonder if Keyhoe, too, might be less sure of himself than he pretended. She saw him watching the door; perhaps, she thought, he already doubted the sense of what he was doing. Yet, knowing him, she knew he would never turn back.

They happened to be at the rear of the hall when a hubbub of sound announced important arrivals. The post commander entered with Colonel and Mrs. Sutter, and behind them came their party—the senator and his wife, the colonel's brother and a young woman Belle judged must be Tom's bride whom she had never seen; a number of others. At once everything stopped. The music broke off, a space opened down the center of the room. Someone began to clap, and the sound of applause grew and preceded them as Jeff Sutter advanced, smiling and nodding his handsome head and shaking hands.

The colonel, as could have been expected, was impeccable from garrison hat to spotless boots; Livy, beside him, looked pretty and flushed with the pleasure of this honor being paid her husband. Now the only man in the hall who took no part in the applause was Frank Keyhoe. He stood motionless, arms folded, a look of sardonic amusement on his face and a cigar between his teeth. And Belle pressed her palms against her thighs and looked at the floor, waiting numbly as the slow strike of bootsoles and rustle of skirts drew nearer.

She lifted her head, then, to find Livy Sutter staring at her, with her mouth forming a round "O" and the color receding from her face. The colonel had halted in front of Keyhoe; he looked at the man and then at Belle and the puzzlement in his face slowly turned to something uglier. In a sudden quiet his voice carried well as he said, "Your joke isn't very funny, Keyhoe!"

"Neither," the marshal answered, "Was your oversight in not inviting me to this affair tonight."

"It was no oversight!" Livy Sutter answered before her husband court speak. Frank Keyhoe looked at her.

"You can't mean, I wasn't wanted?"

"I think you know what I mean!"

The marshal's eyebrow lifted slightly. His mouth quirked. "Always my trumpeter, eh, Livy?" he suggested, with amusement.

A muscle bulged in the colonel's sallow cheek. "You're talking to *me*, Keyhoe!" he snapped. "Not to my wife! Before things go any further, I suggest you take this—this—" His hard blue eyes touched Belle's face as he groped for a word; with a shrug he finished: "Both of you had better leave!"

The other man merely returned his stare and they stood confronted in an unyielding clash of wills, whose significance spread swiftly, now; an eddy of stillness moved out through the room. But one person, at least, seemed unaware of what was happening: The senator had paused at the

171

refreshment table, and he lifted a glass as he sang out, "Who wants to join me in a toast to Colonel Jefferson Wells Sutter—one of the authentic heroes of his generation!" Nobody answered him. All at once sensing that he had no audience, the fat man peered about him into the silence, blinking and looking foolish.

"You were saying, Colonel?" Keyhoe prodded gently. "Something about me leaving...."

There was a curse and Captain Tom Sutter pushed his way forward. "He'll leave all right!"

"Tom! No!"

The young blond woman caught at her husband's sleeve but he shook her hand aside. "Nothing to be alarmed about," he promised. "Even Frank Keyhoe has better sense than to start a row at a time like this!" He shoved past the colonel, and reaching Keyhoe seized him by a shoulder. Cheeks flushed, he said in a loud voice, "You know where the door is!"

The marshal said quietly, "Take your hand off." He allowed Sutter exactly two seconds to comply, and then brought up his forearm, dislodging the captain's grip and striking him a blow across the chest that staggered him.

A grunt of sound broke from the other man as his boots slipped on the waxed floor. After that he caught himself and was charging at Keyhoe with both fists swinging.

A woman screamed. Keyhoe blocked the clumsy attack without any trouble, and then his own fist sliced past the captain's guard and took him solidly on one ear and cheek. Amid a sudden frantic scrambling of people trying to get out of the way, Tom Sutter went spinning, vainly fighting for balance. The senator barely got out of his path as he slammed into the refreshment table, the impact carrying it over and bringing him to the floor in a clatter of glassware; the huge bowl of fruit punch shattered.

A gabble of excited voices rolled through the room; someone at the door sent up a yell for the corporal of the guard. Tom Sutter sprawled there in the wreckage of broken glass and the slop from the punch bowl, shaking his head as though to clear the cobwebs out of it. His cheek was bleeding, whether laid open by Keyhoe's fist or cut on broken glass. He groped a hand across it, looked dully at his palm. And then his face contorted in rage and he came scrambling up off the floor.

Frank Keyhoe had stood as though waiting to see what the captain would do. But Jeff Sutter, moving quickly, got a shoulder in front of Tom. The latter was shouting hoarsely, "I'll kill him! He's been asking for it, and this time—"

"Set him loose," Keyhoe suggested in a fine tone of contempt. "We'll see what he does!"

"I want no more of this!" the colonel snapped. "Tom, I'm giving you an order!" When he brought his arm down the captain stood unmoving, breathing heavily through his nose. The fine dress uniform was a sodden mess.

Apparently satisfied he would behave himself, Jeff Sutter turned back to the marshal. The room, silent now, seemed to hold its breath; Belle Wadsworth could feel the intentness with which it watched. For a moment it looked as though Jeff Sutter would lose control; he actually raised one white-gloved hand, drawn up into a fist, but then he lowered it to his side again. He said clearly, "I don't know what you're up to, Keyhoe, but don't push me too far!"

Before the other could have answered, a detail of enlisted men entered the hall, wearing sidearms and carrying saddle carbines and under command of a man in corporal's chevrons. The noncom sought out Colonel Mackey, the harried-looking post commander of Fort Chase, who returned his salute with a distracted wave of the hand. "Arrest that man!" he ordered.

The corporal of the guard looked startled. He swiveled a glance to Frank Keyhoe and quickly back again. "Sir?"

"Oh, very well—very well!" Mackey grunted. "Just get him out of here! There's been disturbance enough. Escort him to the limits of the post. If he sets foot again in my jurisdiction, I'll have him thrown in the guardhouse!"

"Yes, sir!" The corporal swung to face Frank Keyhoe. The latter stood at bay, as pale as a man in shock. When the noncom said, "All right, Mister Keyhoe—you come along!" he scarcely seemed to hear. The corporal frowned, plainly uncomfortable.

One of the members of his guard was less hesitant. Losing patience, this man closed in at the other side of the prisoner and Belle saw him put the butt of his carbine against Keyhoe's back, to nudge him forward. She could have told him it was the wrong thing to do. In a flash, the marshal whirled. Face contorted with outrage, he caught at the weapon, snatched it from the trooper's hands and flung it aside, end for end, without troubling to notice where it went. The crowd scattered; women screamed and a man tripped and went down as he tried to escape the clumsy weapon that came spinning and clattering toward him. And the corporal of the guard, completely flustered now, drew his pistol and swung the barrel of it across the

174

base of Keyhoe's skull.

The tall man jerked; his tawny head went back, the shoulder-length hair fanning out under the impact of the blow. His knees bent then and Keyhoe fell forward, tried to catch himself upon his hands but dropped full length, with his face against the floorboards.

This was the scene that confronted Rim Adams as he came plunging through the open door and halted on the threshold.

For a moment the tableau held while the newcomer stood stunned—taking in the shocked expressions and the wreckage of punch bowl and refreshment table, and Tom Sutter with his face bleeding and Frank Keyhoe motionless where the corporal's gunbarrel had dropped him. Adams could not have said what he expected, but it seemed somehow, fatalistically, not at all a surprise. The moment they told him at the Novelty that Belle and Keyhoe had left together in a rented rig, without a word as to their destination, he had somehow known this was where he would find them. And that he would find them in trouble.

Merl Brinegar's voice spoke beside him. "Come to collect your boss?" The newspaperman stood a little apart from the center of trouble, where he could observe everything; Adams looked at him and saw the amusement in his narrow face. "You're none too soon. You can see he's been disrupting things."

Adams didn't answer; he had caught sight of Caroline Sutter—a vision in yellow satin, with a little bunch of flowers at her waist. He tore his eyes from her, and walked over to where Frank Keyhoe had pushed up to hands and knees but, crouching there with hanging head, seemed too dazed to move.

175

Keyhoe made no response when Adams spoke his name. Jeff Sutter said, "Unless he had a few too many under his belt, I can't think why he would have acted the way he did tonight. We'll appreciate it, Adams, if you'll get him out of here."

"What I came for." He shook his head at someone's offer of help; bending over the marshal, he searched the back of Keyhoe's skull with probing fingers and near the place where it joined the neck, found a rapidly swelling lump. The skin didn't appear to be broken. Adams gave the corporal, with the gun still in his hand, a scathing look; afterward, touching his chief on the shoulder, he said, "We're going now. I'll give you a hand up. Make an effort...."

His voice must have got through the fog of pain. With no other help than his deputy's hand beneath his arm, Keyhoe came surging up to his feet with a groan. He stood swaying drunkenly and Adams quickly slipped the arm across his shoulder, to take the taller man's weight and help to steady him. In a dead silence, broken now only by the dragging lurch of the hurt man's uncertain steps, Adams got him the length of the hall, past all the curious, staring eyes, and out into the night.

He was standing by his tired horse, still supporting Keyhoe and wondering what to do with him, when he heard someone coming after him—at the sound of light slippers and rustle of satin he turned quickly, thinking insanely that it might be Caroline. But it was Belle Wadsworth, her daring green dress rumpled and her hair disheveled. She pointed. "Put him in the buggy. That's how we came."

Maneuvering the near dead weight took an effort, but with Belle's help Adams somehow got Keyhoe

176

onto the rear seat and propped him there. He handed the woman in, brought his horse and tied it on behind. Then, with the iron weight unsnapped and stowed away, he climbed in beside Belle and unwrapped the lines.

As he turned the horse in a tight circle, almost cramping the wheels, he could see the dark shapes of a few people who had come crowding out of the hall to watch; he cursed them under his breath. Before the buggy was out of earshot, trumpet and fiddle were swinging into action. Already the interrupted ball was getting under way again.

They had no sooner left the post behind than the lights of Chase Center showed against the flat plain just ahead. The stars hung low, dimmed by heat haze; far to the east, heat lightning flickered. The only sounds, now, were the grind of wheels and plod of hoofs, a sawing of night insects in weedy growth beside the wagon track. Frank Keyhoe might have been dead, from any indication that came from the buggy's rear seat.

Until now Adams hadn't trusted himself to speak, stopped by the fury that made him tremble. At last he said roughly, "You going to tell me about it?"

"Why?" the woman countered. "Didn't you see enough?"

"No! I want to know why the hell you thought you had to do this!"

Belle's head whipped around, he saw her face dimly above the dark shawl clutched about her shoulders. "*Me?* You think I dragged him to that place tonight? Oh no, Adams—you're dead wrong!"

He stared at her a long moment and decided she was telling the truth. "All right," he said finally, and turned away. But he had started her talking; suddenly she could not stop.

"It was all his notion. I couldn't do anything with him. I said if he did this to me, I'd never forgive him. And I mean it!".

"It sounds crazy," Adams admitted. "But, when a man's had a couple too-many—"

"He wasn't drunk Had he been, I could have understood. But no, he was cold sober—and that's the worst part of it! I watched him lose all his controls this evening, Adams, and it was a terrible thing. He wasn't Frank Keyhoe—he was like some jealous little boy who couldn't stand it because he got left out at a party. And so he went, uninvited; and when he heard those people applauding Jeff Sutter, he went wild." Belle took a shuddering breath. "You saw how it ended."

Adams turned to look at the motionless figure crammed into the rear seat of the buggy, head rocking loosely to the jolt of the vehicle. "All right," he said again, sourly, and straightening forward gave the rent horse a slap with the reins.

Captain Tom Sutter had left his wife at the dance, temporarily, while he returned to the 11th's encampment for a change of uniform; but with this accomplished he was in no hurry to return. He was in a dangerous mood, and at the best of times he found the company of his fellow officers a deadly bore. The kind of women most of them married were, in his opinion, even worse.

And so, instead of returning at once to Fort Chase, he set out on foot through the familiar layout of the 11th's streets—answering carelessly the salutes of the troopers he passed, as always feeling more at home in this rough male atmosphere of the enlisted man's domain. At the end of a company street, a lantern spread a smear of buttery-yellow light against a tent's canvas, silhouetting the shapes of those within. As Tom Sutter ducked beneath the tied-back tent flap, four troopers squatting about a blanket looked up from their poker game, to greet him with profane welcomes.

Tom, completely at ease here, went down on his ankles beside them. "Looks like you're putting on the dog tonight," a man in a corporal's stripes said, grinning at him.

"Oh, hell yes," the captain said, and pointed. "What's in the jug?"

"We ain't found a name for it yet," one of them answered, passing it over. "But you can try it if you got no regard for your stomach."

Sutter uncorked, slung the jug expertly along his forearm and lifted it to his mouth for a long drag. As he lowered the jug, blowing out his breath, someone saw the glisten of lamplight on scabbed blood on his cheek and said, "Hey, Tom! Had a fight with the missis?"

The captain touched the place and his mouth tightened: "That," he said, "is a little memento I picked up this evening. From Frank Keyhoe…"

At the name, all four of the poker players suddenly grew still, cards forgotten. Sergeant Jud Mannion swore softly through his teeth. "Keyhoe!" he repeated, and touched a hand to his belly. "My guts got a hole in 'em yet, where he rammed his damned gun clear up to the damned trigger guard!" He added, "You holding out on us, Tom? How'd you and Keyhoe come to tangle tonight?"

Sutter belched sightly, rubbed the back of a hand across his mouth. His face wasn't at all handsome just then. He told substantially what had happened over at Fort Chase, though he omitted mentioning the blow of Keyhoe's fist that had sent him to the floor amid the wreckage of the refreshment table. The troopers looked at one another and Corporal Agard, who hadn't shaved that day, rasped a thumbnail through the black beard stubble on his cheek and said, grinning, "So he brung Belle Wadsworth! I'd like to of been there, to see the looks on some of those faces!"

"What I'd like to have seen," Mannion said darkly, "was that bastard Keyhoe on his knees! Too bad the guy with the gun couldn't have hit a little harder…"

Tom Sutter looked at these men, his four particular cronies who had all been in McCord's that day of his humiliation at the marshal's hands— the day he shot the horse. He laid a speculative stare on each of their faces, in turn, and he spread his hands upon his thighs and took a breath. He said carefully, "If I'm not mistaken, there could be a few differences, after what's just happened."

The sergeant shot him a glance. "Different, how?"

"Why, unless I misread the situation," the captain told them, "Keyhoe made a bad mistake tonight. He's lost face with the very people who brought him here—by parading his whore in front of them, he insulted every one of their women, just at a time when they may be thinking they don't really need him any longer."

Mannion asked, "You saying he may get himself fired?"

"His job's all but finished. Chase Center is practically a tomb, now. And with his performance at the fort, he's not going to have many friends. If something bad should happen to our friend Keyhoe, I'm afraid not very much is likely to be done about it afterwards."

Suddenly it was very still in the tent, broken only

180

by the quiet sounds of the camp and the noise of bugs batting against the canvas, as they tried to get in where the lantern was. Finally, pugnacious black eyes never leaving the captain's, Sergeant Mannion reached for the jug, tilted it along his arm and had a drag at the cheap whiskey.

Putting the jug down on the blanket among the forgotten cards and money, he said, "Was it a prediction you just made, about that sonofabitch?"

"Now that he's no longer off limits, who can say?" From a pocket of his tunic, Tom Sutter brought out a billfold and removed several bills from it and dropped them onto the blanket. "Two hundred dollars," he said, with no further explanation as he put the wallet back. "Divide it any way you want."

They were all four staring silently at the money as he rose to leave. About to duck out under the tent flap, the captain was held up by a last question from Mannion. "Tom, what about that deputy? That fellow Adams?"

Sutter returned the sergeant's look. "Nothing about him," he said. "I think he has an eye for my wife, but I don't really care either way."

The other nodded, a barely perceptible movement of the head, and Sutter stepped out into the company street. Straightening, he looked about at the acres of needy aligned rows of tents, the men moving quietly about them on private business. He looked at the sky, and filled his lungs with a slow and tremulous breath.

It was the first time he had ever paid money to have an enemy killed. Aside from the satisfaction of knowing Frank Keyhoe would never have another chance to humiliate him, he was interested to notice that he really felt nothing much at all.

181

CHAPTER 18

Returning from a badly cooked breakfast in the two-by-four diner located hard by the Kansas Pacific tracks, Rim Adams was briefly surprised to find the door of the marshal's office, which he had locked when he left, now standing open. He stepped inside, placed his shoulders against the frame, and looked at Frank Keyhoe seated behind the desk.

For a moment neither spoke, until the silence began to weigh on Adams and to break it he said shortly, "I wasn't expecting to see you this morning."

"It's closer to noon," Keyhoe pointed out.

Adams nodded. It occurred to him it was the first time he had ever seen this man leave his room for the day unshaven. Keyhoe's skin looked ashen, beneath its dark weathering; his clothing hung on him carelessly. One of the hands that lay upon the desk jerked from time to time, spasmodically. Frowning, the younger man asked, "How does your head feel?"

"Like hell." Keyhoe lifted a hand to the back of his skull, and winced visibly. "I don't seem to remember what it was that hit me."

"It was a pistol barrel. In the hands of the corporal of the guard." Adams could have stopped there, but some perverse impulse made him add, "You intend to kill him for that?"

Keyhoe's head lifted and for a long instant his eyes probed the other's face; but then he apparently decided to let the question go. He ran a palm down across his stubbled cheek and across his tawny mustache, and then laid the hand upon the desk again and looked at it as he said slowly, "I gather it was you brought me in to Youngman's last night. You also turned the buggy I rented back to the livery."

Adams gave a short nod.

"And—Belle?"

"I saw she got home."

Rim Adams watched a nerve jump below Keyhoe's right eye; it was the only thing that revealed, suddenly, the immense strain the man was under. "Did she—say anything?"

"She said plenty!" Adams would have dropped it there, but the question was in Keyhoe's eyes and he was angry enough himself that he couldn't resist scoring the man. He shrugged, moving his shoulder against the wood. "She told me she was never going to forgive you. She said it at least three times, during the ride to town. Personally I don't see how anyone could blame her!"

The marshal's eyes were watching him, under the thickets of his lowered brows. "You're put out with me, too...."

"Damn it! Can't you understand you made a fool of yourself—and out of sheer, petty spite!" He pulled away from the door frame and advanced a couple of steps into the room; a night of angry brooding was behind the words that poured out of him. "To put on a show like that in front of—of—"

"In front of Tom Sutter's wife?" Frank Keyhoe finished for him. "That's what really bothers you, isn't it?" And that short upper lip lifted the flowing mustache in a sneer.

Rim Adams felt the tide of warmth flow swiftly up into his face. "We're not talking about her!" he

183

snapped.

"Oh, aren't we?" Keyhoe retorted. His entire manner changed, then; his controls, that had been allowed to slip for an instant, reasserted themselves. "I suggest we let the subject drop," he said and got to his feet, taking his hat from the desk.

Scowling, Rim Adams stood aside as his chief walked to the door to gaze for a moment over such portion of Chase Center as could be seen from here. The summer heat was building; the sun burned down from a sky without cloud, except for a few insignificant streaks of high cirrus. "Town seems quiet," Keyhoe observed.

Adams said nothing.

"On the other hand," the marshal continued, "if only for appearances, it won't hurt to have a look around." He smoothed back his sweeping fall of hair with a palm and drew the hat precisely in place. With the methodical precision of a craftsman he took each of his guns from its holster, in turn, and checked the loads.

He settled the belts in place, adjusted the hang of his coat.

And then he looked at Adams, and saw that the young man stood precisely where he had been, his hands hanging empty, the shotgun still untouched on its pegs against the wall. "You coming?"

Unmoving, his deputy looked back at him. "You said yourself, it's quiet...."

Keyhoe considered him, for a long moment. He nodded. "I see...." If Rim Adams, in a sullen and defiant mood, expected him to make an issue of it, he was mistaken. The tall man did not raise his voice, nor say another word. He turned and walked out of the office, leaving his deputy standing.

Adams listened to the measured sound of his

184

footsteps, moving away and losing themselves in the noontime stillness. Only then did a nagging uneasiness come, with the thought that—for the first time—he was letting Frank Keyhoe start out to patrol the town alone.

Waiting, Jud Mannion was beginning to fight his nerve. Though he appeared to be relaxed—an arm hooked across the back of his chair, stocky legs sprawled wide below the table, garrison hat at his elbow—that was only careful illusion. The vigil had shortened his temper and his patience, and also given him time to remember it was Frank Keyhoe he meant to deal with; this made a danger of the stretching moments, because they eroded his courage.

He drummed blunt fingers on the table top as once more he sized up the arrangements. They were as set and ready as they would ever be: Trooper Liggett, stationed in the doorway where he could watch the street and sing out at the first sign; Trooper Crain, in the chair he had pulled over into the corner at the left of the doorway—a lump of a man, slow moving but with an iron doggedness of will; at the bar, Corporal Agard with a glass of whiskey untouched beside him in case he needed a reserve. Among the four of them, Mannion told himself, they were entirely adequate for the job they had set themselves, even against Frank Keyhoe.

Behind the counter the barman went methodically about his work, with an occasional chatter of glassware to betray the state of his own nerves; only Lew McCord, seated at a table near Mannion's, showed complete unconcern as he turned the pages of an Abilene newspaper. Aside from these six men, the big gambling hall was empty—no customers, no

185

house dealers, no guards. The stage was set, and the somnolent quiet of noontime lay heavy.

Mannion exclaimed, loudly in the stillness, "Why the hell don't he come?"

"He will," McCord glanced at him above the paper as he turned a page, unhurriedly. "He walks up the street every day at this time. He's only missed once, that I remember."

"But after last night," the sergeant said with gruff skepticism, "he might not be in any shape to walk patrol."

McCord shrugged. "That's the chance you take. I only hope you'll know what you're doing when he shows!"

Mannion scowled and ran a palm across his knobby, sunburnt face, and wiped it on his shirt front. There seemed to be no breath of air stirring this morning; the still heat was a burden a man carried about with him.

At the bar Corporal Agard spoke—a small and wiry man, his cheeks raddled by the amounts of booze he got away with, his hair streaked into odd shades by years of fierce prairie sun. "We'll take care of Keyhoe," he said bluntly, "just so Crain don't mess up handling the deputy."

Trooper Crain, from his chair in the far, dark corner, made a scornful sound. "That Adams ain't much!"

"Maybe. I still don't want to mix with no scattergun!"

And then Jack Liggett spoke, from his place at the door: "It's Keyhoe! He's coming—alone!"

"Alone?" Mannion echoed, in disbelief. "Let me see once!" Chairlegs squealed as he pushed to his feet.

Shouldering Liggett aside, he peered with

186

narrowed eyes. Nothing moved at all, out there in the wide and sunsmitten heart of the town, except for one slowly pacing figure, that walked within the narrow circle of black shadow put down by the brim of his own hat. Keyhoe's face was only palely visible, but the high sun struck glints and gleams from the twin handles of the guns, in their holsters, and from the brass that filled the loops of his cartridge belts. He came on with the direct and unwavering pace that had become a familiar sight in the daily routine of Chase Center. The only thing that was different was the absence of a second figure, a pace behind and to the left, shotgun at the ready.

Someone grunted with satisfaction. "That simplifies things!"

Corporal Agard had moved to the dust-filmed window by the bar. Now, in the stillness of the big room, metal whispered against leather as he pulled his gun. "I could drop him from here, and have it over with."

"No!" Mannion whirled from the door. "God damn it, no! I don't want him to get it that way! I want him looking at me—I want him to remember feeding me them two inches of gunbarrel!" His breathing was a trifle shallow as he gauged the marshal's progress along the sunstruck street, while the tension of waiting built up within the room until it became almost a tangible thing.

The sergeant looked around, then, located the faint gleam of a battered brass spittoon. He went and picked it up, hefted its weight. Turning, he raised the spittoon shoulder-high and deliberately let fly with it, in the direction of the bar.

As the bartender ducked wildly, the heavy object streaked past him, to smash into the lineup of bottles

187

and glassware on the back counter. It brought Lew McCord surging out of his chair, the newspaper spiring and scattering. "What in the name of—!"

Jud Mannion grinned. "Your cue, mister. Get out there and tell the marshal you got a drunken dogface busting up your place for you." McCord gave him a furious look, but shrugged wordlessly and swung away. The rest, at door and windows, watched in silence as the resort owner walked outside to intercept Frank Keyhoe.

They could not hear what was said, but McCord's gestures were plain enough. Trooper Liggett remarked, in a tone raised by tension a note or two above its normal pitch, "Looks like he's putting on a good act...."

"I'll help him some more," Trooper Crain said, and picking up the chair he had been sitting in he sent it smashing through the window beside him.

That had the wanted effect. "Here he comes!" Sergeant Mannion warned. "Quick—get back!" They were in position and waiting, facing the doorway, as Keyhoe's prowling step grew louder. He came alone, of course—Lew McCord's deal allowed the use of his place for an ambush, but he would take no part in it.

Just in the entrance, Keyhoe halted as his glance fell on Jud Mannion's face.

It held there a probing instant and then moved on, seeming to take in everything at once: the strained and waiting pose of Trooper Liggett, the half bent crouch of Agard's wiry shape, the way the bartender stood with both hands resting on the counter and the sweat shining on his face. Frank Keyhoe must have seen, too, the barrenness of the long room, and realized what it meant. For Mannion caught the subtle change that came over the marshal—the way

188

his eyes seemed to empty and the planes of his cheeks to draw up, finding himself alone here with these cronies of Captain Tom Sutter.

Trooper Crain was fading out of the shadows now, moving up behind Keyhoe. He clumsily let one bootsole scrape on a sanded floorboard, and Mannion winced; yet the tall man might have been deaf, for any reaction he made. After that it was too late, in any case, because Crain's pistol was dug deep into his back and Crain ordered, in a voice that was strung tight, "Freeze, Keyhoe! Leave the guns alone!"

Mannion watched the color drain from Keyhoe's face, watched it go white and terrible as Crain snaked the weapons out of the marshal's holsters and tossed them aside. Only when he saw Frank Keyhoe disarmed did the sergeant's tension ease a trifle. He dragged a breath into lungs that had become cramped, and he brought up a hand and let Keyhoe look at the Army Colt it held pointed at his chest.

He said, "Walk right in. We've been expecting you..."

When the first popping of guns began, Rim Adams knew from the shocked leap of his nerves that he must have been waiting, keyed up for this. It brought him off the cot in the office, where he had been lying with hands behind his head—staring at the ceiling, hating himself. There were two shots close together, then a space of time while his pulse nearly seemed to quit, and after that a thin rattling of gunfire whose ferocity reached him despite distance and the muffling of walls. By the time he broke free of whatever held him rooted, grabbed up his gun and went running from the office, it was already over.

He had forgotten his hat and he took the direct smash of the sun bareheaded, its glare a punishing dazzle as he ran through the weeds of the empty lot with his heartbeat pounding and filling his throat. Reaching the street he halted uncertainly.

At that moment a pair of horsemen in blue uniforms broke into the open from between a couple of buildings, spurring hard—even a block away he could sense the panic in them. They put their animals into a flat-out run that raised a glittering film of dust, as they headed north in the direction of the fort. Adams watched them out of sight and then, as the flurry of hoofbeats faded, moved on—at a walk, now.

Doors banged open; men began to show themselves and the ragged ends of questions reached his ears. Someone said, "McCord's," and someone else repeated it—the name followed him along the street. Far out on the empty plain the noon westbound whistled. Today, for once, its arrival would not be the signal to pull a straggle of idlers toward the station to watch it rolling in; right now the whole weight of the town's attention appeared to rest on Rim Adams as he turned in before the Kansas House.

No sound came out to him. He faltered a moment, to take a deep breath and run a hand across his scalp—the crown of his head felt hot enough from the sun to scorch his fingers. In dread, then, he walked inside and was met by an overwhelming stench of powder fume, and by darkness that to his unadjusted eyes was almost like a cave.

Momentary blindness seemed to sharpen his hearing, somewhere within this swimming darkness a man was breathing with ragged and pain-ridden

190

effort. Someone spoke in a shaking voice: "Sounds to me he's dying, Adams. This other one's already done for.

A pale glimmer swam into focus and became a man wearing a white shirt. Advancing cautiously, Adams' boot touched a fallen chair and he pushed it out of his way. The speaker, he could see now, was Lew McCord's bartender, motionless, hands dangling uselessly, he stood over a dark huddle that lay sprawled in the middle of the floor. The tortured breathing came from it.

The deputy's eyes were beginning to adjust. Going down on one knee he made out a dark uniform, and a sergeant's yellow chevron. When he touched the hurt man's shoulder the head rolled loosely and he looked at the face of Jud Mannion. The front of Mannion's tunic was a mass of blood; blood bubbled on his lips and stained the drooping mustache.

With a shudder Rim Adams straightened. He looked around and then again at the bartender. He said, "Where—?" and caught the man's gesture; turning, he saw the second one lying against an overturned table he must have taken down with him as he fell. Sightless eyes stared at nothing; this one was plainly dead.

Another trooper. A single blue wisp of powdersmoke drifted in the still air above his staring eyes, at the level of Adams' knee. Scowling in puzzlement Rim Adams swung again to the bartender. "But where is Keyhoe?"

The answer came in a voice rendered toneless by shock. "I dunno! I dunno! He just walked out—like a man in a trance. Or a damned machine…"

At that moment the dying Jud Mannion sucked in a faltering, bubbling breath; it broke, began again.

And then, with a rattling noise deep in his throat, the life ran out of him. A vast stillness seemed to pile up within the room.

Looking down at him, the young man became conscious of the gun he still clutched in his fingers, and shoved it behind his belt. He said, "I think you better tell me what happened!"

The bartender spread his hands and they trembled slightly. "I ain't too sure! I was only going about my business—"

"Why not start at the beginning?" Adams broke in. "It was a setup! They had a trap laid for him—and you knew it!"

The man's broad and hairless features slowly took on color, but he said doggedly, "In my job, you learn not to ask questions!"

Rim Adams shrugged. "All right. I'm not interested in hearing about your job. I want to know what went on in this room!"

"Only thing I can figure, Mannion must have got careless. Four of them took Keyhoe's guns and they had him, unarmed; but they seemed to want something more than just to kill him. He walked right up on Keyhoe, almost like he meant to ram his service revolver down the man's throat. After that, I don't really know what happened—it came too fast for me to follow—but the next thing I knew Keyhoe had the sergeant's gun. He must have took it away from him! And then the shooting started, and a time like that I knew where *I* belonged: On the floor in back of the bar! It was all over in a few seconds...."

"And when you got up off your knees?" Adams prompted scornfully.

"Keyhoe had picked up his guns and was just walking out the door—far as I could see, he hadn't taken a scratch. These two were on the floor. One of the others was wounded but his friend got him on his feet and they ran out the back way, to where they'd left their horses."

That was all the bartender's story. Now he stared past Adams and the latter turned as Lew McCord entered from the street. McCord seemed to have no trouble adjusting to the change of light. He swept into the room, a stocky figure of a man, as untidy and unkempt of appearance as ever. He was coatless, his string tie awry, his waistcoat flapping; his face shone with sweat and his shirt was soaked with dark circles of it under his arms. He looked at the pair of dead men, he looked at his bartender, and then his black eyes pinned Adams.

"Is this your doing?"

The other returned his look. "You know damned well it isn't," he retorted. "Only things didn't go according to plan, did they?"

McCord's face seemed to tighten. "If you're talking to me, you'd better make sense!"

"I make good enough sense. You've had a grudge against Frank Keyhoe, a long time. So today, when you were asked to, you cleared out your hall and let his enemies have a clear field at him. I guess it never occurred to you, they might not be able to do the job!"

McCord's lips worked, rolling the cigar furiously. He jerked his head toward the door. "Get out!"

Rim Adams met his stare as he said evenly, "That's exactly what this town may be telling *you* one of these days, McCord. You might not have noticed, but the place is changing. It may not have room for things like you much longer."

"You think you could put me out?"

"I might have to try. But there's still the man who ran you out of Cheyenne. Keyhoe isn't dead,

193

remember? He'll likely enough be wanting to see you, for your part in this thing today!" Adams thought he saw a brightness of fear flicker in the opaque black eyes. He let McCord chew on the thought, while he walked out into the sunbright street.

He was still too numb to understand exactly what had happened; but with two troopers of the 11th lying dead he sensed that everything had changed, in a moment's time, and there was no way of knowing what the end would be. He ignored the crowd that was already beginning to gather, and set out to look for Frank Keyhoe.

CHAPTER 19

A detachment of a dozen mounted troopers, under command of an officer and a noncom, rode into the head of Main Street and the subdued ruffle of hootbeats in heavy dust ran on with them, announcing their coming. Riding two and two, they had the definite orderly rhythm that meant they came as a military unit and not on casual, off-duty business of their own.

In front of the Novelty, a command from the captain brought his men wheeling neatly out of formation and lined them up along the hitching racks. At another order they dismounted and tied; the officer—it was Captain Tom Sutter, very military and very stern of expression—passed his own reins to the sergeant and swung down, adjusting the hang of his tunic and slowly stripping off his yellow leather gloves as he looked about him

194

at the silent street.

Leaving the noncom in charge, he crossed and entered McCord's and was in there perhaps ten minutes, the time it would take a man to ask questions and gather his answers. When he reappeared he was scowling, gnawing at his lower lip as he came back across the dust. The troopers, who had been lounging against the tie poles, straightened to attention when their sergeant passed the word. Sutter halted before them, took off his campaign hat and smoothed a palm across his blond head of hair and drew the hat in place again. He looked at the sergeant.

"All right," he said curtly. "It's the Novelty. Two of you stay here in case we flush him out. A couple watch the rear...."

The doors were unlocked but, entering, they found things in a state of disarray. The bartender was waxing down the front of his carved cherrywood counter, the old swamper had a stepladder and was hauling it about the big room while he took down the wall lamps to refill them. A couple of Belle Wadsworth's girls, in wrappers and looking hungover, sat in one of the booths having coffee and a smoke."

"Upstairs, Captain, the noncom said.

Sutter nodded curtly. "I know." And he turned without pausing to the steps, halting then as he caught sight of Belle coming slowly down them.

She did not look particularly surprised, from the way she was dressed, her hair and makeup freshly seen to, they might almost have thought they were expected. She stopped, one hand lightly resting on the balustrade, and said pleasantly, "You're a little early, boys. We're not open for business yet, but you can have a drink if that suits you."

195

Tom Sutter answered sharply, "We didn't come for entertainment. We're under orders to bring in the killer who murdered two men of the 11th, today at noon."

For a long moment she looked down at him. "Murder is a strong word," she said finally. "But I suppose you *are* talking about Frank Keyhoe. In any event, you won't find him here."

"This is where he came after the shooting. The building has been watched and he wasn't seen to leave. I think we'll find him here, all right!" Sutter said, nodding. "What likelier place for him to hide? The whole town knows that you're his whore...."

"Sergeant!"

With that summons to the noncom he began deliberately to climb the steps. The woman stood and watched him rise toward her, a look of cold hatred making her almost ugly. Her hand upon the balustrade tightened until the knuckles stood white and her whole arm trembled slightly; but at the last moment, with the captain only a step below her, she seemed to make her decision and drew back against the wall to let him pass.

Two of the troopers, by prearrangement, remained on the lower floor; the rest came tramping at Sutter's heels and, gaining the bleak upper hallway, followed him to the door which they apparently knew was hers, though it was unmarked in any way. Here, for the first time, Sutter seemed to grow cautious. Mouth set hard, he reached over and unfastened the flap of his holster and drew his gun. "Be careful," he warned, "that you don't bunch up in the doorway and give him an easy target. If he makes a suspicious move, don't hesitate to kill him."

"Got you!" the sergeant grunted. Sutter turned the knob, and sent the door crashing open.

196

With nerves strung so tight, it was almost surprising no one began shooting the instant the door slammed the wall. Very carefully Sutter placed a palm against the wood of the door, which had rebounded slightly, and eased it wide again. Cavalry pistol leveled in front of his belt, he slipped into the room and his men fanned out swiftly behind him.

A glance sufficed to show Belle Wadsworth's sitting room was empty. Her carpet smothered the sound of their boots as they picked a way through the clutter of furniture, moving now on the door of the bedroom which, they saw, stood partially open. Sutter looked a signal to the sergeant; the latter, nodding, edged about a small side table with a beaded runner, placed his shoulder against the wall and moved silently up toward the door in that way. When the other three had set themselves, the sergeant eased a bootheel to the hinged edge of the door, and kicked it wide.

Minutes later the captain came storming from the empty bedroom and found Belle Wadsworth standing by the horsehair sofa, her arms folded and her cheeks pale with anger. "Satisfied?" she said crisply. "I tried to tell you. Now, take the army and get out!"

With his men watching, he walked over to the woman; her head lifted defiantly as he loomed above her. "Sergeant!" he said across his shoulder. "You'll take the men we left below stairs, and search every foot of the ground floor. I'll finish up here. I still think he's in the building; but it makes no difference, in the end—we'll hunt through this town till we find him!"

His boiling stare pinned the woman's face as, behind him, the sergeant saluted and wheeled and strode out of the room, about his mission. The remaining pair of enlisted men awaited orders, nervously gripping their service revolvers.

Within an hour of sunset, now, Tom Sutter found himself sweating with the breathless heat and with growing frustration. He stood in the shade under the wooden awning in front of Youngman's, and undoing the top button of his tunic tilted his head as he used a handkerchief to mop his throat and neck. Scowling, he went over again every yard of the futile search he had conducted. Where in this damned town could a man hide from him? Every instinct told him that he had to have been right all along: The man *was* hiding—but, where? Somehow that Wadsworth bitch had to know the answer, yet he had taken her place of business apart and found nothing, nothing at all.

He still had his men going through the motions, but in a lackluster fashion. Meanwhile, in just another hour it would be coming on evening. With darkness, his chances of controlling the situation would drop to near zero. If they didn't find him by nightfall, then the man they were hunting would have everything in his favor for slipping completely out of their hands.

He cursed in thwarted anger, and put the handkerchief away as a couple of his men came up with another negative report. About to give further orders, Tom Sutter sighted the horsemen approaching the place where he stood. One was his brother, the colonel; his companion, a lieutenant from Company D. Tom straightened his tunic and waited as they pulled to a halt and stepped down into the dust.

Jeff Sutter read the look on his brother's face. "I guess you haven't made an arrest..."

"There's no sign of the man! I've gone through this damned town, house by house. Nobody will admit to knowing anything."

Frowning the colonel said, "It would seem to be obvious, then: He's run out."

"I don't believe it! Lew McCord says not, for one thing. He insists the man couldn't have got out of town without him knowing. And he has reason to want to know," the captain added. "He's scared out of his wits!"

"Of Keyhoe? Why should he be? McCord had nothing to do with that shooting in his place. Or—did he?" Jeff Sutter looked at his brother closely. "You don't suppose there might be more to this, than we've been told?"

"No!" Tom said, too quickly. His eyes flickered with panic, then steadied under the colonel's probing stare. "You heard the report. I'm satisfied it was virtual murder—and for one, I'm not willing to let it drop. Keyhoe has gone too far!"

"I've given you full authority to find and arrest him," the colonel pointed out. "But there are limits. If you've let him slip through your fingers, I can hardly let you go hunting him clear across the State of Kansas. This command has more important assignments."

"I still don't admit he got away from me," Tom said doggedly. "McCord says—"

"Damn it, I'm not particularly interested in what McCord says! The man is a blackguard. It would make my job easier if he closed down that gambling trap of his, and moved it someplace a hundred miles from here!"

Tom would have argued, but suddenly his brother was no longer paying attention. A man was coming toward them along the edge of the street, a familiar

199

figure in as ill-fitting town suit and a battered derby. With am expression of stern dislike, the colonel stepped out a pace or two to meet Rim Adams.

The deputy wasn't carrying his shotgun; he had left that in the office, but a revolver was shoved behind his waistband. He came on until the group beneath Youngman's awning blocked his path. He halted, then, with a challenging stare that included the colonel and his brother, and the lieutenant and the pair of enlisted men behind them. "You want something?" he demanded.

"All right, Adams!" the colonel said, with the same withering tone his brother Tom had seen reduce many a junior officer to stammering incoherence. "I'll take no nonsense from you! If you know the whereabouts of Frank Keyhoe, you'll do well to tell me."

But there was no visible trace of awe or respect in the man who stood before him. "I'll say to you what I've said a dozen times already," the young fellow answered. "Even if I knew, I'll be Goddammed if I'd tell the army. I know what you've got in mind to do with him!"

"As commanding officer of the 11th U. S. Cavalry," Jeff Sutter retorted stiffly, "you can't expect me to stand by and do nothing. The lives of my men are valuable to me."

"The lives of your men!" repeated Adams. His voice dripped with heavy scorn. "Don't pull that on me, Colonel! I was in Grant's army, the last months just before Appomattox. I was nothing but a damned buck private, but there wasn't much the likes of us didn't know about. We heard enough to figure the price that the men of your command paid to win you a brigadier's star. And I think you'd be willing to sacrifice every man in the 11th, if you thought you saw a chance to gee it back!'"

The colonel's face had turned white. His brother, choked with anger, took a step toward Adams and a hand lifted as he cried, "You can't talk that way to—"

Adams plunged ahead, ignoring him, carried by the rush of his own anger. "Frank Keyhoe may be just as vain and just as hungry as you for space in the newspapers—but you got to admit he places his own head on the line to get it. He takes his pay and he earns it, risking his life every day on every job. He doesn't ask some other man to do it for him!" He paused for breath, a shade disgusted to find himself trembling.

The colonel meanwhile had regained his color, and now he found his voice and remarked, in an icy tone, "Don't you think you've said enough?"

"Yeah, I'm through," Rim Adams answered, though he didn't sound repentant. "But keep these people away from me! Keep them out of the marshal's office—because I won't take any more off of them!" And with that he moved forward, shoving roughly past the colonel; the pair of enlisted men gaped foolishly as they stepped aside. Without looking back, Adams walked unhurriedly on and turned up the broad steps that fronted the Novelty.

A furious oath broke from Tom Sutter. "By God, there's no call to take such insolence!"

"And what would you do about it?" the colonel demanded. When his brother could only glare, Jeff Sutter shook his head and told him brusquely, "It's not important…Get your horse. I want you to come back to camp with me."

"Now?" The other started a quick protest but the colonel overrode him.

"We've had trouble enough with this town, for

201

one day. One more incident and the whole place might have to be put under martial law."

"But damn it, I haven't finished here!"

"You *have,* Tom. That's just what I'm telling you."

"And what about Keyhoe?"

For answer, Jeff Sutter spoke to the lieutenant—a florid-faced man with a hard jaw and sandy muttonchops, who had stood discreetly silent during this argument between his superior officers. "Swenson, you'll take over here. Give orders to the search detail that they're to keep their eyes and ears open, but leave their pistols in their holsters. If Frank Keyhoe turns up, I want him put under arrest. Give him every chance to surrender peaceably, but take no nonsense off him. Is that clear?"

"Yes sir," Niles Swenson answered crisply.

"If you and your men have turned up nothing by ten this evening, then we'll assume that Keyhoe is gone. You will collect your detail and return to camp." He returned the lieutenant's salute, dismissed him, and turned again to his scowling brother. "Satisfied?"

"You know damn well I'm not!"

"That's unfortunate. You can be a hotheaded fool sometimes, Tom; I don't mean for this to be one of the times. For the rest of the day I want you where I can keep an eye on you. Now, get to your horse."

He would not listen to an argument.

Belle Wadsworth said harshly, "I hope he *has* left—I hope he's gone for good! After the way he humiliated me last night, I never want to see Frank Keyhoe again. And I told him so!"

"All right," Rim Adams muttered, placatingly, scowling into his glass of beer.

202

"That's not all," the woman went on. "I've got no reason to be happy about what the pair of you have done to this town! It used to be a nice, lively little place; but you've flattened all the life out of it. It started to die, that night when the boys tried to burn the jail and Keyhoe turned his guns loose on them. Now it's emptied out so, I might just as well close down."

She indicated the big room. It looked tawdry enough in the last fading light of afternoon, before the wall lamps were lighted and before the music started and the girls appeared in their short, bright skirts and the evening's trade set in. "I hear that one of Timberlake's mule trains got in from Santa Fe an hour or so ago. That should mean some business, when the boys collect their wages and go on the town for a little fun. But take my word for it—thanks to Keyhoe, it ain't ever going to be again what it was."

Adams didn't attempt to argue the point. He knew she was talking for the benefit of the blue clad trooper who had entered the Novelty just behind him and taken a post at the far end of the bar, where he stood now nursing the whiskey he had ordered and carefully not paying any attention to Adams and the woman. It was inevitable he would be watched and followed, Adams knew. They were not apt to let him out of their sight.

He took another drag at his beer. With mouth close above the glass he asked softly, "Where have you got him?"

"Ruby Jerrod's room."

In his surprise he almost forgot to keep his voice down. "They never thought to look there for him?"

"Oh, yes. They all but took this place apart! But he was safe enough."

"How? Where was he?"

For answer she tapped the toe of one slipper against the floorboards. "A trap door," she told him. "Here under the bar—you never know when one can come in handy. After the bluebellies left we had a chance to move him in with Ruby."

Rim Adams shook his head in astonishment, and finished his beer. Putting down the schooner he said, behind the wrist he wiped across his mouth, "Is he all right?"

Her whispered words took on a bitter edge. "If you mean, was he hurt in that battle at McCord's—then, no. He went up against four guns, killed two men and sent the other pair running for their lives, and came off without a scratch. But he's a long way from all right!"

"What do you mean, then?"

"I mean that he's drunk! Helpless, slobbering drunk! He walked out of McCord's and across the street and in that door"—she pointed at it—"and without a word to anyone he came to the bar and helped himself to a bottle and began belting them away as fast as he could pour them out. There was no getting him to quit—when I tried, he turned on me like a tiger. He drank until he was ready to pass out; and then his enemies could have walked in and taken him and he could have done no more to protect himself than if he had been a child!

"Adams, did you ever watch someone you respected go to pieces, right in front of your eyes?"

Hearing her, a great weight seemed to settle upon Rim Adams. "Yet you stood by him. You hid him out—"

"Don't ask me to tell you why I bothered!"

"I think I know why—for the same reason I do. I've known, from the beginning of the summer, that

204

he was going on nerve alone, and it couldn't last. When they laid that trap for him, he walked into it and smashed it apart—but in the process, he cracked! It was going to happen sooner or later."

She shrugged, an angry gesture. "So it happened. It's nothing to do with me."

"I thought you had some feeling for him."

"One time, I did. It died last night. Now all I want is for you to get him out of here!"

"All right." Adams pushed aside his emptied beer glass. "We're all being watched, so it will have to wait till dark. Get him on his feet, if you possibly can. I'll see if I can promote a rig at Weld's livery."

He raised his voice, then, as he turned away from the bar; he knew the watcher at the far end could hardly be fooled into thinking they had been talking about something other than Frank Keyhoe, and for his benefit he told the woman, "I figure I got no choice but to keep the office open and go through the motions of doing his job, until the men who hired him decide what they mean to do about replacing him."

"You don't need to think I envy you!" With her jeering voice at his back Rim Adams walked out of there, hoping he'd given no sign that he even noticed the trooper who had tailed him in.

The town lay in all its ugliness, scattered about this wide scar of a street that had been scratched into the raw Kansas earth. The sun upon the flat horizon; the steady plains wind, blowing out of that quarter of the sky, might have been the blast from the open door of a furnace.

Adams walked along the weedgrown edge of the street with that hot breath against his right cheek, and his face averted from the blinding, unobstructed glare of the swollen sun. Its reflection rolled along the windows on the far side of the street, firing them briefly to burnished gold, keeping pace with Adams as he passed. Almost any place looked its best at this moment of the day, he thought; but there was little beauty in this scatter of slab buildings and dugouts, and hardpan earth that was baked into a pattern of gray and curling scales.

What possible future was there for this Chase Center? Would it die and blow away on the prairie wind, leaving no trace or scar? Or become instead, as its first wildness passed, the town George Youngman envisioned—a busy hub for quiet and fruitful lives? Or would it, after all, live only as a name in the story of Frank Keyhoe: a street where Keyhoe had walked during one short summer, with Rim Adams at his heels, shotgun always ready?

Probably he was too close to it, still, to know the meaning of what had happened on this street and now it was nearly over. Perhaps an era was ending here, a time that could produce a man like Frank Keyhoe and build a legend about him. True or false the legend might have been, but the world would be a grayer place for its passing.

His thoughts thus occupied by that drunken and shattered man in Ruby Jerrod's room, Rim Adams walked and the sun settled lower. When he heard his name, surprise and alarm halted him and swung him full into the sun, and its swollen, swimming fire filled his eyes and blinded him; against the light, the figure he saw there was only a blocky, formless shape.

But out of that black silhouette came the voice of Harry Dowler, saying in heavy triumph, "All right, Adams! They tell me your friend Keyhoe, that warned me off of you, is gone for good. So he can't interfere now—can he?—if you and I settle a little

206

business between us."

"Dowler, I've been waiting a long time for this—ever since the night in Ellsworth!"

CHAPTER 20

The dazzle of sunset turned the trees along the creekbank into black pillars, and spreading across the canvas of the tents made each glow as though with an inward golden light. Tom Sutter saw little beauty in it. Still trembling from an angry scene with the colonel, he ducked through the low entrance of his own quarters and, going directly to a shelf, reached down a bottle and glass he kept there. He pulled the cork with his teeth, filled the tumbler three quarters full. With the bottle returned to its place, he raised the glass and drained off a good part of his drink in a couple of swallows, shuddering as the potent strength of it hit him.

He turned then, breathing deeply and pulling at the collar of his tunic, and saw his wife standing by the bed watching him.

Somehow he had failed to notice her even though the tent, its sides rolled up part way to get the breeze along the creekbank, seemed fairly to swim with the glow of golden light. She had been working at something—a bit of sewing, that she laid aside as she rose from the canvas folding chair. For some reason Tom found he was bothered by her unsmiling expression.

Aware that she did not like to see him drink, he made a small gesture with the glass in his hand as he offered, in gruff explanation, "By God, a man can

207

get so tight wound up, this is the only stuff can loosen his nerves for him! I never knew anyone as stubborn as my brother! Just watch—he'll let that murderer slide right out of his fingers!"

Caroline said quietly, "You're talking about Frank Keyhoe, I suppose?"

"Damned right, I am!" The anger poured out of him, like a dam breaking. "Those were good boys he killed. Jud Mannion was the best sergeant I ever had under me. He was more than that—he was a friend! And there's that cold-eyed, murdering bastard—"

Under the disapproval he read in his wife's eyes, Tom broke off, his face heating up a trifle. It was not a type of language he had ever used in her presence; he had a sudden sense of the poor appearance he was making—face flushed and sweating, tunic awry, whiskey glass in hand. For a moment he almost tried to apologize, but that seemed pointless and he merely shrugged and, raising the glass, drained it off at a gulp.

He thought recklessly, If she had the idea she married a gentleman, it's as good a time as any for her to learn she's only part way right!

He looked at the empty glass, torn between an impulse to fling it from him for the pleasure of hearing it smash, and another to get the bottle off the shelf and pour a second drink. When Caroline spoke he only half heard her, she had to repeat the words before she brought his scowling glance to her face. "I want to ask you something...." She stood very straight, her hands clasped before her. The knuckles stood out white beneath the skin and her cheeks, too, were colorless.

"Yes?" Watching her, seeing the evident distress with which she steeled herself to speak, Tom Sutter found himself thinking, You sure as hell married a fine-looking girl!

"This afternoon," she said, her voice faltering, "there were some enlisted men working around the tent—they were sawing up that big limb, that fell in the wind storm..." He nodded impatiently and she went on, a little steadier now. "Of course, I know they never stopped to think anyone could hear what they were saying—and I never meant to eavesdrop..."

"All right, all right!" he prompted her impatiently. "Get to it, will you?"

She took a breath. "They were talking about the shooting, in town today. I heard them say it was known all over the camp, beforehand, that something of the sort was going to happen. They said it was planned—but, hardly the way it turned out." Her eyes searched his. "Tom, did you know anything about it?"

"I did not! How could I?" he retorted angrily, while he combated the quick chill her words sent through him. He set down the glass carefully, thinking, That sonofabitch, Jud Mannion! Or— which one of the others? Hadn't they had sense enough to keep their mouths shut about what they meant to do? "Even if there was any truth in this wild story, you surely don't think I'd have been aware of what was going on!"

"I don't know, Tom." Suddenly it was hard to meet the weight of her troubled gaze, but he managed. "These men said you were. One said that this Sergeant Mannion you spoke of had told him so. He even said it was your idea. That you—*paid* them!"

"You don't *believe* that?" Fury carried him to her, bootheels sounding on the rough board floor of the tent. "Would you take what you overheard, from

209

some stupid dogface on fatigue detail—against the word of your own husband?"

"Of course not," she answered, facing him squarely. "Even I have learned, by this time, how empty the rumors can be that fly around an army camp. I'd have paid no attention to this one, except for something odd in the way you're behaving now! Tom, it's *you* that's suddenly started me wondering!"

"So?" He waited until he was sure there would be no tremor in his voice before he went on, with icy quiet, "If you think I'm the kind who would pay to have murder done, perhaps you also have some theory why it would be that important to me, to see a cheap gunman like Keyhoe done away with...."

"That was the worst part of all. They said you had hated Keyhoe from a long time back—but mostly because he humiliated you one day a few weeks ago, in that gambling hall in town. You were drunk, and brought your horse inside and deliberately shot and killed it—and the marshal had to knock you in the head with the barrel of his gun to keep you from doing something worse!"

"That is a damned lie!" The cry of outrage exploded from him. "The bastard knew better than to use a gunbarrel on me! It was bad enough that he used his fist!" And then he floundered and subsided, as his wife's face told him how much he had admitted.

Caroline looked then as though she had just watched something die—perhaps it was her love for him. In a leaden voice she said, "I doubt that there's any point in discussing this."

He resorted to hurt innocence. "No, obviously you're ready to believe anything—and anybody, except your husband! Maybe you've even been talking some more to the protégé of Keyhoe's, that nobody named Adams who tags along after him." And then it came pouring out, unchecked: "I always have wondered just what went on, during the train ride you took together. And overnight, at Ellsworth...."

He was unprepared for her quick reaction; the strike of her open palm against his face caused him more surprise than pain. He heard his own voice cry, "You bitch!" and almost of its own volition his own hand swung around. Caroline was staggered by the full weight of the blow; she fell against the wooden frame of the bed and, catching herself there, stared at him while her face drained of color.

Tom could only return her stricken look, quickly sobered by it. "I didn't mean that!" he blurted. "Or what I said just then..."

"Oh, yes," she answered, her voice trembling. "You meant them!" When he tried to touch her she drew back. All the effect of the whiskey knocked out of him now, he stood and watched her move away from him and, for the first time, a hollow fear seized him.

"What are you thinking?"

Looking at him she said, "I'm thinking I have to leave you."

"No!" Catching himself, his fists clenched tight, he went on more quietly, "Not for this—not because we've had a little row!"

"Not for this," she agreed. "But because you've just shown me that all the things I heard were true! You *did* want Frank Keyhoe dead! Why, Tom? Because he caught you out in a piece of drunken stupidity, in front of the gambling crowd at McCord's? Or because last night he knocked you into the punch bowl? Do you really have such a towering ego, that you would plot a man's death over nothing more than a few moments humiliation?

"I'm not saying I haven't anything to blame myself for," she went on, not waiting for his answer. "I'm very guilty. I let romantic notions sway me into marrying someone I didn't really know. Well, I know you now. And I'm afraid I don't like you very much!"

When he found his voice, it had a sharp and ugly edge. "That's unfortunate!" he remarked, under control. "The fact remains that you are my wife— and in this year of 1869, a woman doesn't just walk out on her husband! It would not have mattered if I'd murdered a dozen men—with my bare hands. Legally, you are not very much more than being my property!"

She faced him, unflinching. "I'm aware of the law. I also know that if you try to hold me by force, I'll get away from you somehow. And then you'll never lay eyes on me again!"

She let him think about that, and something in the way she stood up to him convinced him finally that he had lost. He dropped the hand he had lifted, not touching her. He said at last, in a coldly formal tone. "You're going home?"

"I really don't know. That's a long way. Chiefly, I want to get off alone somewhere, where I can think. No need to be concerned—I can look out for myself."

"Will I hear from you?"

"Of course. Whatever I decide."

He drew a long breath into his lungs, and looked about him at the crude interior of the tent. "I suppose now you have no intention of spending another night here...."

"With you? None at all." She added, "But I won't

put you out. That would hardly be decent, since I'm the one that's deserting you. Can you get me transportation into town? I can stay there tonight— Mrs. Youngman can find room for me, I'm sure. Tomorrow I'll take the train. To St. Louis, perhaps; I don't know, yet."

They looked at each other now like strangers, spoke like strangers. With a curt nod, Tom said, "Very well. I'll arrange for the ambulance." But then a flash of his bitterness and anger broke through as he warned her: "I wouldn't take too long making up my mind, if I were you. You just might regret it!" Abruptly he turned and left her.

Alone, Caroline stared after him for a long moment, all the fire and anger draining from her and leaving her weak and spent. She pushed a hand through her hair, her shoulders sagging as she moved to the bed and drew out the suitcase she had stored beneath it. She was putting clothing into it when Olivia Sutter came into the tent.

Dark eyes wide with shock, Livy seemed for once almost wordless. "Carrie! What in the world is going on?"

She tried to manage a smile for her oldest friend. "I thought perhaps I'd take a little trip…."

"Trip, nothing! That was a *fight* you and Tom were having! Honesty, with these sidewalls rolled up, you could be heard all up and down the creek!"

"I'm sorry." Caroline folded a cape and tucked it carefully in the bag. Livy came nearer, seized her by an arm.

"What's happened? You're not really leaving? But—*why*?" Studying the other girl's face she hazarded a guess. "I how, it's not the easiest sort of life following your husband into the field. But I always thought you were a stronger person than

213

this!"

Caroline's mouth set firmly. "It has nothing to do with hardship," she answered, more bruskly than she intended. "Honestly, it's nothing I want to bother you with...."

"But the colonel's not going to like it!"

That caught her up, stunned her, turned her to the other girl in disbelief. "The *colonel* won't like it?" she echoed. "And is that the only thing that matters? Oh, Livy!" she cried as she saw disapproval settle in those wide brown eyes. "I won't quarrel with *you*! I know your sun rises and sets in him. But right now, the very name of Sutter—!" She shook her head, tossing her hands wide, helplessly. "I'm sorry!" she said lamely.

There was nothing in Livy Sutter's face now but cold anger. Turning from her, in silence Caroline closed the fastenings of her suitcase. Outside, wheels ground to a halt, a driver spoke to his team. Moments later he rapped on the tent prop and called inside, "I got orders to drive somebody in to town."

"Yes. Will you take my bag, please."

The trooper carried it out and stowed it into the rig. Caroline turned to Livy, hoping for some response, some decent effort at a goodby. But Livy had been outraged to her soul and she stared straight ahead, lips set tight. Giving up, Caroline kissed her cheek and squeezed her shoulder; afterward she turned blindly away, gathered up hatbox and reticule and hurried out to where the trooper waited to help her into the rig.

The tents beneath the lofty creekbank trees wheeled away behind item, in the last gold wash of light from the swollen sun.

Resolutely she turned her eyes away, facing primly forward as they rolled through the camp with

214

its rows of canvas, its muted and relaxed tempo following retreat.

Then, before a company commander's tent, she caught a glimpse of two men who stood absorbed in talk. One was a major; the other—tall, erect, holding the reins of a handsome bay mount—was Colonel Jefferson Sutter. The pose was one she recognized, for she had seen it innumerable times before one knee slightly bent, polished boot placed slightly forward; yellow-gauntleted fist set on hip, handsome head lifted. The colonel's brother Tom, for one, had learned to imitate it exactly. But Caroline had come to find something so meretricious about these heroic attitudes that she sometimes wondered how she, or anyone, was ever taken in by them.

The ambulance spun on, behind its pair of mules, and her picture of the colonel was swept away. It seemed appropriate, she thought, that it might be the last memory she would ever have of any of the Sutter family.

Rim Adams, trapped, wondered how he could have supposed this moment wouldn't sometime catch up with him. The breach with Harry Dowler had begun to widen from the moment of their first confrontation, in the aisle of a swaying railroad car. Only Dowler's fear of Frank Keyhoe had kept them apart. Now, squinting into an eye-punishing confusion of black shadow and molten, burning light, Adams knew he had heard the voice of his doom.

The brim of a derby was no shield against the direct glare of setting sun. Moving cautiously, he drew back a half step so that a corner of the sod-walled building at his elbow slid between and mercifully cut it away. A dazzling after image

215

seared his vision still, but by squinting he could just make out now the bulky figure of the redheaded yard boss. Dowler had evidently been waiting to let Adams walk up on him unawares. Now he came slouching into the open, stepping up onto the uneven sidewalk; his big fist held a six-shooter as though it were a toy, dangling indolently at the end of one arm.

"Stand still, damn you!" he roared as he saw his victim make another move to back away. He added, his lip curling in satisfaction, "I'm going to kill you. You know that, I guess?"

He possessed the kind of voice that carries. From the corners of his eyes Rim Adams had a glimpse of men who had heard and stopped to stare, but at a safe distance. Across the wide street, there were a couple of blue uniforms—members of the search party hunting Frank Keyhoe. They'd been given their orders, they wouldn't interfere in a private matter.

Harry Dowler had all the time in the world to savor this, and he knew it.

Standing at bay, Adams could feel iron bands tight about his chest. He eyed without hope the gun the big man's fist held engulfed, still pointing carelessly at the ground, and estimated the minutes he might have left to live. And yet, a man couldn't let himself simply give up. He drew air into his lungs, and cautiously pulled his right leg back a trifle, his body making a half turn. This presented a narrower target, and it also shielded his right arm from Dowler. With luck the big man might not be able to see what he was doing, as he began to slide his hand up toward the gun that was thrust behind his waistband, beneath his coat.

Apparently Dowler was too cruelly sure of

216

himself to think there might actually be any danger in his victim. "You might try begging a little," he suggested now, grinning. "I ain't saying it'll do any good, of course, but I'd kind of enjoy seeing it." The gun waggled in his fist, and the barrel lifted. "Get on your knees, mister. Let's see how you look that way!"

A little stooped, head thrust slightly forward, Adams stared into the black muzzle of the gun, and swallowed back the sour taste of fear. In that position the hang of the unbuttoned coat barely screened the careful groping of his right hand. Suddenly, shaking fingertips just touched the unyielding hardness of the gunhandle. He froze, not daring to make any further movement or let his expression warn the big man.

Dowler repeated ominously, "I said, *on your knees!*"

With the implacable eye of that gun leveled at his head, he started down, left hand put out to steady him. It touched rough wood, and his right knee followed; poised in that cramped position, the breath shallow in his throat, he looked up at his tormentor—and with a sudden, despairing move snatched the gun from his belt as he flung himself prone, rolling.

At once the gunmuzzle above him exploded in flame, at point blank range; that the bullet should miss seemed incredible, yet it only chewed splinters from the planking. Adams managed to squeeze off a wild shot and as the big man fired again the roar of the guns mingled in his head. Something like a hot iron skewered his thigh and he felt a shout distend his throat, at the sudden pain of it. Then he had reached the edge of the sidewalk, still rolling, and went on over to land in deep dust.

Harry Dowler, cursing, dropped the hammer on another cartridge; yellow dirt erupted in a geyser that made Adams blink and duck his head, half blinded. Sprawling on his belly with his gun extended in both hands, he made out the dark shape of the man looming directly above him.

He braced his elbows against the ground, and shot the big man in the chest.

The leg wound was hardly more than a gouge, that had bled very little. Rim Adams thought he would be limping for a while, favoring that left leg; what he could scarcely believe was that he had come through at all. Working by the lamp in the marshal's office, he washed out the glistening red trough with whiskey from the desk bottle, gritting his teeth at the burn of it. When the job was done he upended the bottle and took a long drag at the fiery stuff, hoping to settle his nerves.

Nearly an hour after the killing of Dowler he was still shaking. He shuddered as the raw alcohol hit home, considered a second drink but instead made a face and, ramming the cork solidly with the heel of his hand, dropped the bottle back into its drawer.

Having bound the wound and pulled on his only other pair of trousers, he was reloading his gun when a footstep outside caused his nerves to leap. He slapped the cylinder shut and pointed the gun at the open door. But when his visitor emerged from the darkness, Rim Adams let out his breath in a sour grunt and laid the weapon down.

"It's you again!" he said.

On the threshold, Merl Brinegar tilted his head on one side and gave the deputy an appraising look.

A plume of smoke trailed from the stem of his pipe as the newspaperman took it from his mouth and pointed with it. "You, my friend," he said pleasantly, "have really had yourself a day! First, to tell off Jeff Sutter and put him in his place; and then to stand up to that tough redhead!" He wagged his narrow head. "It's really been something to watch!"

"You've been watching me?" Adams scowled at him. "I never noticed you!"

"The mark of a good newspaperman—intrusive only when he has to be. And after all," the man added, his lips quirking, "would I be apt to make myself conspicuous when lead threatened to be flying?"

Brinegar came on into the office, as far as the desk, where he halted to stand looking at the deputy while he sucked thoughtfully at the pipe stem. "I wonder," he said suddenly, "if you know what Lew McCord is doing, at the moment?" He waited for the other's brief shake of head. "He's closing down his gambling hall. The doors are locked, and rumor has it he's got his men busy packing, to pull out by tomorrow morning. On top of everything else, I think that's rather interesting. You didn't happen to suggest, did you, that he ought to think of leaving Chase Center?"

"I may have," Adams admitted shortly. "But if you think he's going on my account, you're crazy! It's Keyhoe he's afraid of."

"That's where you're mistaken. The whole town knows by now that Frank Keyhoe's lost his nerve and run for it." Merl Brinegar half turned and hitched himself onto a corner of the desk, making himself comfortable; he looked at Adams through the fog of smoke from his pipe. "Maybe it's time somebody brought you up to date. You don't seem to realize it, but this town doesn't care too much about Keyhoe now. You've given them something

219

new to talk about."

"Me!"

"It's human nature: Better a new hero walking around where they can see him, than an old one that's all of a sudden lost his nerve and gone into hiding…"

Rim Adams stared. His lips scarcely moved as he said tightly, "You're talking pure nonsense and I'm getting a little sick of listening to it!"

"All right." Calmly, the other turned and tapped his pipe against the open windowsill, brushing the dottle away with his fingers. He put the pipe into a pocket and swung to his feet. "I've got a story to write. Since the big one on the burning of the jail, I can't send my editor enough copy from Chase Center. Oh, yes indeed!" he went on, seeing Adams' look. "You and Keyhoe have ready been putting the town on the map, this summer. With a little help from me, naturally!"

Rim Adams found his tongue. "You been writing about us? In that damned newspaper?"

The man seemed to miss the danger in his tone. He said blandly, "Of course—I hope I know a news story when I see one. I believe I have a cutting or two with me," he went on, as he dug a wad of papers from a bulging pocket and began to shuffle through them. "Take my word for it, you and Keyhoe make just the sort of team that catches the public's fancy: An older man going down, a younger one at the very start of his career.…"

Adams cut him off. "I'll bet you got a real good story out of last night, didn't you—Keyhoe being humiliated in front of all those people! A real chance to drag a man's reputation through the dust!"

A faint flush tinged the other's bony features, but he answered stoutly enough: "I do my job, and my

220

editor thinks I do it well!" Still fumbling with the papers, he added, "I got a wire here somewhere from the publisher himself, promising me a better line rate if I can keep the stories coming—"

With a sudden fury, Rim Adams reached and knocked the papers, scattering from the fellow's hands. Leaping up, then, he circled the desk and gathered the little man's coat and shirtfront into a hard grip as he said in a voice that shook, "You damned scavenger! I don't want anything at all written about me—is that clear? And from now on, lay off of Frank Keyhoe. Haven't you cheap penny-A-liners done him enough hurt?"

Brinegar tried for indignation, but Adams' hand at his throat reduced his voice to a hoarse whisper. "It was people like me made Keyhoe famous!"

"And the worst hour of his life," Adams retorted, "was when he decided he had to live up to the stuff you wrote about him! All I got to say is, don't try that on *me*! Don't try to persuade me I'm as good a man as Frank Keyhoe—because I never was, and never could be!"

He shoved the man from him, to bring up against the wall with the beginning of fear showing now in his sweating face. "Now go on—get away from me!" Adams ordered. "Get clear away!"

For a moment the man returned his angry look. But something he saw in it at last caused Brinegar to drop his eyes; without a word he went down on his knees and began to scoop up his clippings, with fluttering hands.

Long after he was gone into the darkness Rim Adams remained as he was, leaning against the desk, still tasting the brassy aftermath of violent anger that made his whole body tremble.

CHAPTER 21

The stars were out, the full spreading mesh of them, but dimmed by the heat haze of a summer night. A lantern on its hook beside the stable doorway swayed gently, putting a moving circle of light across the street dust. Lamplight burned in the cubicle, partitioned off at the front of the team, where Bert Weld sat working on his books; when Rim Adams came, limping slightly, through the wide street entrance, the livery owner put down his pen and stepped out to meet him. His manner seemed cautious and unusually respectful. "Adams!" he said. "How are you feeling? How's the leg?"

"All right," the young fellow said shortly.

"I wish you'd step into the office for a minute."

Puzzled by the man's new attitude, Adams took the chair he offered him while the liveryman eased into his place at the rolltop desk, with its crammed and untidy pigeonholes. Weld picked up a pencil and tapped the desk nervously with the point of it. Finally he blurted the question that was troubling him. "Will you answer me honestly: Do you know where Keyhoe is?"

Adams hesitated a fraction, then spoke the literal truth. "At the moment—no, I don't."

"I see." Weld shook his head, scowling, and tossed the pencil aside. "Then it should be plain enough. The man has sneaked out of town, and there's no point expecting him back again. I've been talking to George Youngman and some of the others. Sooner or later they've got to come around to my point of view."

"And, that is—?"

"That we have no choice but to declare his post vacated."

"What you really mean," Rim Adams interpreted coldly, "is that you're grabbing the opportunity to fire him—without having to tell him to his face, or even hear his side of the story!"

The man's cheeks turned slowly red. "We have to do what we consider best for the town! I'll ask you bluntly: Do *you* think Frank Keyhoe will ever show his face here again—to answer the charges the army has brought against him because of the men he killed?"

"To answer you honestly," Adams said, "then, no."

"Then what choice do we have? We still need a marshal, here—enough has happened today to prove that." The man paused, his eyes on Adams' face; he seemed to be choosing his words, or debating their effect. "I've been wondering if you'd consider taking the job."

"*Me?*" Surprise jolted the exclamation out of him. "Mister Weld," he pointed out, "at first you didn't even want me for a *deputy*! You'd as soon have hired somebody out of McCord's place! And even if you've changed your own mind," he went on as Weld shifted his shoulders, "what about Asa Timberlake? He's not going to favor the idea, at all. I've killed Harry Dowler—and Harry was his man…"

"Harry Dowler was a tough and a bully. He was one of the things that was wrong with this town. Now that he's gone, Timberlake is going to learn there's been a change." The liveryman continued,

"Those of us who really want a town here are going to go ahead and get Chase Center platted and filed, and elect us some kind of honest-to God, legal government. If the obstructionists, such as Timberlake, find it cramps their style to obey ordinances and pay taxes to enforce them—then, like Lew McCord is doing right now, they can damn well pack up and go elsewhere. This time we mean business!"

"Now that you've actually *got* a town—thanks to Frank Keyhoe!" Rim Adams got to his feet, stood looking down at the other. "If you're seriously offering me his job, I'll give you my answer: I'm not interested."

The liveryman frowned. "You're passing up a real opportunity, for a fellow as young as you. You've made a good start here."

"And now I'm making a good finish! I decided, less than an hour ago—I've had all I want of this place. I'm getting out."

"So, between you and Keyhoe, you're leaving us without any law at all!"

Adams hesitated. "All right," he said reluctantly. "I'll give you two weeks. I guess that's customary—and it should give you time to find your replacement.

"Right now," he added, not caring to prolong the argument, "if that rig you rented Keyhoe last night is handy, I'd like to get rid of the smell of this town for a few hours at least. I'll be back—but I've got some thinking I want to do...."

In an ill humor, Weld shrugged and pushed to his feet. "I'll hitch up."

"I can manage the harness. Just tell me which horse to take."

"The gray, in the third stall," the man told him

stiffly; as Adams thanked him with a nod and walked out into the barn, the liveryman stated blankly after him.

A moment later Bert Weld blew the lamp and came from his office, with a hat set squarely atop his head. Adams watched him stalk out through the street door, and guessed he was on his way to find George Youngman or some of his other colleagues and report the unsatisfactory results of his talk with the deputy marshal.

A week ago, Adams thought with heavy irony, it would never have entered his head to leave his place of business open and unguarded....

The buggy was stored in a rear corner of the barn near the alley door. He got the gray from its stall and backed it between the shafts and began putting on the harness, working hurriedly and with a mounting nervous tension. When that rear door creaked faintly on its hinges, he jerked about and almost went for the gun behind his belt, before he saw Ruby Jerrod's face in the wash of the team lantern.

She said, "Didn't mean to give you a start! But Belle's gettin' anxious. She sent me to try and find out if you're ready yet."

Adams said gruffly, "Soon as I finish here."

"I'll tell her." But the girl stayed where she was, watching him work with the straps and buckles. She asked, hesitancy, "When Mister Keyhoe leaves— does that mean you're going, too?"

"That's right."

Silence, for a moment. "Don't reckon there's—" She started again. "Don't reckon there's any way I could get you to take me with you?"

That made him turn to look at her. She was barearmed and short-skirted; her hair was piled up, but in lanternlight the rouge and rice powder only made her look younger and less mature. She read his look and suddenly there was a glint of moisture in her haunted eyes. "I guess you think that's crazy!" she blurted out. "But I can't help it! You been nice to me—nicer than about anybody I ever met. I—I don't want to see you go because I know it'll be forever. I'll never see you again!"

He found himself sweating a little, as he saw the naked hurt in her face; she misread his silence for she said defiantly, "Whatever you're thinking, I ain't no bad girl. Honest I ain't! Belle doesn't—I mean, she ain't ever insisted on—"

His face burning, Adams said quickly, "That's not what bothers me. There's a couple of reasons I can't do what you're asking. One is that—there happens to be somebody else."

"Oh." Something seemed to die in her voice. Her shoulders drooped and her eyes fell away from his. She stared at the toe of her slipper. "Somebody you got a real feeling for, I guess?"

"That's right..."

They both fell silent The gray horse stomped a hoof in the straw litter. Adams felt he had to try again, to give her a better answer. "For the second reason, I don't really think you'd want to go where I'm heading."

Her head jerked up quickly. "Oh, I wouldn't care! Any place you said—Denver, or Sacramento, or— Well, it couldn't help being better than *this*!"

"But that's just the point. I'm not going any of those places. What I got in mind, when I leave Chase Center, is finding myself a piece of land somewhere. Something I can farm."

"Farm!" Ruby's eyes widened, almost in horror. "*You*?"

Her expression forced him to smile a little, but

226

then he nodded soberly. "Just yesterday I walked into a wagon camp, and heard some immigrants talking about the land they were hoping to take up, and what they hoped to make of it. And, Ruby, ever since that moment I realize I've been on the wrong track, for a long time. I came off the land, and I'll never really be happy until I get back to it. That's the thing that's been wrong with me. It's why I've been restless, hunting everywhere because I didn't know what I was missing."

She could only shake her head, her red mouth pulled into a shape of pure distaste. "My pa's a farmer. Him and my five brothers—it's all they ever knowed or want to know. It was to get away that I up and left Missouri!"

"If I did take you away from here," Rim Adams warned her, "it would be in order to see you got back to your family. That's a promise!"

Ruby studied his face during a long moment, reading the sober earnestness in him. At last she looked away and said, in a toneless voice, "All right. What am I supposed to say to Belle?"

"Tell her I'll only be a few minutes...."

She left him without another word, the door creaking shut behind her. When Adams returned to his work, he knew that the thought of Ruby Jerrod would bother him for a long time to come. But there was nothing he could have done for her.

When he had finished he went to the forward door and checked the street. All seemed quiet; but knowing that the men of the 11th were still on the prowl, Adams could not be easy in his mind until he was free of this place. Returning to the buggy, he swung the alley door open and led the horse outside, into the darkness. And he saw the pair who stood just at the edge of lanternlight, in the weeds by the stable's rear wall.

Frank Keyhoe had his back against the rough, unfinished boards. His face was lost in the shadow of his hatbrim; he neither turned his head nor made any answer when Adams said anxiously, "Keyhoe? You all right?"

"He's walking, at any rate," Belle Wadsworth said in a tone of deep bitterness. "I propped him on his feet and got him this far. Now, take him away from here, so I can be rid of fretting about him!"

He looked at her, and then at the marshal. "All right," he said, and laid hold of Keyhoe's arm above the elbow. "Let's go."

The tall man let himself be led to the buggy—stiffly erect, moving carefully yet not entirely in control. Once he stumbled and Adams was sure only the grip on his arm kept him from going down. But Adams managed to help him onto the seat, and then the woman was there to say, "Take this." He recognized the cracked leather bag that held Frank Keyhoe's worldly belongings. He stowed it beneath the dashboard and afterward turned back for a word with Belle.

"No need to worry," he told her, keeping his voice down. "I have friends I'm sure will take us in tonight. If by tomorrow he's sober enough to decide what he wants—"

She cut him off, with a violent shake of the head. "No, no! I don't want to hear!" She actually raised both hands to her ears, shutting out the sound of his voice. "I don't want to know anything more about Frank Keyhoe, ever!"

Rim Adams looked at her in silence, and finally nodded. "All right." He touched the narrow brim of his hat to her, and went around to the other side of the buggy and climbed in, taking the reins.

Keyhoe's body gave loosely as the rig shifted and settled, but he seemed to have a good grip on the ironwork. Adams slapped the leathers along the horse's back, and put the rig in motion.

Once across the Kansas Pacific tracks they would be free of the town and, likely enough, safe from pursuit. Rim Adams pointed them in that direction, hugging the dark backsides of the buildings while the buggy's wheels lurched over uneven ground. With perhaps a hundred yards still to go, the alley swung to join the lower end of the street; now a lantern showed, burning on the wall of the depot. The liquid glimmer of steel rails reflecting its glow seemed to beckon, yet drew nearer with the most maddening slowness.

He heard a yell.

A man in trooper's uniform had stepped into the roadway, just ahead, an arm upraised as he repeated the command to halt. Face grim, Adams said between his teeth, "You go to hell!" and gave the gray a slap with the leathers.

As the buggy picked up speed the trooper came running forward, pulling his holster gun but apparently still not sure enough of the situation to open fire. Adams cut a glance at Keyhoe, to see how his passenger was faring. Glassy-eyed in a vagrant gleam of lanternlight that probed the darkness under the buggytop, Keyhoe showed no awareness of what was going on. The younger man gathered both reins in his left hand as he freed his own revolver.

The trooper set himself, pistol raised; but as the gray horse came abreast of him he did a very foolish thing: He tried to grab the animal's headstall, evidently meaning to pull it to a halt. Rim Adams saw in time, and gave a hard yank at the reins that jerked the animal's head up and away from the reaching hand. Thrown off balance, the man couldn't catch himself. A wheel of the buggy struck and flipped him, rolling, into the street; the gun flew from his fingers.

Adams, leaning from his seat, peered back and saw him bring to a halt, reach his hands and knees and then drop flat again. After that a haze of lifted dust settled between; but he thought most likely the trooper was, for the moment at least, stunned and badly shaken.

It was enough. Everything had gone quickly and seemingly unnoticed, and with luck it could be minutes before the trooper recovered enough to raise an alarm. Already they had passed Timberlake's warehouse and freight yard, and now they took the jolting crossing of the steel tracks. On their far side, Adams swung the gray's head toward the east. Nothing rose to stop them; they left the clapboard station building behind, and the scattered lights of Chase Center dwindled and drew together and gradually fell back into the immensity of the dark plain.

Now there were only the stars, and the warm wind, and the slog of hoofs and singing of ironshod wheels through rank weeds that grew alongside the roadbed. Rim Adams kept the gray moving through the late summer night.

CHAPTER 22

Unexpectedly, and in a completely sober voice, Frank Keyhoe spoke: "She was much too good for me..."

230

Adams whipped his head around in astonishment. "You mean, you heard all that?" When Keyhoe made no answer, after a moment the young fellow added, "You must have hurt her pretty bad."

"I always have. At least she knew what to expect, in taking up with me again."

"Well, she's through with it now—all through. And I ain't sure I blame her!"

Keyhoe seemed to take no exception. He said, mildly enough, "It's all right. I won't be bothering her any more." He abruptly changed the subject. "It wouldn't look as though we're being followed."

"No." Adams had been alert to any unusual sounds coming from the darkness. "It's my guess the fellow I spilled, back there, was pretty much shaken up. Likely as not it would of took him time to get his head clear and sound the alarm—even if he was dead sure who he'd tangled with."

"And so, Jeff Sutter really wants to nail my ears to the barn door!" Keyhoe shifted his weight on the padded leather seat, braced one boot upon the dashboard. "I'm surprised," he muttered, as though half to himself. "We've clashed before, but it never came to anything serious."

The younger man hesitated. "From what I heard, I got an idea it was Tom who really stirred this up."

Keyhoe nodded. "I could believe that. In his own fashion, Jeff Sutter is by way of being a rather big man—I can't deny it, though I'd like to. But his brother Tom is nothing, nothing at all. In any event, I expect it will all blow over."

He sounded confident enough; he sounded very much like himself as he sat there beside Rim Adams, talking quietly, with the warm summer night about them and the dimly seen quarters of the gray horse moving easily and rhythmically between

231

the shafts. But somehow the younger man knew, more surely than ever, that this was not the same Frank Keyhoe. He had pushed himself too hard, had driven himself once too often to look upon the face of death. The special thing that had set him apart from other men was used up and gone.

The wagon circle looked a peaceful place tonight, a few fires wavering and throwing their wash of light over treeboles and the underside of the leafy canopy overhead. There was less of the air of an armed camp than there had been yesterday; when he was recognized, Rim Adams drew some friendly greetings and was allowed to find his way directly to the Hawkins wagon, unhindered.

Dave Hawkins appeared to be mending, and would have made the effort to get to his feet if Adams hadn't waved him back. Leaving Keyhoe in the rig, he got out and, having shaken hands, went down on his ankles beside the wounded man to talk for a little. He had wondered just how he would explain things; he decided the best explanation was the simple truth, and he told it as briefly as he could.

Apparently the people here had got no wind as yet of the day's events. Hawkins listened intently, not interrupting. When the other was finished he said without hesitation, "Tell me what I can do to help."

"Would it be asking too much, to lay over here till morning?"

"Consider it settled. I guarantee nobody will bother you—I'll have Billy hide your horse and rig back in the trees, just in case. And now," Hawkins added, "How about supper? We've already eaten, but Beth can dish up something."

Adams was hungry enough, but Frank Keyhoe said he wanted nothing. "When the younger man

232

had explained the arrangements to him and helped him out of the rig, he barely nodded to Hawkins and his wife and then seated himself gingerly on a straight-backed, wooden chair. At Adams' insistence, he accepted a cup of coffee from Beth Hawkins but he drank little. His hand when he lifted it held a distinct tremor. If these people noticed, however, they didn't comment. Keyhoe, for his part, said nothing at all.

The food was plain enough—beans and biscuit and salt pork—but it tasted fine to Adams. As he ate he kept a corner of his attention for the sounds of the deepening night, but already he was beginning to let himself relax as he felt the peace of his surroundings. The baby woke in its bed in the wagon and fretted a bit; its mother settled it and afterward came to take the dishes as the guests finished with them. Through it all Frank Keyhoe sat like a lump, holding his silence while the others talked of neutral matters—soil, and weather, and the activities of Hawkins' friends in scouting around looking for possible homestead land.

After awhile others of the company began drifting up—sundarkened men, and a scattering of half-grown boys. Not interfering, they hung at the edge of the firelight to listen to the talk and watch the visitors. Adams knew it was Frank Keyhoe who intrigued them, but no one ventured to intrude upon the tall man's moody silence, until presently Billy Hawkins came riding in, bareback, on one of his brother's wagon horses.

Hauling at the rein, the youngster peered at their guest, took a second look and came piling off with a yell that made everyone turn. He hurried forward, exclaiming, "Frank Keyhoe! It *is*, isn't it? Hell! You look just like your pictures!"

His brother said gently, chiding him, "Now, Billy..."

The boy's enthusiasm wasn't to be quelled. "Aw, Dave! I ain't ever met a *famous* man before!" Impulsively he swiped a palm across his jeans and thrust it out. "I'd purely like to shake your hand, Mister Keyhoe!"

Adams held his breath, not knowing what to expect. Keyhoe eyed the youngster for a moment, without expression; then, surprisingly, he reached up and gravely shook with him. And the older Hawkins said quickly, "All right, Billy. Stop bothering the company. You go tell Beth to serve you up some coffee and grub."

"Sure." But Billy couldn't seem to tear himself away. Gangling frame hipshot, arms akimbo, he said, "There's a good chance we may be neighbors of yours, Mister Keyhoe."

"Is that so?" the latter said politely. They were almost the first words he had spoken.

"I been looking over a quarter section of railroad land we just might buy for ourselves—that is, if Dave likes it, and we can make a deal."

The elder Hawkins was frowning. It occurred to Adams he might not like too much to see his brother making over a gunfighter in this way. He said now, with an edgy abruptness, "Mister Keyhoe ain't going to be around here himself much longer, kid."

"Oh?" That took some of the wind out of the boy's sails. "Why not?"

"You might say," Rim Adams put in dryly, "that he did his job too well!"

Slowly, a grin spread across the bony face. "Showed he was too tough for them, huh?" Billy turned again to Keyhoe. "We heard what you done to that mob that tried to tear down the jail! Now

234

you've made a tame pussycat out of Chase Center, I bet you already got some other tough job waitin'. Ain't that so?"

"Why, yes, as a matter of fact," Keyhoe answered, and touched a pocket of his coat. "I happen to have a letter here, from the top people at Ellsworth."

"Ellsworth?" Billy Hawkins echoed eagerly. "We come through there. Looked like a pretty rough place, to me!"

"It may get rougher. They've got the Texas cattle trade coming in, next season, and they want me to take over as marshal. Not that it's likely to be too great a problem, for an experienced lawman," he added carelessly. "But anyway, I'm heading there now to look the proposition over. If I can get the right price for the job, I suppose I'll decide to take it...."

With a cold thrill of disbelief Rim Adams realized that this man, whom he had never actually known to boast, was boasting now—merely to impress a bunch of sodbusters and a gawking, teenaged boy. To have to see Frank Keyhoe brought to this, his spirit so broken that he must try by such a means to pull the tatters of his reputation and his self respect about him, was somehow the saddest and most frightening experience of all.

The morning promised a day as hot as any. The sun, half way up a brassy sky, turned the steel rails of the siding to molten brilliance, and caused a man to jerk his hand away when he happened to touch the ironwork or the canvas top of the rent buggy. Restless with waiting, Rim Adams had climbed out to limp about in the brittle weeds, grasshoppers snapping and leaping from under his boots. He stood and looked awhile at the immensity of the plains, idly hunting for some sign of life anywhere in all those sun-smeared distances. Afterward he returned to where the gray horse dozed, droopheaded, between the shafts.

He said, "Then you're really going to Ellsworth?"

Keyhoe, in the scant shade of the buggy roof, nodded without looking at him. Adams scowled. So far not a word had been said by either man, to suggest that he ought to go along to serve again as deputy on this new job. Perhaps Keyhoe was waiting for Adams to volunteer. Perhaps he was just as reluctant to ask for help, as the other was loath to offer it.

And so, the words that were not said hung between them like a wall. And now a vibration of the rails began, hardly sensible at first, but growing to a thrumming that swelled steadily as the oncoming train became blackly visible against the western rim of the sky.

The train grew in size, took on the shape of a single day coach and a baggage car and caboose, and the engine with woodsmoke pluming from its diamond stack. As it slowed for the siding a brakeman dropped off one of the cars to throw the switch. The engine rolled onto the siding and halted in a sigh of escaping steam, a curtain of heat waves shaking above the whole length of its boiler.

Rim Adams said, "Well..."

Still not speaking, Frank Keyhoe climbed out and got his luggage, and Adams followed him through rank weeds toward the train. A man in a conductor's blue coat and billed cap had stepped down onto the right of the way, to check his watch against the sun; Keyhoe spoke to him about a ticket and was waved aboard. Mounting the iron step, the tall man carried his leather bag up the aisle to the front end where

236

there was a vacant seat, and here stowed his belongings in the rack and seated himself. He seemed unaware that Adams had stayed with him until the latter leaned and put out a hand.

"Take care of yourself, Frank," the younger man said gruffly, realizing it was the first time he had ever called him by that name. Keyhoe slowly lifted his head—that finely sculptured head, with its hawklike nose and tawny mane—and gave a younger man a long look. He took the hand, then, in the briefest of farewells. For all the August heat, his palm felt clammy and Adams could see clearly the tic that jerked at the muscle in his cheek.

Turning away, he knew somehow he would never see Frank Keyhoe again....

As he blundered back along the aisle he was stopped short by Caroline Sutter's voice speaking his name; he might have walked right by her, unnoticing. She sat alone, attired as he first remembered her—in the gray traveling dress and the hat with the bird on the brim. Sight of her swamped all thought of Keyhoe, or awareness of anyone else on the train; it turned his knees unsteady and dropped him into the empty seat beside her.

"Hullo!" he blurted. "You off on a visit?"

Her nod seemed hesitant. Adams thought now that she looked pale and tense—he wondered if perhaps the heat had made her ill, and asked.

"Oh no," she said quickly. "I'm fine...."

But he sensed in some way things were very wrong. He was sure of it when, impulsively, she placed her hand upon his and the cold touch of her fingers shocked through him. "Mister Adams!" she began, then as suddenly withdrew her hand as she added, "I'm sorry! If you aren't careful I'm apt to unload all my troubles!"

237

"I wouldn't mind a bit," he insisted hurriedly, but got no answer. He found his glance drawn to the hands that were locked together now in her lap; it took him a moment more to realize what it was about them that appeared somehow strange.

All at once it hit him: The gold wedding band was missing from her finger!

Startled eyes lifted to search her own, as a hundred questions crowded into his throat. Yet he could scarcely ask, Does this mean you've left your husband? So instead, lamely enough, he stammered out, "You know, if there's anything at all you want to tell me...."

By the way she hesitated, while the tip of her tongue came out to touch her lower lip, Rim Adams felt certain she was on the verge of confiding in him. But even as he watched, something changed within her eyes and she resolutely shook her head. "I couldn't impose on you—you've been far too kind already."

"It wasn't kindness! Believe me, if I—" It was no use—he had to let it go, unable to break past her reticence.

He fumbled with the derby, turned it between his palms, and in an expressionless voice heard himself saying, "Anyhow, I hope you have a good trip. I'm going away, myself."

"To another town as bad as Chase Center?"

Plainly she'd misunderstood when she saw the two men enter the car together. "Oh, no, ma'am. Keyhoe and I are splitting up. What he does is his business; but personally, I'm heading West from here. Colorado, maybe Oregon. Something different from this..." He indicated the blast of light and shimmering, empty land beyond the car window. "I've got a hankering for greenery, and running

238

water—maybe a hill or two. And no more marshal's jobs! I've had enough to last me a long time."

"I'm glad," Caroline said. "Now I won't have to worry about you."

Despite himself, such evident concern brought him close to blurting out to her his earnest thoughts about returning to the land, where he belonged. But he stopped himself, thinking, What the devil! How could anyone like her—a genuine lady, with her wholly different background—give a damn about a dirt farmer's ambitions? So instead he said gruffly, "I saved most of my pay this summer. I suppose I'll knock around awhile, until I find something else."

"I hope you find every single thing you're looking for," she told him, as though she meant it.

Somewhere in the distance the lonely whistle of an engine haunted the stillness. Rim Adams got to his feet. "That'll be the westbound, that you're sidelined for. So, if I don't happen to see you again—" He reached for her hand once more and it slipped into his—that hand without a ring. Her eyes were on him, serious and intent. Once more, for just a moment, the two of them seemed almost on the verge of real communication....

The moment passed. The other train thundered nearer, drivers pounding and sending their pulse along the rails. And Rim Adams said goodby, and turned away from her eyes and walked out of the coach, into the smash of the sunlight.

He stood watching as the westbound passed, hooting its signal to the sidelined train. He watched the brakeman reset the switch, and now the other engine steamed again to life. A last moment, he saw Caroline at the window; he lifted his hand in salute, and let it fall with an aching sense of loss.

Afterward there was the fading sound of the train

239

moving away from him, the pungent smell of woodsmoke and heated metal passing on the sweep of the steady wind. The hum of the rails thinned to silence and he was alone in the vastness of the plains.

He turned and, favoring his hurt leg, limped through sunbrowned prairie grass to where the horse and rig stood waiting.

We hope that you enjoyed reading this
Sagebrush Large Print Western.
If you would like to read more Sagebrush titles,
ask your librarian or contact the Publishers:

United States and Canada

Thomas T. Beeler, *Publisher*
Post Office Box 659
Hampton Falls, New Hampshire 03844-0659
(800) 251-8726

United Kingdom, Eire, and
the Republic of South Africa

Isis Publishing Ltd
7 Centremead
Osney Mead
Oxford OX2 0ES England
(01865) 250333

Australia and New Zealand

Australian Large Print Audio & Video P/L
17 Mohr Street
Tullamarine, Victoria, 3043, Australia
1 800 335 364